Escaping From School

"How do you feel about being a student at Whittaker?" Kate asked.

William shrugged.

Kate leveled an intense stare directly into his eyes. "Let's try that again. How do you feel about that?"

William's smile faded away. He blinked for several seconds. "I hate it," he said at last.

Kate favored him with a kind look. "I know what you mean. We hate it, too." She stopped to look at George. "Or at least I do."

George protested, "Wait a minute! I hate it, too. I want out of there."

Molly added, "I hate it, and I don't even go there."

"I'm going to find us a way out," Kate said. "I don't know how yet, but I believe a door will open and we will be able to escape through it. Are you with us, William? Do you want out, too?"

William was now in tears. He assured Kate, tom of his heart, "Yes, I want out. I'd have quit lo parents woulda let me."

"We all need to keep our eyes and ears open, Whittaker, for every weird thing that happens. We prepared to act."

Story Time

Story Time

EDWARD BLOOR

Harcourt, Inc.

ORLANDO   AUSTIN   NEW YORK
SAN DIEGO   TORONTO   LONDON

www.HarcourtBooks.com

First Harcourt paperback edition 2005

The Library of Congress has cataloged the hardcover edition as follows:
Bloor, Edward, 1950–
Story time/by Edward Bloor.
p. cm.
Summary: George and Kate are promised the best education but instead
face obsessed administrators, endless tests, and evil spirits when they
are transferred to Whittaker Magnet School.
[1. Schools—Fiction. 2. Ghosts—Fiction.] I. Title.
PZ7.B6236St 2004
[Fic]—dc21 2002151503
ISBN-13: 978-0152-04670-5 ISBN-10: 0-15-204670-4
ISBN-13: 978-0152-05222-5 pb ISBN-10: 0-15-205222-4 pb

Text set in Janson
Designed by Lydia D'moch

ACEGHFDB

Printed in the United States of America

For Amanda

WEEK ONE

I

A Carefree Evening

Kate was flying. She was thinking beautiful thoughts, and she was flying.

She sailed across the backyard in a graceful arc, ten feet above the dirt, rising over the fence at her apogee near the kitchen window and dipping below it at her perigee near the back gate.

Kate's uncle George, a slight, bespectacled boy, ran along the ground below her like a disembodied shadow. He had a length of rope tied around his waist. It ran up to a system of pulleys that were screwed deeply into the oak branch, threading through them and connecting, finally, to Kate. He was Kate's ballast, scurrying back and forth beneath the big oak branch, grunting and tugging in contrast to her effortless aerobatics.

He called up to her, "How does the bodice feel?"

Kate thought for a moment about the Velcro-and-wire brace wrapped around her body. "It's killing my armpits on the turns," she shouted, "but it's worth it! I'm flying, Uncle George. I'm sprinkled with fairy dust and I'm flying!" Spontaneously she broke into the first big number from *Peter Pan*, lustily singing "I'm Flying."

As she sang, Kate dipped one arm and one leg left, executing a smooth glide across the length of the yard and then back again. Her auburn hair wafted on and off her forehead, and her green eyes shone in the sunset.

On the ground, George hustled to keep up with her. He was two years younger than his niece, Kate. He was twenty-two years younger than Kate's mother, his sister, June.

Theirs was an unusual, although not unheard of, family arrangement. George and his parents, Kate's grandparents, lived in one-half of a gray-shingled duplex, with this fenced-in yard, while Kate and June lived in the other half. This is how things had always been, for as long as George had been alive.

George was red and sweating when he called up, "Let's try a landing."

"No," Kate shouted back. "Please, Uncle George. Let me sing 'Never Never Land,' and then I'll come down."

George paused for a moment to check his invention. The pulleys were still securely attached to the tree. The rope was gliding smoothly through them. The bodice was a good fit, except for Kate's armpits. With a satisfied nod and a sigh, he took off running once again as the warm early-September evening faded slowly into dusk.

Kate scooted her arms and legs outward, ballerina-like, and sang "Never Never Land."

With each move, Kate gained more confidence dancing on the air, coordinating her arms and legs in sweeping jetés, grand gestures for the audience in the back row of the Lincoln Middle School auditorium. That was where, in two months' time, she hoped to be starring in the fall production of *Peter Pan*. But for now her performance was for George alone.

Kate and George's duplex sat in a row of such double homes. Most were occupied by two unrelated families, and their facades clearly demonstrated this. Home owners up and down the street painted their front porches in colors that seemed deliberately at odds with their next-door neighbors'. But that was not the case at Kate and George's house. Their front and back porches extended from one side of the duplex to the other in uninterrupted gray.

The back porch sagged slightly as a plump, muscular woman stepped onto it. She wore bright red boots, a yellow cowgirl dress with red stitching, and a white cowgirl hat decorated with a multitude of feathers, mirrors, and sequins.

She was joined by a thin, craggy-faced man. He was dressed all in black, from his boots to his hat. His black shirt, however, had yellow stitching in a pattern similar to the woman's red stitching.

The two stood together, tapping the heels of their boots lightly and surveying the scene in their backyard, not the slightest bit surprised by what they saw. Their granddaughter, Kate, was flying through the air and singing, and their son, George, was huffing and puffing beneath her, keeping her up in the air with some crazy contraption that he had probably just invented.

The woman smiled wide, held up a letter, and let out an earsplitting whoop. The man joined in, whooping along with her, startling George and snapping Kate out of her happy reverie.

George stumbled and fell, catapulting Kate into a wild arc over the garbage cans toward the trunk of the tree. She quickly pulled her legs in and managed to bounce off the tree, unharmed, while George struggled to his feet.

"Georgie!" the woman screamed. "Where's my little genius boy?"

The man beckoned. "Come on, Georgie. Come on over here and look at this letter."

Kate snarled at them. "Ma! Pa! George is attached to me right now."

Ma laughed. "Then get yourself unattached, Georgie, and get over here."

George had by now strained his small body to the limit. "Kate," he panted, "I'll let you down."

"No! I don't want to come down. I want to keep flying."

George looked at his parents and back to Kate in despair. "You heard them. I have to go."

"Fine. Then go. Just let me swing back and forth."

"You can't. You need a ballast."

Kate completed two slow passes over George's head, then told him, "Tie me to the railing."

George carefully undid the rope around his waist and struggled to tie it to the porch railing. Kate was now confined to a small arc, but she stubbornly continued to practice her moves.

Ma waved the letter high. "Georgie! This letter says that you are a genius and that you are invited to go to the genius school, right here in town."

Pa echoed, "Right here in town, son, down at the Whittaker Building. They got a school for geniuses just like you. Did you know that?"

"It's called the Whittaker Magnet School, Pa. We all had to take a test for it."

Ma started to whoop again. "You sure did! And you passed it!"

Pa said, "You're on your way now, son."

George shook his head. "It's sixth grade, Pa. I'm only going into sixth grade."

"Not for long, though. Eh, Georgie boy?"

"Well, I'd say for about a year."

"Then you'll be going to a genius college."

"No, then I'll be going to seventh grade."

George's parents doubled over in laughter at that re-mark, so he turned to check on Kate. Her momentum had wound down almost completely. She drifted slowly in place above the yard. George shook out his arm muscles, took a firm grip, and began to unknot the rope.

The door to the other side of the house opened, and a thin, bony woman with unnaturally bright blond hair walked out onto the porch. Next to her overdressed parents, she looked particularly drab in a shapeless blue housedress.

"Lookit here, June," her mother said, pointing at the letter in the fading light.

June muttered, "I didn't bring my glasses. What does it say?"

"It says your brother, George, passed some big test and he's going to that genius school in town."

June looked at George and told him, "Congratu-lations."

That set George's parents off again. They danced back into the house, making a syncopated sound with their boots.

June looked out at her daughter, Kate, who had by now come to a complete halt. June slowly reached into the housedress and pulled out an identical envelope. "Kate," she said quietly, "you got a letter, too."

Kate's jaw clenched, and her eyes focused in on the envelope.

George's hands froze in their effort to untie the rope. He and June stared up at Kate hanging limply in the fading light, like a fairy who had run out of flying dust.

2

A Mutant Octopus

"Get me down! Get me out of this thing!" Kate snapped at George.

Her mother asked, "What is this about, Kate?"

Kate's arms and legs flailed outward, like an angry marionette. "How am I supposed to know what it's about? I'm hanging in a tree!"

George told his sister, "It means we've both been accepted into the Whittaker Magnet School, June. It's an experimental, college-prep charter school."

"Where is it?" June asked, a quaver in her voice.

"It's in the Whittaker Building downtown. Along the river."

"By-by the library?"

"It *is* the library, June. It's in the same building. The Whittaker Building, that big brown thing."

The rope suddenly slipped through George's hands, burning his palms. Kate's feet dropped to the ground and she pitched forward, breaking her fall with her hands and elbows. She pushed herself up, then clapped the dirt away and struggled to unstrap the bodice.

When she spoke, it was directly to George. "It doesn't matter where it is. We're not going there." She rolled up the Velcro-and-wire outfit and deposited it in his arms. Then a thought occurred to her. "You don't want to go there, do you, Uncle George?"

George hesitated, then smiled. "No. I hear it's all geeks and nerds like me. And, anyway, if I change schools now, I'll miss all those kids who've been picking on me for six years."

Kate looked down into his bespectacled eyes. "Listen: It's okay if you want to go there. I'm just telling you that there's no way on earth I'm going there. I am going to Lincoln Middle School."

George stashed the bodice and the length of rope in a metal utility shed along the fence. Kate watched him suspiciously. "Anyway, I thought you had invented the flying machine for me, for *Peter Pan.*"

"I did."

"Well, Lincoln is the school that's doing *Peter Pan*

this year. If you don't go to Lincoln, you can't be in the Stagecraft Club and we can't use the flying machine. Is that what you want?"

George exhaled loudly. "No, that's not what I want. But maybe the Stagecraft Club isn't my ultimate dream, either."

June spoke up. "You should do what you want to do, George."

Kate shot an angry look at June. Most of Kate's looks at June were angry ones. Kate bitterly resented that her mother seemed fearful of everyone and everything; that she was unable to look people in the eye; that she always left it up to Kate to solve their problems. For this last reason, specifically, Kate no longer addressed her as "Mom." Instead, like everyone else, she called her "June."

Kate turned away so that June disappeared from her field of vision. She told George as reasonably as she could, "That's right. You should do what you want to do. And you don't have to run the flying machine, you know. Maybe somebody heavier, in fact, would give me more ballast. You could actually be *in* the play. You could be one of the Lost Boys or one of the Darling children. You could be the small one. His name is Michael."

George nodded and answered with mock gratitude, "Yes. Yes. You're right. It is very important to me, upon entering middle school, to demonstrate to everyone exactly how small I am."

"That's not my point, Uncle George."

"I know. Listen, Kate, let's not disturb the order of the universe. You be the star. I'll be backstage."

June cleared her throat and brought up another topic. "Kate, why don't you let somebody else be the lead in the play? That's a lot of rehearsal time. Your homework will suffer. Why don't you be one of the Darling children? Or an Indian?"

"An Indian?" Kate scoffed. "That's a chorus girl part. I've done my time in the chorus, two long years. No way. That lead role is mine."

June was about to say something else when the back door banged open and Kate's grandparents emerged. Her grandfather carried a portable CD player. Her grandmother's voice boomed out: "Who's ready for some clogging?"

June protested quietly, hopelessly, "Ma, Pa, not right now, please. We're discussing something imp—"

The sound of banjo and fiddle music blared from the little machine. Kate's grandmother and grandfather started to hop and shift their boots forward and back, like Russian dancers. Ma shouted over the music, "Georgie! You eat dinner with your sister tonight. We're having the Tri-County Cloggers over for some practicin'. We got that big clog-off comin' up over in Anchorsville."

George replied as loudly as he could, "Ma! Pa! This porch was built eighty-seven years ago, with substandard timbers, by striking miners. You could go crashing right through the wood!"

"Ah, Georgie, we've been cloggin' in this house since before you were born! It ain't come crashing down yet."

Kate's grandparents switched from their warm-up routine to a choreographed, noisy dance number, clapping the cleated heels of their boots down onto the trembling porch in time to the bluegrass music.

Kate and June ducked inside the house, followed by George. Kate went directly to the refrigerator, opened it, and peered in. She shouted to June, "You know, Molly's coming over."

June closed the screen door and the wooden door to muffle the clogging. "No, I didn't know that. For dinner?"

"Yes."

"I wish you had told me this before, Kate."

"Molly comes over every week. Do I have to tell you about it every week?"

"Yes. That would be nice."

"Sorry. But it would be nice if I could go to her house sometimes, too."

June opened the pantry and removed a box of spaghetti. "You can go to her house. You have gone to her house. I've driven you there."

"Twice, June. Twice in two years. Once in sixth grade; once in seventh grade. And then only until nine o'clock. First graders have better curfews than that."

June filled a pot with water. "Please, Kate, we've been over this too many times."

"I can't sleep over at anyone's house, and I'm not allowed to know why. And I'm not supposed to be the star of the play or to make a spectacle of myself in any way, but I'm not allowed to know why."

June exhaled. "Should I defrost some meatballs?"

Kate gritted her teeth and growled. Then she stomped up the kitchen stairs in rhythm with the back-porch clogging.

George answered the question. "I could go for some meatballs, June."

The kitchen stairs rose to a broad landing, where they met the front parlor stairs. Kate's computer was set up on the landing in a rickety pressboard hutch.

Kate slid into the chair and logged on. The obsolete computer struggled to download Kate's e-mail, clicking and whirring through a maddening series of pop-ups, asking her off-the-wall questions, one after another, like a brain-damaged reporter.

By the time Kate determined that she had no mail, George had appeared on the landing.

Kate snapped, "Have I mentioned that I hate this machine?"

"I don't think you've said it yet today."

"Do you want to check your mail while I have it up?"

"No. I want to get into the school district website."

"What for?"

George shrugged.

Kate stood up to let him have the chair. "I told you before, you can go to that school if you want to. Just leave me out of it."

George sat down and worked the mouse. "I just want to see the website." He quickly accessed the King's County School Districts website and clicked through it until he and Kate were staring at a very curious map.

George pointed. "Look at this, Kate. Most school districts look like little rectangles or trapezoids. Lincoln Middle School's, for example, forms a nearly perfect parallelogram from the county line to the boundary line of its neighboring school district."

Kate nodded tentatively, unsure of her geometric terminology.

"Now look at this thing." George put his finger on the screen and traced a narrow looping shape. "This is the Whittaker Magnet School District. It's not a definable shape at all. It's a mutant octopus. Look, it runs along the river and then reaches out, like a tentacle, into every other school district."

Kate followed her uncle's small finger over the screen. "Where's our house?"

His finger moved to the lower right. "Here."

"We're not in that octopus thing?"

"No. We're solidly in the Lincoln Middle School District."

"So that's it, then. For me, it's case closed."

"But what about the letter from Whittaker?"

"I'll say, 'No thanks.' I've been at Lincoln for two years, Uncle George. All of my friends are there. I've worked hard for the lead in the play. It's a *no-duh*. I am going to Lincoln."

George studied the screen for another moment. "How can this be? The lines don't run along streets, or parks, or natural boundaries. It's like this district shoots its lines out to individual houses, like it's lassoing them in with a rope."

George paused, tapping lightly against his temple. "Sorry. That's redundant. If you're lassoing something, you're already using a rope. You don't need to add 'with a rope.'"

Kate tried to change the subject. "Is dinner ready?"

"It's almost like if they find a street with a smart kid on it, it becomes part of their district. But if the next street has a dumb kid on it, it doesn't."

"Yeah, whatever." Kate's head turned at the soft *dingdong* of the doorbell. "That'll be Molly."

3

A Father without an Address

Kate tramped down the front stairs, through the parlor, and into the vestibule.

She opened the door to a short girl with black hair, which, although completely natural, fell in such unnaturally straight lines that it looked like a wig. The girl was accompanied by an even shorter old lady with gray hair, tied up primly in a bun. Kate said, "Hi, Molly. Hi, Mrs. Brennan."

Molly reached up to hug Kate. Then she squeezed in past Kate and turned back toward her grandmother. "Good-bye, Grandmom."

But Mrs. Brennan was not so easily dismissed. She stared Molly down. Then she redirected her gaze to Kate and asked, "How are you, dear?"

"I'm fine, Mrs. Brennan."

"Looking forward to starting school?"

"Oh, yes, ma'am. I can't wait."

"That's nice to hear." She looked past Kate's shoulder and asked, "Is your mother here?"

Kate blinked. "Yes, of course. She's making dinner."

Molly said, "Ms. Melvil will be driving me home, Grandmom."

"Who, dear?"

Molly exchanged a look with Kate. "Kate's mom."

Mrs. Brennan's cheeks flushed. "Oh. I'm sorry. I thought your mother was"—she gestured at Kate—"Peters."

Kate shook her head. "Nope. I'm the only Peters now." She tried to sound matter-of-fact. "Well, just my dad and me. The rest of them are Melvils."

"I see. I'm sorry, Kate. It's not my business to pry." She continued anyway. "But wasn't your mother named Peters, too?"

"She was. Until the divorce became final and she went back to her maiden name."

Molly said, "Anything else, Grandmom, like Kate's blood type?"

Mrs. Brennan stared her down again. "Don't be snippy, Molly. I need to know how to address Kate's mother properly when I see her."

Molly answered with practiced contrition, "Sorry."

Mrs. Brennan looked at Kate. "I'll be going now. Tell Ms. Melvil I said hello."

Kate closed the door. Molly told her, "Sorry she was so nosy."

"That's no problem, no problem at all. I really like your grandmother." Kate led the way through the parlor. The floors and walls were now shaking perceptibly. Kate added, "At least your grandmother doesn't clog."

They climbed up to the landing just as George was clicking out of the website. He asked Kate, "Do you want me to leave the map? So you can show Molly?"

Kate's face lit up with a fake, perky smile. "Molly? Do you have any interest in seeing a map of the King's County School Districts?"

"Do I look like a hopeless geek?"

"I'll take that as a no."

Yet Molly did lean forward and squint at the screen. "You're looking at the Whittaker Magnet School site." She spoke like someone familiar with the topic. "That is a very weird, ultra-geeky school. It's down in the basement of the county library." She bulged her eyeballs at Kate. "Seriously, it's in the basement, like some indoor mushroom farm. They say the kids there never see the sun."

Kate poked George. "Sounds great, eh, Uncle George?"

"I never said it sounded great."

"I haven't heard you say it sounds horrible. Which it does. It sounds like the most horrible school in the U.S.A."

"Actually, it has a reputation as one of the best schools in the U.S.A."

"See! You *do* want to go there. Admit it!" Kate grabbed him, playfully but firmly, by the earlobe.

George winced. "I'm just saying that if we had to go to some other school, there are worse places to go."

Kate demanded, "Name one." When George hesitated, she announced triumphantly, "Aha!" and finally let go of his ear.

Molly told Kate, "My grandmother says the Whittaker Magnet School gets written about in a lot of magazines."

"Like what? *Geek World*?"

"No. Like education magazines."

"Same thing."

George cupped one hand over his reddened earlobe. "The Whittaker School is modeled on a Japanese *juku*, an after-school program where kids go to cram for exams. Except at Whittaker, they cram all day long, too."

Kate started into her bedroom. "Like she said, it's a very geeky school."

The girls closed the door on George and his web

search just as he spotted a curious hypertext link: "See also: *Haunted Buildings of the Midwest.*" George scratched his chin thoughtfully. Then he looked over both shoulders, to ensure that he was alone, and clicked on it.

"We have our first band meeting scheduled already," Molly said. "Can you believe it? The first day of school? We're supposed to get the sheet music for *Peter Pan.*"

Kate flopped back on her bed. "Have you heard anything about auditions?"

"Nothing official. But Lisette told me that Derek Arroyo is definitely trying out."

Kate let her tongue drop down like she was dying of thirst. "He is *so* hot. It'd be almost worth it to play a girl so I could kiss him onstage."

"Lisette said he wants to be Captain Hook."

"Captain Hook? Does he kiss anybody? Like, Tiger Lily?"

Molly frowned. "No. I don't think Captain Hook kisses anybody. I think he's gay. At least that guy who played him on TV was gay. I think all of the pirates were gay."

"Then why would Derek try out for it?"

"You don't have to be gay to play Captain Hook. I'm just saying that the guy who played him on TV was."

"Great. The guy I love wants to play a gay pirate. Where does that leave me? Are there any straight guys in it?"

Molly scratched her head. "Well, yes and no. The boys are, like, John and Michael Darling. But what kind of last name is that? And they wear these gay pajamas all the time, you know? Like ladies' pajamas? Except they wear black top hats with them. Nice touch."

"How about Peter Pan?"

"He's not gay, although he was played by a lady on TV. But he's supposed to be a guy. Except in that scene where he's pretending to be a lady. It's all very compli-cated. Think about it, Kate. Let's say Derek plays Cap-tain Hook, and you have to kiss him. You'll be a girl pretending to be a guy, dressed as a lady, kissing a guy who may be gay. It'll ruin any relationship you two could ever have." Molly fell silent. She raised her hand to the wall to feel it vibrate. "You may as well go to that geek school."

"No way. I don't care if I have to kiss Nana the dog. I'm going to Lincoln."

"Well, what about your father? Couldn't you call him? Maybe there's something he could do."

Kate's eyes drifted to a framed photo of her father in his wedding-day tuxedo. He looked tall, handsome, and confident. "He doesn't have a phone number."

"No? Well, then, maybe you could write to him?"

Kate pressed her lips together. "He doesn't have an address."

"How can he not have an address? Everybody has an address! What, is he one of those homeless guys who lives in a big cardboard box? You know, like refrigerators come in?"

Kate's eyes flashed angrily. "He doesn't live in a cardboard box. And he's not homeless. He's a teacher."

"You never told me he was a teacher."

"You never asked."

The girls fell silent until Molly explained, "I didn't want to sound like my grandmother. I knew your parents were divorced, but I didn't want to pump you for information. I figured you would tell me when you wanted to."

"And I've been waiting for you to ask. You should have asked."

Molly placed her hand on the vibrating wall for a long minute. Then she tried, "So, your father's a teacher?"

Kate answered evenly. "He is. He is a teacher."

"What's the name of his school?"

Kate pointed to a brochure wedged into the side of her mirror. "It's not a school. It's a company that runs foreign schools. The American Schools Abroad

Program. I write letters to that company's address, and they forward them to him wherever he is."

"Like where?"

"I never know. It could be, like, Korea, Japan, Thailand." She added, "I haven't heard back in a while." Kate pointed to the photo. "I look totally like my father." Then she frowned and looked at the door. "I don't look a thing like June."

4

Agoraphobia

Dinner was spaghetti, meatballs, and garlic bread. June sat silently among the children as they talked. The conversation, inevitably, turned to the Whittaker Magnet School.

"My grandmother used to work there," Molly said, "back when it was only a library. She still goes to County Commission meetings at the Whittaker Building."

June looked up.

Molly went on, "I don't know if you've heard the stories, but lots of people say the Whittaker Building is haunted."

June looked back down.

"The building itself has a bloody history," George said. "Lots of people have died there."

Kate turned to June. "So you want me to leave Lincoln, where all my friends are and where I'm set to star in *Peter Pan*, to go and be killed in a haunted library? Is that the plan?"

June swallowed hard and answered, "No, Kate, that is not the plan. But as far as that play goes, you're not certain to get the lead part. It could go to someone else. Right, Molly?"

Kate snorted. "Who? No one else will even audition for the lead. Everybody knows I'm perfect for Peter Pan."

Molly mumbled, "LoriBeth Sommers will."

"LoriBeth Sommers! Please, I'm trying to eat. She can't dance. She can't act. All she can do is stand next to the flagpole and sing the national anthem. So what? She hits her one high note; then all the guys yell, 'Play ball!'"

If Kate expected enthusiastic agreement from George and Molly, she did not get it. Instead, George informed the group, "I learned this, too: The Whittaker Magnet School is ranked number one in the United States in standardized testing."

Kate reached over and pinched his cheek. "Great. Have fun there. Alone. I will be at Lincoln Middle School."

Molly asked, "Have you ever seen the place?"

"No," Kate said, but then turned to June. "Have I?"

June seemed offended. "Of course you have. Many times. I used to take you there when you were little."

She was offended further when Kate replied, "Oh? Was that back when you took me places?"

"That's not fair, Kate. I drive you everywhere you want to go."

"Okay. Let's be fair." Kate leaned forward. "Take me there now. I want to see this haunted building."

"It's-it's Sunday night, Kate. I'm sure it's not open."

At that moment, a familiar vibration began in the floors and walls, three times as strong as before, as all six members of the Tri-County Cloggers started practice.

Kate offered a compromise. "Let's just drive over and look at it from the outside. If I ever went there, I must have been two years old. I sure don't remember."

Molly was enthusiastic about the idea. "It's cool looking. Like Frankenstein's castle."

"Do you mean Baron von Frankenstein?" George asked. "Or Frankenstein's monster?"

"Uh, the monster."

"Frankenstein's monster didn't have a castle. He lived in a shack in the woods. With a blind guy."

"He did? What, was he like his guide dog?"

"No. He was his friend. The blind guy didn't know the monster looked like a monster."

"Uncle George!" Kate snapped. "Does it really matter?"

George backed off. "No. I guess not."

"The point is that Molly thinks it looks like a scary castle, okay?"

"Okay."

June stood up. She steadied herself with both hands on the table, then stammered, "How about if we make ice-cream sundaes and sit on the front porch for a change? The clogging won't sound so loud there."

Kate stretched her neck, trying to make eye contact. "We're leaving the house, June. That's what normal people do. They leave their houses and they do things."

June exhaled. "Then I have to go to the bathroom." She hurried out of the kitchen.

"Maybe this is a bad idea," Molly whispered. "If you really want to go, my grandmother could drive us there tomorrow."

"No. June can drive us there now. There is no reason why she can't." Then, in a sudden moment of reflection, she turned to her uncle. "Is there, Uncle George?"

George swallowed a final bite of garlic bread. "There may be. June may suffer from a mild form of agoraphobia. That's from the Greek. Literally, it means 'fear of the marketplace.' It means you are terrified to go out in public."

"If my hair looked that bad," Kate muttered, "I'd be afraid to go out in public, too."

June emerged from the bathroom, pale and sweating.

Kate told her, "Okay. We don't have to go, June, if you're not up to it."

"Nonsense. You kids want to go, so we're going."

George scrutinized her face. "Are you sure, June?"

"I'm positive."

"It's okay if you're afraid to go. Lots of people are afraid of movie monsters, and ghost stories, and haunted buildings."

June opened the door and started out. "I'm not afraid. I just had to go to the bathroom."

George continued. "But, really, there are no such things as monsters, and ghosts, and haunted buildings."

June laughed, a queer, brittle laugh. She said, "I know that. Everybody knows that. Anybody who doesn't know that is crazy."

5

A Fearsome Building

June clung to the steering wheel of her Geo Metro like she was lashed to a boat wheel in a storm. George sat in the front seat, occasionally flashing a worried sideways glance at his sister, while the girls gossiped in whispers in the back.

As they approached downtown, George noticed a billboard and called out, "Hey, Kate! Look. It's the guy from the aquatic park!"

Kate looked out at the billboard. It showed a heavy-set man holding up his thumb beneath the message: "Now *your family* can live in the #1 school district in America! Reserve your homesite in Bud Wright's Ivy League Estates today!"

"He's talking about the Whittaker School District," George said. "Do you know that home values near the Whittaker Magnet School have tripled in the past five years?"

Kate replied, "Like I care."

The little car rounded a bend and struggled up a steep hill to its destination.

Kate and George were both taken aback by their first sight of the Whittaker Building. It was a truly massive stone structure—eight stories high and a full city block wide. It dominated the puny buildings around it like a fearsome giant.

June started to pull over, but Kate urged her along. "Keep going, June. We want to get a close look at this place!"

"Can't we see it from here?"

"No, we can't. Drive right up to it."

June silently obeyed.

Kate pressed her face against the window and stared up. "I think it looks creepy. Like Dracula's castle." She directed a withering glance at her uncle. "Shut up."

"Dracula *did* have a castle," George assured her. "Of course, his name wasn't really Dracula."

"Shut up."

"It was Count Vlad."

The little car crept closer as George continued.

"They may as well make a horror movie about this place, so many people have died here."

"How many?" Kate asked.

"Dozens. Going back almost a hundred years. In all kinds of ways, too: electrocuted in the basement, run over at the loading dock, dismembered by power saws. More people have died in that building than in the state penitentiary at Milton, where they keep the electric chair."

"Sounds like a real nice place to go to school."

The building had a large drop-off area in front, curving off the main street like a crescent moon. Kate directed June to turn into the drive and pull over.

A large poster dominated the entranceway. It showed a girl and a boy above the caption, "Story Time at the Whittaker Library Changed Our Lives!" The girl was seated. She wore a frilly white dress and had her hair done up in long blond ringlets. The boy was standing. He was short and skinny, dressed in tan slacks, a blue blazer, and a purple-and-yellow striped tie.

Kate leaned out of the car window and stared at the poster with distaste. "They can't be serious. Is this a joke?" She was soon distracted, though, by a bright red flash from high above. A light was emanating from a room at the top of the building. Kate strained forward to see. She cried out, "Look! Somebody's up there! Maybe this is the haunted part."

George and Molly leaned out to see, too.

A windowpane on the eighth floor was glowing an eerie, pulsating red. Intermittently, a shower of hot sparks bounced off the glass.

Kate whispered, "What's going on up there?"

"It looks like the spray from a power saw," George said. "Someone must be sawing metal."

"At this hour?"

They watched the flickering window, puzzling over it silently, until a shadowy figure appeared. Kate saw it first and screamed. George and Molly screamed right after. The figure—thin, black, and tall—seemed to be staring down at them.

"What is that?" Kate cried. "A woman?"

George could not speak, but Molly answered, "Yeah. A crazy woman. Maybe, like, a power-saw killer!"

The figure vanished as rapidly as it had appeared, leaving the three children staring at the darkened window for another half minute.

"Okay," Kate finally announced. "I think we've seen enough of Uncle George's dream school."

June didn't respond, but she did manage to get the car turned around and moving back toward home.

They drove for several minutes in silence until the pull of the Whittaker Building finally faded away. By the time they got back to the house, Kate and Molly were once again laughing and joking. They called

Lisette and carried on a merry three-way conversation about hot guys at Lincoln. But Kate's merry thoughts kept getting interrupted by dark ones. Kate ignored the thoughts as best she could, but they kept beeping into her head like messages from a shadowy caller, phoning with a singular purpose from a darkened upstairs room.

6

The Whittakers

On Tuesday, at 10:30 A.M., June and the children climbed into the Geo Metro and followed Ma and Pa's VW camper downtown. Kate was sullen, George was nervous, and June was as terrified as she had been two nights before.

They pulled into a parking space on the River Road. June locked the car, took a deep breath, and followed Kate and George up the steep hill to the Whittaker Building.

No one spoke until George spotted an inscription over the glass double doors. "Hey! I didn't see that the other night. It's in Latin. *Id pen—*"

Kate cut him off angrily. "This can't be happening.

This is a nightmare, right? We'll wake up in an hour and get ready to go to Lincoln."

Ma and Pa stood waiting outside the entrance. Kate's anger quickly turned to mortification when, upon seeing them, her grandparents broke into a sidewalk clogging routine. Kate hissed, "Ma! Pa! Cut it out! People can *see* you out here."

Her grandparents whooped and laughed, but they did stop clogging.

Then Kate, George, Ma, Pa, and June entered through the glass doors. They walked past a tile mosaic full of fiery colors and scenes of a small, bearded man writhing in agony. The mosaic was followed by two portraits of men with large heads. Brass nameplates identified them as CORNELL WHITTAKER I and CORNELL WHITTAKER II. The plate below a third, smaller portrait identified its subject as DR. J. KENDALL AUSTIN.

The entranceway opened onto a cavernous lobby. Kate looked up into a vast center space, at the top of which was an ornately painted ceiling depicting scenes from American history. The ceiling had a ragged square hole cut into its center, through which unpainted plywood boards protruded. Ringing the empty expanse were seven floors of metal shelves filled with books.

Kate turned her attention back to the lobby. It was filled with bookshelves and display tables. A series of small, functional offices ran along the wall to her right. The lobby was illuminated by four chandeliers that plunged on steel chains all the way from the ceiling eight flights above to the second-floor landing.

Aside from the entranceway behind her, Kate noted six means of escape—an elevator in each corner and two stairwells, centered on the walls to her left and right. Then she became aware of other children milling around her and of her own family arriving at a desk designated NEW STUDENT REGISTRATION.

Behind that desk sat a fearsome-looking woman. A mink stole barely stretched across her broad shoulders, and within her large head, her jaws seemed to be continually grinding. A turban of thick blond hair added nearly a foot to her height. Her face bore a strong resemblance to the portraits of Cornell Whittaker I and II. Next to her, in a white dress, sat a blond girl with the same harsh features.

George whispered, "That's the girl on the poster."

The woman addressed George in a deep voice. "Congratulations on your selection to the Whittaker Magnet School. I am Cornelia Whittaker-Austin. Yes, I am one of *the* Whittakers. Do you have your official letter of acceptance?"

Ma pulled out the letter, waved it in the air, and whooped mightily.

Cornelia Whittaker-Austin hissed, "Keep your voice down! This is a library! You are to conduct yourself with dignity within its walls!"

Ma froze in midwhoop. "Sorry."

Pa added, "We're real sorry, ma'am."

Cornelia Whittaker-Austin took the letter and demanded, "Have you made an appointment for your personal assessment with Dr. Austin?" Ma just stared at her dully, so she answered for her. "No? May I ask why not? You were clearly directed to do so in your letter."

"Well, Georgie's the genius in our family. Not us."

Cornelia pushed back her chair, planted her elbows on the table, and stood up. George watched her rise, and rise, and rise until she blocked everything behind her from view. Then, seemingly from nowhere, she turned on a bright smile. "You are in luck! We have an opening later, after Dr. Austin returns from Washington, D.C. You may come here at eight o'clock."

Ma laughed noisily. "Eight o'clock!" Then she lowered her voice. "You mean tonight?"

Cornelia looked down at her. "That is what I mean. Bring a checkbook or a major credit card."

"That doctor of yours, he must be a hard worker."

"We Whittakers are all hard workers. That is how we built this county. My husband is made of the same stuff."

Cornelia swiveled and pointed to a table piled high with copies of a book. "I have written this acclaimed profile of my grandfather and my father. It's titled *The Whittakers of King's County: A Biographical History.* It is required reading at the school. You may purchase your copy now for twenty dollars." She held out her enormous hand and waited.

Ma gave Pa a meaningful look. Pa smiled nervously, reached into his wallet, and handed over a twenty-dollar bill. Cornelia in turn handed him a copy of *The Whittakers of King's County: A Biographical History.*

Pa stared at the alternating purple and yellow letters of the title. He dared to ask, "Now, who were they again?"

Cornelia's jaw ground silently for several seconds. She finally explained, through clenched teeth, "They were the founding family of King's County. Your local royal family, if you will. They donated this great library to you, the common people."

George looked up at her. "I just read an Internet article about the Whittaker family."

Cornelia's smile returned. "Did you? How nice."

"It said the library wasn't really donated. It said the county got stuck with it in a bankruptcy foreclosure."

Cornelia's smile vanished. "It was wrong."

"But the Internet article—"

"The Internet is a very *un*reliable source for anything except pornography." Cornelia looked George up and down. "You're very small, aren't you? Unhealthily so. We'll have to get you started on protein shakes right away."

Ma interjected, "Let's not forget about little Kate, ma'am. Our granddaughter is here, too. Kate Peters." Cornelia looked at Kate as Ma added, "She's a singer. A real good one."

Cornelia returned to her seat. She smiled at the girl in the white dress, and they exchanged a smug look. "Is she? Where has she sung? In New York, perhaps?"

Ma laughed. "No. In the backyard."

"Oh? Yes, of course. In the backyard." Cornelia picked up a list and checked it. "Has she been accepted into Whittaker, too?"

Kate had a desperate flash of hope. She thought, *Please, please, no.*

But Cornelia found her name. "Ah, I see. She lives at the same address as George Melvil."

Ma confirmed, "She sure does!"

"So that's how she got in." Cornelia looked Kate up and down. "How very fortunate for you. Like a poor ragamuffin girl in a fairy tale who has no hopes and no future, but who suddenly gets a magical opportunity." Cornelia pointed to the next child in line as she told Kate, "Do try to make the most of it."

7

A History Lesson

A skinny boy walked into the lobby from the glass elevator closest to the entrance, designated Elevator #1. He was dressed in tan slacks with a blue blazer and a purple-and-yellow striped tie.

"That's the other kid on the poster," George whispered.

The boy announced, "I am ready now, Mother."

Cornelia smiled at him. Then she looked over at Kate and George and scowled. "Remember: Dr. Austin will see you two tonight at eight o'clock. Now take your seats with the other new students. It's time to start."

Kate and George joined the flow of children and parents into a cordoned-off area of the lobby. Approximately one hundred children and parents, all well dressed and enthusiastic, hurried to find seats. Kate and George took two chairs up front, letting Ma, Pa, and June fend for themselves.

Cornelia stood behind the podium, and the girl and boy from the poster sat behind her. As soon as the noise subsided, Cornelia addressed the crowd. "Let me begin this meeting by saying congratulations to all of you. You have been identified as the academic elite of King's County. The crème de la crème. You must forgive my husband, Dr. Austin, for not being here to greet you personally. He is in Washington, D.C., meeting with representatives of the United States Department of Education." She paused, which compelled some members of the audience to applaud weakly.

"You may applaud if you wish. I am used to being interrupted by applause. Often. But in order to communicate more effectively, I find it useful to have a signal that indicates when applause is appropriate and when it is not. This is the signal." She turned the palm of one large hand over and flurried her fingers in a "Gimme, gimme" gesture.

Kate looked around for Ma and muttered, "I guess a flashing APPLAUSE sign in the library would be too undignified."

Cornelia continued. "It is my great pleasure to introduce the president of the Whittaker Magnet School student body—who also happens to be my son—Cornell Whittaker Austin. We all call him 'Whit.' Whit is, at this moment, being actively recruited by representatives of Princeton and Harvard."

Kate muttered to George, "For what? The varsity geek team?" But George would not laugh. Or smile. He stared straight ahead.

"Whit is also the leading science student in the school and the inventor of an astonishingly lethal new superweapon that would make his grandfather and great-grandfather proud. Ladies and gentlemen, boys and girls, with no further ado, let me present my son, and Dr. Austin's son, Cornell Whittaker 'Whit' Austin!"

Cornelia gave them the applause signal.

Whit stepped up to the podium. His face showed no emotion. His eyes betrayed none of the intelligence so recently ascribed to him. He began to speak in a clipped, precise voice. "It is my duty to inform you today about the great library in which we sit and the great family that built it.

"Schoolchildren learn at an early age about the man President Ulysses S. Grant called 'the Thomas Edison of death.' They learn how Cornell Whittaker Number One took rusting Civil War cannons, melted them down, and turned them into modern weapons of mass destruction, including the first cluster bombs and the first aerodynamic nerve-gas canisters."

Kate leaned toward George. "I wonder if that's how

they ask to go to the bathroom here: 'I have to go Cornell Whittaker Number One' or 'I have to go Cornell Whittaker Number Two.'"

George ignored her. But Whit did not. He suddenly stopped, narrowed his eyes, and studied her for a long moment, making Kate fidget in her chair.

Whit then resumed. He pointed behind the audience to the entranceway. "A brief history lesson: Andrew Carnegie, the nineteenth-century robber baron, near the end of his life, decided to build a series of public libraries as monuments to himself."

Here Whit looked up, apparently reciting by heart. "When Andrew Carnegie came to King's County, waving his money around and expecting the people to grovel before him, Cornell Whittaker Number One told him that we neither wanted nor needed his money to build a library. Indeed, we would build our own library and, I quote, '*We* will pay for it.' These words are now inscribed in Latin above the library entrance, '*Id pendemus.*' We will pay for it."

Whit left the podium and strolled toward the entranceway, forcing the audience members to turn with him. "My great-grandfather spent his own fortune constructing the Whittaker Library, the great building in which you now sit. He vowed that it would be twice the size of any library Carnegie had ever constructed. It would contain books on every subject known to man *except* the subject of Andrew Carnegie. Finally, it would contain a four-thousand-foot mosaic, the mosaic that you passed today on the way in here, depicting Andrew Carnegie burning in hell." Whit looked at his mother, and the audience followed his gaze. She was blinking back tears.

"My great-grandfather donated his magnificent library to King's County. The county changed the name to the King's County Library Building, but to young and old, rich and poor alike, it will always be the Whittaker Library Building."

Cornelia leaped to her feet and gave the applause signal with both hands. Whit bowed slightly, then sauntered back to his seat. He looked at Kate and cocked up one eyebrow.

Kate looked away, appalled. She whispered to George, "Can you believe this kid?"

Cornelia returned to the podium. She informed the audience, "It is genetically astounding that the same family should be blessed with both a spellbinding orator and a gifted dramatic actress. Unfortunately, you will not have the privilege of watching Heidi Whittaker Austin in one of her acclaimed Story Time performances today. But many who have seen them swear that they are as good as anything on Broadway, in New York."

George finally spoke. "Isn't that redundant?"

But Kate was no longer listening. She became aware, in her peripheral vision, of anonymous teachers scurrying around. Kate thought she glimpsed her music teacher from Lincoln among them, but she dismissed that thought as impossible.

Cornelia Whittaker-Austin finally finished speaking, gave the applause signal, and adjourned the meeting.

As soon as they got back to the house, Kate dragged George to the computer hutch and commanded, "Pull up that school district website again."

George accessed the site without difficulty and soon had an updated version of the district map. He was not at all surprised by what he saw, but Kate was shocked. The brave face she had put on at the library crumbled as she stared at the computer screen.

The Whittaker Magnet School's boundaries had changed. The octopus had grown. And their house— indeed, their entire block—had been swallowed by its longest black tentacle.

8

The Blue Shower Curtain

Eight hours later, at 7:45 P.M., Kate, George, Ma, Pa, and June returned to the Whittaker Building. They again traveled in two cars. June parked in the same spot by the river. Ma and Pa, however, parked in the library driveway.

As soon as she saw the VW camper, Kate rounded on June. "Please explain to us, June, why we are walking up Mount Everest again when there are parking spaces right in front of the door?"

"I couldn't have known that, Kate. I knew we could park by the river because we did it this morning."

"Yes. Yes, so let's do it again tonight. Even though there are no cars around for blocks."

George was not listening to their squabbling. He was entranced by the building looming before him. He spoke with a touch of fear. "Check out the library now."

Kate and June looked up. As the sun set, the Whittaker Building took on a dark aspect, as if it had been carved out of one huge rock from the netherworld. June recoiled visibly and stopped walking.

George stopped with her. He whispered, "It's only a building, June. Admittedly, it's a scary one, but it's only a building."

But June would not move. George turned to Kate. "Please, Kate. We can't do this without you."

Kate, who had stopped five feet ahead of them, muttered, "There's a news flash." She walked back and told her mother, "Come on, June. Like he said, it's just a building. It's not like it's a... Greek marketplace or anything."

George gave her a piercing look.

Kate added, "And we'll all be together, the whole time. You'll be perfectly safe in there."

June breathed deeply and began walking again.

Kate led them to the driveway, where they picked up Ma and Pa. Then she led the entire group inside, through the glass doors, past the fiery mosaic, and into the empty lobby.

They bunched into Elevator #1. Kate pressed the button for the top floor and silently read the sign, 8TH

FLOOR—PRIVATE OFFICES. They rode up quietly, watching through the elevator's glass walls as the floors passed. When the doors opened, the group stepped out into a wide carpeted hallway. To her right, Kate saw a bright light pouring out of a doorway and heard a high-pitched electrical sound.

Kate glanced at her family. Ma and Pa wore clueless grins. George now seemed as frightened as June. He and his big sister were clinging to each other like two-year-olds.

So Kate led the way to the open door, leaned forward, and peered inside. There, sitting on a high stool, was Dr. J. Kendall Austin. Or his head, anyway, just like in the portrait hanging in the lobby—a large head with neatly groomed gray hair and a neatly trimmed gray beard. But the rest of Dr. Austin was gone, hidden beneath a blue shower curtain that extended all the way to the floor.

Around him fluttered Cornelia Whittaker-Austin, still wearing her mink stole. She was picking away at his beard with a buzzing electric trimmer.

Kate waited a moment and then cleared her throat with a timid sound, a sound many decibels below that of the trimmer. When she got no response, she leaned farther into the room, into the man's peripheral vision, and tried to get him to notice her.

He noticed her.

Dr. Austin let out a startled shriek and snapped his head left, causing the trimmer to plow through his beard like a runaway lawn mower. Cornelia shrieked, too, and pulled madly at the electrical cord until it popped out of the wall socket.

Kate was still frozen in the doorway when the man gained control of himself enough to bark at her, "How dare you sneak in here! Who are you? What do you want?"

Kate stared, petrified, at the disembodied head above the shower curtain. Then she took two small steps forward, like Dorothy advancing toward the great and powerful Oz. She managed to say, "Eight o'clock appointment."

Dr. Austin regarded her coldly.

Cornelia, who had been brandishing the unplugged trimmer like a stun gun, now lowered it. She looked Kate up and down and demanded, "Where are the others?"

Kate turned and saw, to her dismay, that she was alone in the room. She held up one finger in a "Wait a minute" gesture, stepped back out into the hallway, and hissed, "Get in here! All of you!"

George moved cautiously into the room. Ma and Pa followed. June was too frightened to move at first, but she was also too frightened to remain outside. She finally sidled in, but just barely, and hung back by the door.

Dr. Austin made a hand gesture that created a rolling billow under the plastic curtain. "Come closer. I am, of course, Dr. Austin. I believe you have already met my wife, Mrs. Cornelia Whittaker-Austin."

Cornelia told him, "This is the little boy who made the perfect score on the entrance exam."

Dr. Austin's gray eyebrows arched ceilingward. He smiled broadly, revealing a row of square white teeth. "You're George Melvil?" He evidently raised one finger and pointed at George, because a narrow blue fin emerged from the shower curtain, like the sudden appearance of a shark.

"I have been looking forward to meeting you, George Melvil! You are the kind of student that the Whittaker Magnet School was created for. A single superlative student can make a great difference. Am I right?"

Cornelia answered for George. "Of course you're right."

"The Whittaker Magnet School first came to national attention because of a single superlative student, Ashley-Nicole Singer-Wright." He turned to Cornelia. "Show them the photo."

Cornelia, with some reluctance, took down a photo

from a bookcase shelf and handed it to her husband. He gripped it through the blue plastic and explained admiringly, "This shows Ashley-Nicole posing with my father-in-law, Cornell Whittaker Number Two."

He turned the frame to reveal a little girl dressed in a plaid skirt and white blouse with her blond hair tied back in a ponytail. She was accepting a plaque from a very large, round-shouldered old man in a black suit.

"I was the first to identify her genius. I administered her first standardized test, the PSAT." A dreamy look appeared on his face. "She was, of course, off the chart."

Dr. Austin handed the photo back to his wife. Then he pushed his arms straight out, causing the blue shower curtain to fall in a crumpled semicircle at his feet.

Kate and the others could now see the rest of his body, clad in a natty cream-colored suit and seated atop a high stool. He said, "Now we have you, George Melvil," and he slid down from the stool to the floor.

Kate's gaze slid down with him. Down and down. She tried not to look surprised, but he wasn't even five feet tall. Barely taller than George! Yet poise and self-confidence radiated from him at such high wattage that he managed to be just as intimidating as his giant wife.

Cornelia picked up the shower curtain and shook it out. Then she pulled a Dustbuster vacuum from its wall socket, switched it on, and started to clean up.

Dr. Austin snapped the lapels of his suit and checked himself in a wall mirror. He gingerly touched the sparse patch where the razor had slipped. Then he turned his attention back to George, shouting over the sucking noise of the vacuum, "Are these people your parents?"

George nodded. Ma and Pa stepped forward with big grins on their faces.

Dr. Austin read the message on their matching T-shirts. "Now what does this mean, 'Un-clog your arteries'?"

Ma cackled. "It's a joke. We're cloggers. And cloggin's good for your arteries."

Dr. Austin spoke as if thinking aloud, "You clog. That means that you take part in some sort of...folk-dance ritual that requires shirts."

"And shoes! Don't forget the shoes."

"And for how long have you participated in this activity?"

Ma looked at Pa for help with the question, but no help was forthcoming. She finally answered, "Since about a year before Georgie was born. The day after I delivered him, we competed in the Midwest Clog-off."

"And we took third place," Pa added.

"So, do you engage in this clogging activity still?"

"All the time, Doc. We're part of the Tri-County Cloggers. We do it all—Appalachian flatfoot, modern clogging, buckdance, pitter-pat, you name it."

"I would if I could." Dr. Austin smiled his square-toothed smile. "Anyway, congratulations to you both. I'm sure you are very proud of your son."

Ma whooped at that, and Pa joined her.

Cornelia clicked off the Dustbuster and shouted, "Good heavens! Don't do that in here! Find yourselves a barnyard."

Ma looked down. "Sorry, ma'am. Sorry again." She turned to Dr. Austin. "But you'll see. Little Georgie ain't like us. Never has been. He's smart, just like June used to be when she was little."

Dr. Austin suddenly noticed June. He bowed his head and said, "Madam."

Ma gestured sadly toward June, as if she were a dent in the side of a new car. "June used to be a genius, too. Least we thought she was. Her and that Charley Peters she married. They was both real smart. They knew everything about everything."

"Charley worked at Technon," Pa added. "Like me. He had a real good job there."

"Then he ran out on June and the baby."

June began to shrivel in the doorway, but Ma kept talking. "That's when she broke down and all. And became an invalid. That's when she moved back in with us."

Dr. Austin turned away, clearly hoping to change the subject. His gaze fell upon Kate. He looked at her quizzically, then he said, "I'm sorry. We don't usually include other children in the personal assessments."

Kate turned both open palms toward him. "No problem."

But then, to Kate's surprise, June spoke. "She's supposed to be here, too. She got a letter."

Dr. Austin looked over at his wife. She explained, "The girl lives in the same duplex as George Melvil."

Dr. Austin nodded. "Well, we do have some cases such as yours. And they have worked out very well. You will be exposed to the finest teaching methods in the United States. That can't help but change you for the better, can it?"

Ma said, "Her father ran off. He was that Charley Peters I was telling you about. Last we heard he was over in Korea or someplace."

Dr. Austin looked at June. She stammered, "He-he is employed by the American Schools Abroad Program. In Asia."

Dr. Austin raised his eyebrows. "Ah, yes. I am aware of it. A fine program."

Ma cackled. "I guess they'll let anybody teach them kids over there."

"On the contrary, madam. They have very high standards. We can learn much from the Asian continent. Their students outperform American students with depressing regularity, particularly in math and science. They don't outperform Whittaker students, though." He gestured to his wife, who selected a book from the bookcase and held it up. "Ten years ago, I implemented a revolutionary plan for education, explained in my groundbreaking book *TBC: Test-Based Curriculum*. You shall hear more about it later in our interview."

Cornelia set the book back down.

Dr. Austin walked toward the door. "For now, let us take a quick tour of the top floor. Would you like that, George Melvil?"

George mumbled, "Yes, sir."

Dr. Austin's eyes flicked over to Kate. "And of course you, too, miss."

9

A Short Tour,
with a Long Lecture

As on the floors beneath it, a black iron railing lined the inside perimeter of the eighth floor, protecting pedestrians from an eight-story plunge to the marble lobby. Dr. Austin led his small group along that railing and down the hallway, stopping at a pair of tall oak doors bearing brass plaques. Dr. Austin paused to read the first: "Cornell Whittaker Number One, 1851–1942." He added, "The man was a genius, a great inventor. Are you interested in inventing, George?"

George gulped. "Yes, sir, I am. In fact, I have invented a flying machine."

"Excellent! Then you must enter our science fair."

Kate clenched both fists as George said, "Yes, sir, I would like that."

Dr. Austin said, "Excellent," again. Then he read the next plaque: "Cornell Whittaker Number Two, 1901–1998." This time, he didn't add anything.

They turned right and continued around the railing, passing a long wall without doors. Dr. Austin asked, "Do either of you have questions?"

Kate did, and she spoke up. "Yes. I was wondering: How does your school district map work? Why doesn't it have a normal shape, like every other district?"

Dr. Austin laughed heartily. "Because it is not like any other district! The County Commission, in its wisdom, has given us the permission—nay, the mandate— to draft talented students from any part of King's County we like."

Kate glanced at George and asked, "What if they don't want to come?"

Dr. Austin laughed again. "What student would not want to attend one of the finest schools in the United States?"

They walked in silence for a moment, until George, too, thought of a question. "Do your students have just one teacher, like in elementary school? Or do they change classes, like in middle school?"

"They change classes, like in college." Dr. Austin stopped to look George in the eyes. "Let me tell you about the teachers here. They are known for two things: being well paid and being anonymous.

"Teachers at the Whittaker Magnet School make four times the salary of other King's County teachers. As you can imagine, we have a tremendous backlog of enthusiastic applicants."

George's curiosity was piqued. "But why are they anonymous?"

"Within our system," Dr. Austin explained with pride, "your teachers will be known to you only by subject and grade level: Science Six, Math Seven, and so on."

George said, "They don't have names?"

"Of course they have names! But their names, and indeed their lives, are not relevant to your academic achievement. Their names are, in fact, a distraction. Teachers have no business cluttering up my carefully designed curriculum with anecdotes about...oh, how they forgot to feed their goldfish the night before! This is one of my many innovations."

Dr. Austin stopped to point out the County Commission Room. It took up one entire side of the eighth floor. The group peered through a long Plexiglas window at a cluster of flags, a white dais with a long wooden table, and thirty rows of folding chairs.

"You will be privileged to watch social studies come to life in this very room, to watch democracy in action. This is where the county commissioners debate and ratify the bills that affect all of our lives."

The tour of the eighth floor ended back at Dr. Austin's door, where Cornelia was waiting. She asked her husband, "Did you show them the ceiling murals?"

"Not specifically. No."

"May I?"

"Certainly."

Cornelia leaned against the railing. "Ignore the unsightly hole in the roof. It's still under construction. The murals, of course, will be professionally cleaned afterward. For now, let me point out my favorite part. This scene right above us shows George Washington, on a horse, presenting Cornell Whittaker Number One, also on a horse, with a book." She paused and added proudly, "That sort of thing never happened to Andrew Carnegie."

George said, "It never happened to Cornell Whittaker Number One, either. He was born more than fifty years after Washington died."

Cornelia bristled. "Perhaps when you have written and published a book about the Whittaker family, you'll be able to discuss the topic with me."

Dr. Austin favored George with a sympathetic smile. Then he led the group back into his office.

Cornelia positioned herself in front of the exit. "Of course, all of the extra benefits of a Whittaker education mean extra expenses. Are any of you wealthy?"

Ma and Pa guffawed loudly. June shook her head.

"Well, the County Commission has estimated the costs at about ten thousand dollars per year per child."

June gasped. Ma and Pa guffawed again, like they thought Cornelia was joking. But the stern look on her face assured them that she was not.

Pa found his voice first. "I'm afraid we don't have that kind of money."

Dr. Austin joined his wife. He smiled warmly. "I understand, sir. Many families of gifted students lack the resources to educate them properly. That is why the County Commission, in its generosity, has developed the Leave No High-Scoring Child Behind Program. Through this program, the county pays the expenses of indigent children." He looked at Ma, Pa, and June. "All the county asks of you in return is some voluntary work, here at the school."

Cornelia handed contracts and work schedules to Ma, Pa, and June.

"As luck would have it, we have a low-level clerical job available for June Melvil. We may also be able to find her some domestic work—dusting and that sort of thing. Ma and Pa Melvil, of course, are suited to custodial work only."

Ma and Pa obediently signed their contracts, but June hesitated. She tried to make eye contact with her daughter, but Kate looked away. So June whispered to herself—"This is for the best"—and signed.

Kate's attention soon snapped back, however, when Cornelia added, "As far as the children's jobs... George Melvil will work at the after-school preparatory. And since Kate Peters wants to learn to sing, she will be the personal assistant to Heidi Whittaker Austin."

Cornelia collected the contracts from Ma, Pa, and June.

Dr. Austin smiled. "So, your next question is, What will I be getting in return? I can tell you in three words: Test-Based Curriculum. Your children will soon understand the intricacies of standardized tests better than the people who write them. They will be *the* top test takers in America."

Ma, Pa, and June nodded tentatively, clearly unsure of the bargain they had just made. Kate shook her head at them slowly, in disbelief. Then she leveled a withering look at George.

George struggled to think of something to say to his niece. He actually opened his mouth to speak, anticipating that the words would come, as they always did. But this time his jaw simply hung open.

Dr. Austin turned to George. "You should score some impressive numbers here, my boy. A logical, level-headed young man such as yourself makes the best kind of tester."

George finally thought of something. He raised his hand—more to attract Kate's attention than Dr. Austin's—and asked, "Is the Whittaker Library Building haunted?"

June squeaked like a mouse.

Dr. Austin froze.

Cornelia, however, erupted with rage. She took two giant steps and loomed over George. "How dare you ask that! Where did you ever hear such a thing?"

George, thoroughly cowed, ducked his head and hunched his thin shoulders. He mumbled weakly, "A website."

"A website! You had better forget about your websites, little boy, and start reading books. Books like mine! Only people who are jealous of the Whittakers, people like Andrew Carnegie, would say such a thing."

Dr. Austin restrained his wife with a firm hand and placed the other on the quivering shoulder of George Melvil. He assured him, "That kind of talk is nonsense, George. Absolute palaver. I have worked in this building for my entire adult life, and I give you my word, as a nationally renowned educator, that nothing abnormal, paranormal, supernatural, or preternatural has ever occurred within these walls."

He clapped George on the shoulder, signaling an end to the discussion. Then he turned to include Kate. "I know it's late, but I have one more treat in store for you young people. While my wife runs some credit checks on the grown-ups, you two will enjoy my personal tour of the building."

10

Mysterious
Miss Pogorzelski

A flight of cement stairs took them down to the seventh-floor landing. The seventh floor, and every floor beneath it, contained rows of bookcases. Each case bore a sign on its endcap describing the topics and the range of Dewey decimal numbers to be found there.

Dr. Austin explained, "Our head librarian, Mrs. Hodges, is in charge of the seventh and the sixth floors. The books here are dedicated mostly to theology and philosophy."

Kate spotted Mrs. Hodges at the end of an aisle, removing an old book and carefully dusting it. She was thin and angular and dressed in a high-buttoned black dress. Her dark hair, pulled tight and hanging down her back, had a wide streak of gray in the middle, creating a skunklike effect, like someone had set out to make a coonskin cap but had used the wrong animal.

Dr. Austin led them down two more flights. "The fifth and the fourth floors are the realm of Miss Pogorzelski." Kate caught sight of a furtive figure in the stacks. She also wore a long black dress, but it was too large, and dirty, as if she had been outside jumping in puddles.

Dr. Austin's eyes searched the stacks for her. "We call her Pogo. She won't object if you call her that, too. Because to object would require her to speak, which she does not do. Pogo's sections are history and the applied sciences."

As they descended more stairs, he added, "Here's an interesting tidbit, George: Pogo and my wife, Cornelia, both grew up in this building. Pogo's father was the custodian here for fifty years, until his death."

George said, "That is interesting," without really seeming to mean it.

Kate, however, was eager to hear more. A distant glimpse had been enough for Kate to recognize the mysterious figure from two nights before. The woman at the top-floor window, outlined by the fiery red glow; the woman with the snarling power saw. It had been Miss Pogorzelski.

Dr. Austin described the third and the second floors as "literature and biography, the provinces of Walter Barnes." He then lowered his voice, as if approaching a sleeping zoo animal. "There's Mr. Barnes now."

Ahead of them, slightly to the right, was an old wooden desk bearing the sign BOOK RETURN. Behind the desk, in a padded chair, was the snoring figure of Walter Barnes. He was dressed in a dark brown, shiny suit. His nearly bald head was resting on a green blotter, on which was spread the half-eaten remains of a peanut butter and jelly sandwich. They watched him sleep for a few seconds, then moved downstairs again.

Dr. Austin inhaled deeply as he entered the main lobby, as if to take in its vast expanse. He turned to George and challenged him. "How would you calculate the volume of this great square, George Melvil?"

"Actually, sir," George replied, "it's a great rectangular prism. To calculate its volume, I would multiply its length times its width times its height."

Dr. Austin smiled tightly. "Yes, of course. We really must get you into the science fair." He changed the subject. "The first floor is devoted to children's literature. Ten years ago we began a program called Toddler Time; it has evolved into the present Story Time with phonics. This program is, like Test-Based Curriculum, poised to become a model for the entire country."

Dr. Austin caught his own reflection in the window of the library office. He smoothed his hair and beard. Then he pointed at one last stairwell. "And now, would you like to take a look at your school?"

Dr. Austin started down to the basement without waiting for a reply. He turned right at the bottom of the stairs and led the way through a hallway of whitewashed cement walls tinged green by fluorescent lighting. He stopped at a room bearing the sign PROTEIN LAB. "This is Mrs. Hodges's kitchen, from which you will receive your delicious and nutritious protein shakes."

They then walked past a series of classrooms with signs such as MATH 6 and SOCIAL STUDIES 6. Kate thought, *This is it. This is the mushroom farm.*

When Kate spotted a door that said WORKROOM, she spoke for the first time on the tour. "Is this where old Mr. Pogorzelski died?"

Dr. Austin appeared surprised that Kate was still there. "Yes," he answered cautiously. "Yes, it is. Mr. Pogorzelski died right in this room, on the job."

"From what?"

Dr. Austin's eyes shot to the door. "From old age. The poor man was nearly sixty when Pogo was born. He was in his nineties when he died."

They retraced their steps to the lobby with no further talk and ascended from the basement just as Cornelia, Ma, Pa, and June descended in Elevator #2.

As they waited for the elevator, Dr. Austin commented, "This building is distinguished both for what you see and for what you don't see."

Kate was startled by this sudden admission. She mouthed the word, "Ghosts?"

But Dr. Austin meant something else entirely. "Unlike many formerly great American libraries, this one has not been converted into a flophouse for the homeless."

The elevator doors opened. Ma, Pa, and June walked out ahead of Cornelia, like robbery victims. Kate and George fell in step with them, and the five family members took off, without another word, toward the exit.

Kate's brief interest in the building's mysteries vanished as soon as she hit the night air. Shortly into the ride home, she turned around in the front seat and leveled another piercing look at George. "So, George Melvil? Did he win you over? Are you going to be one of Dr. Austin's little super test takers?"

George was offended, but he tried to hide it. "No. But you must admit, he was nice to me. He treated me like somebody important."

"So what? You don't think the same thing would happen at Lincoln?"

"No, I don't think it would," George answered sincerely. "I think I'd be just another geeky little sixth grader. Someone to make fun of and to push into the lockers. Then I'd be a geeky seventh grader, and then a geeky eighth grader."

Kate couldn't think of anything to say to that. She told him, "Fine, then. You should go to the Whittaker Magnet School, for ten thousand dollars a year. If it's the best school for you, you should go there. Lincoln's the best school for me, so I should go there. For free."

George replied bluntly, "But you can't go there. You no longer live in the Lincoln school district. You live in the Whittaker district now."

"I live exactly where I've always lived!"

"But the district lines have changed, and there's nothing you can do about it. It's over, Kate. What's done is done."

Kate stared at him angrily for five more seconds, then she turned away. As they drove along next to the dark river, she thought about her uncle's words, *What's done is done.* She answered them silently: *And what's done can be undone, too. Some way. Somehow.*

II

The First Class, the First Test

The first day at the Whittaker Magnet School began with an assembly in the lobby. Dr. Austin made some remarks about the school's "national championship test scores." He read aloud e-mails from the state's governor, two senators, and seven representatives congratulating Whittaker on its success. He urged everyone to "keep Whittaker's winning streak going."

Kate wasn't really listening until she heard him say, "It is especially important for indigent students, such as Kate Peters and George Melvil, to use every minute here wisely. Their parents will be performing menial tasks right here in front of them in hopes that young Kate and George can someday lead better lives."

Kate could only look down at her feet, so complete was her humiliation. George whispered, "It's going to be okay, Kate."

"No, it isn't. Didn't you hear him? He just made us the poster kids for poverty."

Dr. Austin next introduced the school's teachers, but not by name. He called them simply "the Dozen." The Dozen stepped forward and formed a straight line in front of the students. Each teacher wore an identification badge showing his or her subject and grade. Each held out a list of names at arm's length, like a medieval proclamation.

The returning Whittaker students knew what to do, and George followed their lead. He approached all the teachers with 6s on their badges—MATH 6, SOCIAL STUDIES 6, READING 6, and SCIENCE 6. He found his name on each teacher's list and noted when he was scheduled to attend each class.

Kate remained sitting in her chair amid the swirl of students. George knew better than to talk to her at that moment. Instead, he approached the teachers with 8s on their badges and compiled Kate's schedule for her. Then he sat down and asked her gently, "Are you going to be okay?"

"No."

"What can I do to help you?"

"Uncle George, what if I just walked out of here and took a bus to Lincoln?"

"They wouldn't let you register at Lincoln. Taxpayers' dollars for the education of Kate Peters go to Whittaker now."

"This can't be happening. I'm supposed to be at Lincoln. With normal kids. There must be a way out of here."

"There might be. But for now, you're stuck. You have to accept that."

The lobby grew quiet as students poured down the stairwell, like grain down a chute. George pressed Kate's schedule into her hand. "You start with math eight; I start with math six. Then we move to social studies eight and six, reading eight and six, and science eight and six. After that, we go home. Okay?"

Kate looked at the empty lobby and the gaping hole of the stairwell. "We wouldn't go home at Lincoln. We'd go to play practice, or band practice, or soccer practice." She sighed deeply and then trudged down to the basement with George.

George spotted his math 6 classroom and ducked inside. Kate continued down three corridors, under sputtering fluorescent lights, until she found math 8.

She walked in and took the last available seat, all the way in the back, in the row farthest from the door. She looked around at the room. The walls were white-washed rectangular blocks, completely bare. Then she looked at her classmates. The lights gave them all an unhealthy greenish pallor. Aside from a big goofy boy who had to move his feet to let her pass, none made eye contact with her. She decided that she would have no friends here. These were not her people. These were Mushroom Children.

Kate heard a rattling sound out in the corridor, joined by the squeak of metal wheels. Then Dr. Austin entered, talking rapidly. "Good morning, students. It is nearly time to begin today's testing. But, first, whenever you see this rolling refrigerator, you know that you are in for a treat!"

He pointed to the open doorway. Kate could barely make out the stiff figure of Mrs. Hodges, posed with her hands atop a steel coffinlike contraption.

"Mrs. Hodges and her assistant, Pogo, make delightful energy drinks for you right here in the basement's Protein Lab. Here at Whittaker, we are pioneering the use of herbal derivatives—ginseng, Ginkoba, gotu kola— just to name a few. The human brain is a unique machine. It needs its own special fuel to keep it running smoothly." He faced the doorway and called, "Thank you, Mrs. Hodges," prompting her to push the rattling refrigerator farther down the hall.

Dr. Austin turned again to the class. "Let me explain your seating arrangement. It has been worked out with mathematical precision, again to optimize your performance on assessments.

"You will sit in four rows; each row will have four desks." Dr. Austin came to a stop at the head of the row closest to the door. "Traditionally, this first seat in the first row belongs to the student who achieves the highest test scores the preceding week. Conversely"—Dr. Austin pointed to the seat that Kate had chosen—"the last seat in the last row belongs to the student who received the lowest test scores."

Then Dr. Austin addressed the teacher for the first time. "Now, Math Eight, I will leave you to your duties."

Kate turned her attention to her first-period teacher. She was pretty, Kate thought. She was dressed in a dark blue blazer with matching skirt and a white blouse.

Kate relaxed a little, expecting to hear about classroom procedures, rules, objectives, and so on. Instead she heard, "Please take out two sharpened number-two pencils." Math 8 then passed out a pile of booklets.

When Kate got hers, she read the cover: *The New Jersey Test of Basic Math Skills.* She leaned toward the goofy boy and hissed, "What's this? We have a test on the first day?"

He shot a fearful glance at Math 8. Then he whispered, without moving his head, "Well, yeah. We have a test every day. In every class. That's what we do."

Kate broke into a grin. "You can't be serious."

The boy did not respond.

Kate's grin faded slowly. Then, like every other student in her classroom and every other student in the school, she opened the test booklet and began to bubble in answers.

The students worked in silence for fifty-five minutes, after which Math 8 announced, "Your time is up. Put down your pencils." She led them back through the test, page by page, revisiting each question and demonstrating how to find the correct answer.

Then a soft bell intoned, and Kate got up and filed next door, in step with the Mushroom Children.

12

Democracy in Action

A well-dressed woman in the next classroom briefly introduced herself as Social Studies 8. Then she announced, "We will not be testing today. Instead, we will be taking a field trip upstairs to the County Commission Room. Before we do, please make note of your first essay topic. The essay, in five-paragraph format, is due to me on Friday." Social Studies 8 held up an index card and read out: "Why the Homeless Should Be Banned from Public Libraries."

Kate dutifully wrote down the topic, as did fourteen other members of her class. One did not. A skinny boy in a blazer and tie was not writing. He was leaning forward and leering at Kate. She realized then that one of the Mushroom Children in this class was Whit Austin himself.

The students rode upstairs together in the steel-lined service elevator. Whit stood right behind Kate, too close for Kate's comfort.

Upon arriving on the eighth floor, they formed a line outside the County Commission Room. Kate looked through the Plexiglas and saw Cornelia Whittaker-Austin inside speaking to a group of adults.

As the students waited, Whit casually removed a book from a case marked PRIVATE COLLECTION—DO NOT TOUCH—THIS MEANS YOU! He perused the contents for barely three seconds then shoved it roughly back into the case, still opened, breaking its leather spine.

Then the students filed inside and sat on folding chairs, except for Whit, who took a seat upon the white dais. Cornelia asked everyone to stand while Whit led them in the Pledge of Allegiance, with one modification. It now ended, "... with liberty and justice for all in this great building erected by the Whittakers."

The center seat on the dais was occupied by a flitty birdlike woman whose silver jewelry clanked when she moved. A sign on the table in front of her read CHAIR, KING'S COUNTY COMMISSION. The four remaining seats on the dais were occupied by men in suits. Signs in front of them indicated only that they were representatives of Technon Industries.

The chairwoman gaveled the meeting to order. "I am Susan Singer-Wright, chair of the County Commission. Before we begin today, my husband wants to say one little old thing. What is it, Bud?"

A portly man in a loud sports coat stood. "I just want to say a quick word to these Whittaker students. You're gonna hear about an audition that's coming up. We're looking for the right girl to play that big, lonely fish Orchid the Orca in a very special performance."

Susan rattled her wrist jewelry at him. "Now, Bud, we're going to hear more about that very special performance in just a few minutes. First, we have some exciting news from the director of Library Services for King's County and the distinguished headmaster of our wonderful Whittaker Magnet School, Dr. J. Kendall Austin."

Dr. Austin rose from his seat and stood before the students and adults in attendance. He spoke as if he were narrating a historical documentary. "On Monday of this week, Dr. J. Kendall Austin received two FedEx letters from the White House in Washington, D.C.

"The first was from the chief of staff of the First Lady of the United States." He lifted up a letter and read, "'Dear Dr. Austin: The First Lady accepts your invitation to tour the Whittaker Building on Tuesday, October sixth. The Secret Service will contact you this week to make arrangements for a preliminary security screening. We look forward to a mutually beneficial visit. Signed, Rosetta Turner.'"

He shuffled the papers. "The second letter was from the Secret Service. 'Dear Dr. Austin: The president of the United States is considering your school, the Whittaker Magnet School, to be the site of a major presidential address on education. You will be contacted soon about potential security arrangements. Signed, Special Agent James J. McCoy.'"

Cornelia leaped to her feet and started to applaud. The county commissioners followed suit. But Dr. Austin raised the letters high, a signal to quiet the celebration. "Please! Wait for the official announcement. The White House and the Secret Service like to do things their own way."

"Thank you, Doctor," Susan Singer-Wright said. "We'll all hush till we hear that announcement. Now let's move on to old business. As you all recall, we faced a lawsuit from the families of those construction workers who died here a couple of weeks back. Our county coroner has determined the facts of that case and is ready to present them to us today. Dr. Cavendar?"

A gaunt old man rose from a chair in the back. Dr. Cavendar, the King's County coroner, could have been mistaken for one of his autopsy subjects. He was ancient and unhealthily thin. He wore a threadbare black suit that looked like it had been robbed from a corpse several decades before.

The doctor made his way to the front, stepping spryly for someone his age. He faced the commissioners, moving his mouth only as much as needed. "I have completed the coroner's report on the three workers who allegedly fell to their deaths in the lobby of the King's County Library Building."

Dr. Cavendar removed an index card from his suit pocket and read from it. "The autopsy revealed that the oldest of the three men had a simple heart attack, a coronary occlusion, totally unrelated to his work on the library roof. My examination confirmed that he would have died of that heart attack at that hour, of that day, regardless of where he had been or what he was doing.

"Unfortunately, in his desperation, he clutched at two innocent coworkers. Once he latched on, he would not let go. The three of them crashed through a hole in the roof. It was, of course, entirely the first man's fault.

"Earlier this morning, the county prosecutor tried him in absentia before a grand jury. He was found guilty and convicted of two counts of first-degree manslaughter. Because of this conviction, the families of the other two workers are barred from suing King's County for damages."

Susan peered around the room. "And are any of those people here today?"

"No. I suspected a touch of tuberculosis in one of them. I had their homes quarantined until we can be sure that none of them are contagious."

Susan nodded appreciatively. "Of course. We certainly can't take any chances with the public health. Then, if there are no objections, this case is closed." Susan banged her gavel, and Dr. Cavendar started back to his seat. "Thank you, Doctor. Good work.

"Next, for you students, we have a special treat. As you know, the county commissioners select a best essay every week from the students here at Whittaker. Well, the commissioners got together over the summer, looked at all of those prize essays, and selected the best essay for *all* of last year. Once again, it's that rascal Whit Austin who won. That boy sure can write!"

Whit stood up and surveyed the crowd casually. Then he stopped. Kate realized, with a sudden chill, that he was staring at her again. He held out his hand, took a piece of paper from his mother, and read from it flatly, "'Why Higher Test Scores Mean Higher Real Estate Values,' by Cornell Whittaker Austin.

"The higher the test scores, the more people who want to move into your school district. The more people who move into your school district, the higher the tax revenues. The higher the tax revenues, the more money to invest in the schools. The more money to invest in schools, the higher the test scores." Whit handed the paper back to his mother and sat down.

"That was so compact and eloquent," Cornelia commented. "Just like Abraham Lincoln's Gettysburg Address. It combined—"

Susan pounded the gavel. Cornelia glared at her, but she stopped talking. Susan said, "Now on to new business. Our first petitioner today is Mr. Bud Wright."

Bud Wright walked forward to the dais, but he swiveled so that he could address everyone. "As all of you know, I purchased that big community swimming pool three years ago. Nobody else wanted it, so I bought it. I turned it into an educational destination, a place that fulfilled our students' science requirements and that doubled as a fun family attraction.

"Well, now Bud Wright's Swim-with-a-Dolphin Aquatic Park is officially dead. It died two weeks ago, when my old male dolphin went belly up, and my new female dolphin, as you all know, turned out to be an orca. A damn killer whale. She's swimming around that big pool right now, sucking down about a ton of seafood every day."

Susan interrupted gently. "Can the commission do anything about this?"

Bud nodded. "Yes, darlin', it can. I need a new direction for the aquatic park. Nobody wants to swim with an orca. I can tell you that. They got a bad reputation that way. But! If we could get another orca, a male mate for this here female one, we could save the park. I know we could.

"People would pay to see a married fish couple like that. And I figure, the way nature works, they'd have a baby orca soon, and that'd be real big news."

Susan pointed to the others at the dais. "Bud, tell the commissioners exactly what you want."

"I want another orca. A male. The Japanese are ready to sell me one. He's a beauty, too. Even does a jumpin' trick, so they tell me. But the U.S. government is blocking the deal."

"Why, honey?"

Bud threw his hands into the air. "They say I'm violating some cruelty-to-animals law. Like me feeding a ton of food to an orca every day is a cruel thing to do. I wish someone would feed *me* free shrimp all day. When I'm down at the Stuckey's salad bar, I gotta pay for my own."

Bud held out his arms, pleading. "I am asking the County Commission to pass a resolution stating that Bud Wright is not cruel to animals. The dolphin that died was old and sick when I got him. It's not like you get American Kennel Club papers when you buy a dolphin, you know. I thought I was buying a young dolphin. Turns out he was on his way to the tuna fish factory already." He looked out into the audience. "Where's old Doc Cavendar?"

Dr. Cavendar stood up at his seat.

"Now, Dr. Cavendar here did an autopsy on that dolphin. And he's prepared to swear that it had never been abused one day in its long, full, happy life. Ain't that right, Doctor?"

Dr. Cavendar nodded darkly.

Susan looked left and right along the dais. "Well, there it is! If our own county coroner is willing to swear to it, who are we to disagree?"

The other commissioners nodded their assent, and Susan pounded the gavel with finality.

Kate wished her uncle George were there, so she could share a sarcastic remark with him. She had to settle for the boy with the big feet sitting next to her. She muttered, "There you have it. Democracy in action."

But he replied with total sincerity. "Yeah. Gosh, isn't it great?"

Kate stared at him briefly, hoping he was kidding. Then she rolled her eyes up to the ceiling. *I am alone here*, she thought. *I am as alone as Orchid the Orca.*

———

Kate's class left when second period ended. The next stop on their schedule was a high-protein lunch in the basement, but the students were blocked by a noisy altercation in the hallway. One of the librarians was upbraiding another, loudly and angrily. Kate pushed up front to see.

Mrs. Hodges was waving a book in Miss Pogorzelski's face and yelling about "Mr. Whittaker's collection." Kate recognized the book as the one Whit had mishandled.

Kate stepped forward. "Wait a minute. She didn't do it!"

Mrs. Hodges drew back, clearly unused to such talk from one of the Mushroom Children. She studied Kate's face with severe attention, like she had recently seen it on a WANTED poster.

Just then Cornelia emerged from the County Commission Room with Whit at her side. She observed the standoff and snapped, "Mrs. Hodges! What on earth is going on here?"

Mrs. Hodges held up the antique book. She cantilevered its spine, making it flap slowly, like a dead bird.

Cornelia flew into a rage. "Who did this to my father's book?"

Mrs. Hodges looked at Kate, so Cornelia did, too. Kate raised her arm and pointed at the true culprit. "It was your son, Whit. He's the one who did it."

Cornelia instantly snapped at her. "That is not true! That is impossible. He was with me the entire time."

"No, he wasn't. He did it right before the meeting."

Mrs. Hodges held her hands out toward Kate, with her fingertips splayed, as if she were sensing Kate's aura. She announced, "I have a feeling about this one. A bad feeling."

Cornelia rounded on Kate, but she addressed Mrs. Hodges. "You do?"

"Yes. There is something wrong with this one. Something evil. Something that begins in the home."

"Do you think that *she* did this to my father's book?"

"I wouldn't be surprised."

Cornelia looked at her watch. "Fine, then. I must leave the building to run some errands. But I have an idea of what do to with such a student. A good idea. If this girl confuses priceless books with trash, let's give her some time working with real trash." Cornelia looked through the small crowd around her. "Where is your teacher?"

Social Studies 8 timidly raised her hand. "Here, Mrs. Whittaker-Austin."

"This student will spend her lunchtime hauling trash with Pogo. I think it will teach her a valuable lesson."

Social Studies 8 replied, "Yes, I agree." She turned to Kate. "Go on. You heard Mrs. Whittaker-Austin."

Kate scanned the faces of the crowd—the Mushroom Children, Mrs. Hodges, Cornelia, Whit. She answered with dignity. "Fine. I'd rather haul trash with Pogo than eat lunch with any of you."

Kate held her head high as the others trooped past, leaving her and Pogo behind. Kate turned cautiously, not knowing what to expect. Pogo was staring at her curiously, tilting her head from left to right and shifting from foot to foot.

13

An Unfortunate Encounter
with a Shopping Cart

Pogo crooked a finger, indicating that Kate should follow her. The pair took off on a long walk down eight flights of stairs, across the lobby, and down another flight to the basement. There, Pogo turned right and ducked into the Protein Lab.

The Protein Lab was the same size as a classroom. It contained a wall phone, a long metal table, a sink, and two horizontal refrigerators on wheels. Pogo took hold of a large plastic-lined trash bin, also on wheels, and pushed it toward Kate. She grabbed a second bin for herself. Then, to Kate's utter surprise, she spoke:

> "Sippity sup, sippity sup.
> Sippity, sippity sup."

Kate said, "What was that?" but it was a question that was not to be answered. Pogo wheeled her trash bin out the door and turned left. Kate did the same, pushing the noisy, smelly container down the eerily lit hallway. They arrived at a steel door to the outside, which Pogo quickly opened. A man who had been sitting on the loading dock jumped to his feet.

The man was tall and thin, with long brown hair and a straggly brown beard. He was dressed in a clash of styles and colors, as if his clothes were from a Goodwill store.

He and Pogo rummaged through her trash bin expertly, like they had done it many times before. They extracted aluminum cans and tossed them with perfect accuracy into a supermarket shopping cart parked below.

Kate waited for her turn to push her bin forward, but it never came.

Kate heard a now-familiar voice bellowing, "Get that disgusting cart out of my way! You're blocking the exit! I have things to do! Important things!" Cornelia Whittaker-Austin was leaning out the window of a red Hummer H2, revving the engine angrily.

The can man scrambled down to the ground and grabbed hold of his shopping cart. He tried to pull it back toward the loading dock to clear a path for the big vehicle. In his panic, though, he stumbled just as the

Hummer roared forward. Cornelia slammed on the brakes, but the cart collided noisily with her left front fender and cans went flying everywhere.

The can man leaped to his feet and ran forward to retrieve the cart. Cornelia, enraged by the collision, hit the gas just as he gripped the cart's handle. The can man flew into the air, as lightly as one of his aluminum cans. He landed directly in front of the Hummer, and it rolled over his leg as if it were a skinny speed bump.

Cornelia hit the brakes again and turned off the engine, leaving the can man writhing in pain in the gap between the front and rear tires. She climbed out of the Hummer yelling, "This is not my fault!" She checked the damage done to the left front of the vehicle and then the damage done to the can man. Once she determined that he was alive, and likely to stay that way, she yelled down at him, "You do not belong here! Most of you people have gotten the message! Why do you keep coming back?" Cornelia turned and hurried into the building.

Pogo jumped up and down in front of Kate, waving her arms frantically, a look of desperation in her eyes. Kate took charge. "There was a phone in that Protein Lab, wasn't there?"

Pogo nodded, still bobbing crazily. Kate pointed to the writhing can man. "You stay with him. I'll go call nine-one-one."

Kate sprinted back through the hallway to the Protein Lab. She snatched the phone off the wall, dialed, pleaded for an ambulance, and ran back to the loading dock all inside of one minute.

Pogo was cradling the can man's head in her lap, rocking him back and forth. Kate watched from the vantage point of the loading dock, praying that the ambulance would arrive before any "help" from inside.

It turned out to be a tie. The ambulance rolled into the parking lot just as Dr. Cavendar emerged from the building with his medical bag. He gestured to Pogo to get out of the way. She lowered the can man's head onto the asphalt and ran up the side stairs of the loading dock. Dr. Cavendar then gestured to the paramedics to drive away, but they would not. Instead, they hopped out of the ambulance and ran toward the can man.

"His color is good," Dr. Cavendar announced to all. "He is making good, strong sounds. I do not believe he is injured at all. It is probably an insurance scam."

The paramedics rolled their eyes at each other. One of them said, "Nice to see you again, Dr. Cavendar." They brushed past him and loaded the can man onto a stretcher. They gently slid the stretcher into the ambulance, hopped inside, and drove away.

Dr. Cavendar shook his head, as if completely puzzled by their behavior. He then climbed into the seat of Cornelia's Hummer H2, pulled it slowly to her parking space, and walked back into the building.

Kate turned to Pogo for an explanation and got back another stare. But this stare was not merely curious. It was intense. As intense as the fire from a welding torch.

Pogo then spun away and jumped down from the loading dock, her black dress billowing outward. She began to collect aluminum cans, piling them first into a fold in her dress, and then into the battered shopping cart. Kate watched in silence for a moment. Then she jumped down, too, and started to pick up the far-flung cans.

14

The Juku Warriors

Near the end of fourth period, Science 8 handed Kate a note instructing her to report for her after-school job as "personal assistant to Miss Heidi Whittaker Austin."

Before the watchful eyes of the boy with the big feet, she crumpled the note, popped it into her mouth, and chewed it slowly, like a belligerent cow. The boy's jaw opened and stayed open.

When the bell rang, Kate stood with the other students and gathered her belongings. The students filed out in order of their test scores, meaning that Kate left last. She took out the soggy wad of notepaper and tossed it across two rows, creating a wet thump in the trash can.

Kate followed the Mushroom Children upstairs, but

at the entranceway, she detoured and walked into the lobby. She spotted Heidi at a table in front of the library office. Heidi was dressed, as always, in a white crinoline dress with puffy sleeves. Her golden ringlets ran down both sides of her head like thick ropes.

Kate stood in front of the table while Heidi wrote in a notebook. As she waited, Kate noticed an announcement taped to the office window: "Dr. Austin has decided that a Whittaker Magnet School student will read a scene from Cornelia Whittaker-Austin's classic children's book *Orchid the Orca* for the First Lady of the United States. Auditions to select that student will be held in the County Commission Room tomorrow at 4 P.M."

Heidi finally informed Kate, without looking up, "My mother, Mrs. Whittaker-Austin, has assigned you to me. As you will soon learn, I am three times busier than the average sixth-grade student. In addition to my schoolwork, I sing, dance, act, and serve as a goodwill ambassador for the Whittaker family."

She pointed to a stack of books with handwritten compositions sticking out of the sides. "Take those papers out and put them in a pile. Then put the books back on the shelves where they belong."

Kate stood in her place for a moment longer. Then she said, a bit louder than library volume, "Hey, look at me!"

Heidi looked up. Her eyes stretched open wide.

"I sing, dance, and act, too. In fact, I will be starring in the Lincoln Middle School production of *Peter Pan* this fall. I am busier than the average eighth-grade student. Maybe two and a half times busier. And I serve as a goodwill ambassador for the Peters family. There are only two of us left now, my dad and me. He's a teacher, in Asia. Good-bye."

Kate picked up the books, piled up the compositions, and set off toward the stacks. After a few minutes, she spotted a familiar figure walking across the lobby. She called out, "Mr. Kagoshima! Mr. Kagoshima! It's Kate Peters, from Lincoln! Remember? I was Minnie in *Annie Get Your Gun.*"

The young man looked around. He whispered, "Yes. Yes, I remember. But please do not shout out my name like that. I have agreed to be Math Six here, nothing else."

"I thought I saw you the other day, but I figured it couldn't be. Not with this"—she pointed to his clothing: a loose-fitting white suit, no shoes, a white-and-red headband—"this..." She finally gave up. "What is this called?"

"It is called a *gi*. It is a Japanese martial arts uniform."

"You're a martial arts instructor?"

Mr. Kagoshima smiled nervously. "Partly. I'm mostly a math instructor. That was my minor in college, you know." He leaned closer to Kate. "Just between you and me, I fake the martial arts stuff. Watch this." He waved past Kate to a pair of small children who were waiting nearby with their mother. The children were dressed just as he was. He bowed at them; they bowed back. "They're only six," he muttered to Kate. "What do they know?"

More parents approached from the entranceway, and the group of small children in *gi*s quickly expanded to seven.

"What about music?" Kate asked. "Don't you teach them any music? They'd be perfect for that Suzuki violin thing, wouldn't they?"

Mr. Kagoshima said, "No. No violins. There are no musical instruments here at all. They got rid of them."

Suddenly, to Kate's surprise, he jumped into an awkward stance, like a frozen jumping jack, and yelled, "Ha! Position one!" The children nearby looked up at him; then they tried to imitate his stance. Kate turned and saw the reason for his abrupt change from Mr. Kagoshima to Math 6.

Dr. Austin was walking toward them, and he had George by the elbow.

Kate whispered, "Bye," and took off with her books.

Dr. Austin was telling George, "All local elementary school children are eligible to attend the Whittaker After-School Preparatory. They are divided into the Juku Warriors, grades one and two, and the Cram Crew, grades three through five. Members of the Cram Crew actually interact with their counterparts in Japan via instant messaging."

Dr. Austin clapped George on the back. "This is your after-school job. You will assist Math Six with the Juku Warriors. I'll leave you to it. You can start by passing out those worksheets." Dr. Austin pointed to a pile of papers and then walked away.

George nodded respectfully to Math 6, who was apparently performing martial arts stretching exercises with the Juku Warriors. He picked up the worksheets and waited for his chance to pass them out.

But after the stretching, Math 6 said, "Let me see one of those." He looked it over quickly and decided, "No. Not today for that one. We'll save that for another day."

Dr. Austin reappeared from behind a bookcase. His face looked troubled. "Why aren't these children doing the worksheets?" he demanded.

Math 6 explained, with professional pride, "It's good that I previewed those worksheets. They are not ready for pre-algebra. Their brains are not developed enough for the abstract reasoning required."

Dr. Austin eyed him as a cobra might eye a mongoose. He asked slowly, flatly, "Is that so?"

Mr. Kagoshima clearly did not pick up on Dr.

Austin's tone. "The worksheets they did yesterday made them cry. That is why I decided to check more carefully today."

Dr. Austin bared his teeth and spoke through them. "I, at this moment, am on the short list for a presidential commission concerned with what our children *are* or *are not* capable of doing. You, at this moment, are an unemployed karate instructor. Leave immediately."

It took Mr. Kagoshima several seconds to figure out what had just happened to him. Not knowing what else to do, he bowed awkwardly and left.

Dr. Austin turned and addressed the startled parents. "Part of my job as headmaster is to fire those who would settle for less than the very best."

He turned to the Juku Warriors. "But enough grown-up talk! We are here to have fun, aren't we? To learn and to have fun." He selected a second stack of papers from the desk and handed them to George. "Perhaps we'll start with these, instead."

George passed out the worksheets to the children and helped them arrange themselves on the floor. Dr. Austin said, "Let's start with some Bubble Time. Do any of you know what Bubble Time is?"

None of the seven Juku Warriors replied. A helpful parent bent over and whispered to a little boy, who then shouted out, "Play with soap bubbles!"

This prompted a little girl to say, "Blow big bubbles!"

"No, nothing like that." Dr. Austin chuckled. "Much more fun than that." He reached into his suit coat, pulled out a handful of sharpened No. 2 pencils, and leaned into the crowd. "Now, everybody will need a pencil and an answer sheet. This is the good part. Take your pencil and bubble in one empty circle on each line. Just one now! One circle on each line."

Dr. Austin smiled benignly and backed away. He told George, "You take it from here. Have them fill in one circle, only one, in each of the twenty lines."

Then Dr. Austin disappeared. George looked at the Juku Warriors, and they looked back at him. He was utterly clueless as to what to do next. He tried to show a few of them how to fill in the circles, but he soon abandoned this idea as, one by one, they started to cry.

That night, over a meager dinner of frozen potpies, Kate had a desperate conversation with June. "We have to move to another school district! Or to another country, I don't care. But we have to move!"

June pushed down the crust in her pie. "We can't do that."

"Fine. Then can I move in with my father?"

"Yes. If you can find him."

"That's a mean thing to say," Kate snarled.

"No, Kate. That is the truth. George told you the truth the other night, and you didn't like it. Remember? He said, 'What's done is done.'"

"Great. Thanks for the reminder. I didn't know you were listening."

June sighed. "I am listening, Kate. I want you to talk to me. I want to talk to you."

Kate tried another approach. "All right. Talk to me about my father."

"What do you want to know?"

"Everything."

June set her fork down. "All right. Here is the story about your father: He wanted to get married; we got married. The minister gave us a Certificate of Marriage. He wanted to have a baby; we had you. The doctor gave us a Certificate of Live Birth. Then he wanted to get divorced; we got divorced. The lawyer gave me a Certificate of Dissolution of Marriage.

"I put the papers in a safe-deposit box at the King's County Savings and Loan. They all look basically the same."

After a long pause, Kate asked, "That's it? That's the story of my father?"

"Yes."

Kate exhaled a long breath of air. "I am going upstairs now. I am going to write a letter to my father asking for his help. I am also going to ask if I can go live with him."

"I understand why you might want to do that. And I wish you well."

"Do you?"

"Yes." Then June added, as kindly as she could, "But don't get your hopes up."

Kate laughed ruefully. "I don't think you need to worry about that."

15

Alpha Brain Wave Time

By Thursday both Kate and George had established their positions in the Whittaker Magnet School student hierarchy. In each of their classes, George sat in the first seat in the first row, and Kate sat in the last seat in the last row.

As Kate settled into her third-period reading class, she was surprised to notice a decoration on the wall. Someone had taped a Folger Shakespeare Library poster on the cement blocks next to her. Before she could read it, however, she heard the rolling refrigerator clatter to a halt outside.

Dr. Austin entered, and his gaze fell immediately on the poster. "Here is a question for your teacher: If information is not tested in any of the fifty United States, is there any reason for a United States student to learn it?"

Reading 8, a forty-year-old man with a salt-and-pepper beard, stood very still by the chalkboard.

Dr. Austin approached him slowly, asking, and answering, in his predatory voice, "Can you cite for me one example of a question about Shakespeare on a state test? No? What about a county test? A district test? No, no, and no again."

Reading 8 blinked rapidly and nodded in complete agreement. He broke away from his spot, hurried to the back, and ripped down the offending poster.

But it did him no good. Dr. Austin said, "You can take that with you. You are fired."

Kate watched Reading 8, or whatever his name now was, redden with humiliation. He rolled his wrinkled poster up, hung his head, and walked out of the classroom.

Dr. Austin then turned to the students. "What I just did, I did for you. Whittaker is your school as well as mine. We are all in this together. One mediocre teacher can undermine the efforts of eleven others. One mediocre student can undermine the efforts of one hundred ninety-one others.

"*I* cannot do this alone. I will root out the under-achieving teachers, but it is up to you to tell under-achieving students to get to work; to try harder; to stop pulling *your* class average down."

Dr. Austin walked to the teacher's bulletin board and studied the test scores from the day before. He shook his head sadly and muttered, "Tsk, tsk, tsk." Then he shouted, "Mrs. Hodges!" and the door flew open.

The black-clad Mrs. Hodges shot to the bulletin board like a clump of iron filings to a magnet. Her hawkish face followed Dr. Austin's finger down the list as he pointed out certain scores. She counseled, "Ginkoba capsules, five hundred milligrams," for one; "Siberian ginseng root," for another.

Mrs. Hodges exited just as rapidly and yelled instructions at someone in the hallway.

Pogo entered the classroom, her eyes averted, carry, ing a twelve-ounce plastic cup. The cup had the name KATE PETERS written in large block letters around its perimeter. Pogo walked back to Kate and handed it to her, whispering:

"Sippity sup, sippity sup.
Sippity, sippity sup."

Everyone watched while Kate stared at the vile-smelling liquid. Then she pinched her nose, raised the cup, and took the smallest possible sip. Her whole body, from head to feet, wriggled like an electric eel. Kate exhaled loudly, trying desperately to expel the foul taste from her mouth.

Dr. Austin cast his gaze over the rest of the class as he addressed Kate. "There, there. You'll get used to it."

Kate looked up at the Mushroom Children. To her surprise, she saw only sympathy in their eyes. Then, as her classmates watched, Kate took a breath and bravely chugged the contents of the cup.

Dr. Austin then called out, "William Anderson." The large boy next to Kate raised his hand. Mrs. Hodges entered with a green canister marked OXYGEN. She spotted the boy and rolled it toward him. She then produced a clear plastic mask and attached it to his face with a rubber band.

Dr. Austin said, "A few minutes of pure oxygen will awaken your sleeping faculties, William."

Kate handed her cup back to Pogo, believing that her torment was over, but she was wrong. "Kate Peters, come up here," Dr. Austin said. "Mrs. Hodges, prepare her for the treadmill."

Mrs. Hodges snapped, "Pogo!" and Pogo hurried back outside. While she was gone, Mrs. Hodges attached a sticky round patch to each side of Kate's neck; then she connected the patches to a set of long wires.

Pogo returned with a truck dolly bearing a large contraption that, when set up, became a health-club-quality treadmill. Mrs. Hodges plugged Kate's wires into outlets on the control panel. She turned to Dr. Austin, gave him a thumbs-up sign, and started the motor.

"Surely you slept through yesterday's test." Dr. Austin held up a student booklet. "A few minutes on the treadmill will certainly improve this abysmal reading score."

The treadmill began to pick up speed. Kate struggled to keep pace. Everyone in the room, including the aspiring William Anderson, was again staring at her. Soon the machine was humming along at five miles per hour, and Kate was running for her life.

Dr. Austin checked his watch sporadically until three minutes had passed. Then he indicated to Mrs. Hodges that she should turn off the oxygen canister. After another minute, he walked around to the control panel to monitor its readings. When Kate's heart and respiration rates were to his liking, he pressed the stop button and announced, "Excellent. That will do." Kate grasped the handrails to keep herself from being catapulted off the treadmill. "You have reached alpha brain wave time. That is the optimal time to start testing."

Mrs. Hodges ripped off the sticky patches and pushed Kate toward her seat. Kate had to steady herself against the desks on her way there. As she plopped down, William Anderson turned to her and whispered, "Come on, Kate. We have to do better."

Kate rallied her strength enough to whisper back to him, "No. Actually, we don't."

William Anderson's bright oxygenated eyes stared at her in amazement.

Kate did not even notice when the new teacher materialized. But there she was, standing before the class, dressed for the job and ready to go. As Dr. Austin, Mrs. Hodges, and Pogo packed up and moved on, the new Reading 8 passed out copies of *The Georgia Reading Proficiency Assessment*. Kate could only stare at her booklet, overcome by a combination of exhaustion, humiliation, and Ginkoba.

Before Kate's fourth-period class began, Science 8, a short bald man, read a note aloud. "Science class today will be preempted for a special meeting in the County Commission Room. All Whittaker students will be privileged to hear a legal brief presented by Cornell Whittaker 'Whit' Austin to representatives of the Stanford Law School."

Kate studied her classmates' faces as they filed out into the hallway. Under the fluorescent lights, they all exhibited a green tint. Kate expected the tint to vanish once they entered the lobby, but it didn't. They rode up together on Elevator #1, a glass jar full of Mushroom Children.

As soon as she entered the County Commission Room, Kate felt the hairs on the back of her neck rise. She looked around to see why. Whit was again staring at her from his perch on the dais. He was sitting to the right of Cornelia, who was wearing a padded cervical collar around her neck.

Once the last student was seated, Whit rose and began. "I speak to you today on a sad occasion for all residents of King's County. My own mother, Mrs. Cornelia Whittaker-Austin, the granddaughter of the benefactor of this great library, was assaulted on this very property.

"The said Mrs. Cornelia Whittaker-Austin was attacked in broad daylight, in front of witnesses. She was attempting to leave these premises in her motor vehicle when the criminal leaped out of the shadows and unlawfully restrained her from leaving. The offense can clearly be identified as false imprisonment, which, I need not remind our distinguished visitors from the Stanford Law School, is the tort, or wrongful civil action, of unlawfully restraining another person.

"The initial tort was then compounded when the criminal, by his unlawful act, damaged the motor vehicle, causing extensive repairs and lost time to the same Mrs. Cornelia Whittaker-Austin."

Suddenly, Kate could not listen to any more of

Whit. She felt a surge of herbal supplements rising in her throat, about to spew out. She leaped to her feet and ran to the door, regardless of who might try to stop her.

No one did.

Kate staggered down the hallway, unsteady on her feet, until a strong hand cupped her under the right elbow. The hand guided her toward the stairwell.

It was Pogo's hand.

Pogo led Kate step by step, up to the roof exit, and out into the fresh air.

Kate breathed in and out deeply until her nausea passed. Then she straightened herself and looked around. A large wooden stage, nearly completed, stood just to her left. Scattered remnants of construction tarps, lumber, and wire lay to her right. Pogo gestured outward with both arms, encompassing it all. Then, to Kate's amazement, she produced a wrench from beneath her black dress.

Pogo indicated that Kate should follow her. She led the way to an air-conditioning vent, creeping up on it as stealthily as a cat. The vent was shaped like a mushroom cap, two feet high and two feet in circumference.

Pogo crouched down, loosened two bolts, and bent the metal cap backward. Kate leaned over and peered down. She saw the top rung of a ladder; the rest was but a dark hole.

Pogo bounced and nodded eagerly, and motioned for her to climb down. Kate hesitated. She looked into Pogo's eyes, trying to decide whether to trust this mute, mysterious woman. She saw only childlike eagerness looking back. After a quick mind-clearing shake of her head, Kate slid herself feetfirst into the hole.

Kate descended eight rungs in the darkness before she felt a floor beneath her feet. Pogo closed the metal cap and descended behind her. After some scraping around, Pogo turned on a battery-powered lantern, and a dim green light filled the space.

Pogo pushed on a wall directly behind them. It spun open on a hinge, and Kate gasped. She wanted to shout out, "A secret passage!" but she kept as silent as her guide. Then she followed Pogo through the wall.

16

The Secret Room

Pogo shone the light on a narrow space, two feet wide, bounded by a low bookcase. Beyond lay what looked like an office, one that had not been used in many years.

Against the right wall lay an antique wooden desk and chair. The office had no windows, but air from the rooftop blew in and out through a hinged wall flap behind the chair.

The room's middle space was taken up by a magnificent floor-to-ceiling bookcase. Its shelves were filled with leather-bound volumes, photos, and other papers.

To the left lay a wooden trunk and a short, square machine made of metal and glass. Kate could make out the words HOLOGRAPHIC SCANNER on its side.

Pogo led Kate into the center of the room. She held the lantern up to the books so that Kate could read the titles: *The History of Spiritualism*, Volumes I and II, by Sir Arthur Conan Doyle; *The Works of Aleister Crowley*; *The Key to Theosophy*, by Madame H. P. Blavatsky.

Pogo pointed to a leather-bound volume with no title. Kate opened it and saw the handwritten words "The Diary of Cornell Whittaker II." She scanned it and whispered, "Wow. This guy really thought he was important. He recorded every meal he ever ate; what time he got up and went to bed; everything."

Pogo whispered back to her:

"One misty, moisty morning,
When cloudy was the weather,
I chanced to meet an old man
Clothed all in leather."

Kate returned the diary. She bent to read the initials on the old trunk. Pogo moved the lantern closer so that she could see CWII.

Kate then turned to the Holographic Scanner. It resembled a supermarket checkout scanner. Two books were sitting on top of its glass face—an old edition of *The Three Billy Goats Gruff* and an even older edition of *Mother Goose*.

Kate slid the books aside and saw that a bronze plaque had been affixed to the face of the scanner: ASHLEY-NICOLE SINGER-WRIGHT, SIXTH-GRADE SCIENCE WINNER.

Pogo whispered:

"Little Polly Flinders
Sat among the cinders,
Warming her pretty little toes."

Just then, Kate and Pogo were startled by the sound of a door opening. Pogo killed the lantern light, and they scurried back behind the bookcase.

They heard a rhythmic, metallic sound, like a suit of armor approaching. A wooden bookcase on the left wall started to move, rotating on a hinge. Kate thought, *Another secret passage! One from the front, and one from the back!*

Susan Singer-Wright entered, her metal jewelry clinking. She turned on an overhead light, causing Pogo and Kate to cower even deeper into the shadows. Then she sat in the chair next to the opening-and-closing air flap and lit a cigarette.

At that very moment, eight floors below, June was attempting to enter the building. She tried inching her way along the wall of the entrance, but she soon froze, unable to move any farther. She looked, to any outside observer, like a lost soul inside the *Andrew Carnegie in Hell* mosaic.

George spotted her while walking three of the Juku Warriors back to their parents. He delivered his charges and then hurried back to the mosaic. June had not moved. He took her by the elbow and whispered, "Take one step at a time, June. You can do it."

June answered through clenched teeth, in a high voice, like a bad ventriloquist. "I don't know. I thought I could. But now, I don't know."

"You've done it before, June. It's just the Whittaker Library. That's all."

"I-I'm scared."

"To tell you the truth, I'm scared of this place, too. But I know I shouldn't be. It's an irrational fear." George applied some gentle pressure to the elbow. "If we both take it one step at a time, like this, I'm sure we'll see that there's nothing at all to be scared of."

George helped his sister move forward, through the glass doors and into the lobby. June grew calmer and more assured with each step, until she and George were both jolted by Cornelia's booming voice. "There you are! I've been looking all over the building for you!"

Cornelia glared down at the pair. George, assuming that he was the object of her anger, began to stammer, "I was—"

But Cornelia directed a long manicured finger at June. "You! Dr. Austin will be making several important announcements today during Heidi's Story Time performance. You are to be standing in the lobby with this." She thrust forward a white envelope, which June took in hand. "This envelope contains today's test results."

June nodded stiffly.

"Dr. Austin will signal you, like so, during the Story Time." Cornelia demonstrated a hand gesture similar to the applause signal.

"Upon receiving this signal, you will walk up to Dr. Austin and hand him the envelope. Do you understand?"

June squeaked, "Yes," in her ventriloquist voice.

"Afterward there will be a very short audition up on the eighth floor. I doubt that anyone but Heidi will show up for it. She will be reading from my book *Orchid the Orca*. You can stick around and clean up after that."

By this time, Susan Singer-Wright had finished smoking two cigarettes, turned out the lights, and vacated the secret room. Pogo turned the green lantern on and led Kate back out through the mushroom cap.

Kate rode down alone in the service elevator and walked out into the lobby. She already knew her work assignments for the day. First she visited the children's bookshelves and located a copy of *Brown Bear, Brown*

Bear, What Do You See? Then she walked into the office, thumbed through the phonics file drawer, and pulled out a copy of the *b*-sound worksheet. She was standing at the photocopy machine when she heard the distinctive sound of someone retching on the other side of the wall, in the ladies' room.

A moment later, the door opened and June walked out. Kate felt a pang of sympathy for her mother. She wanted to ask June what was wrong, but she hesitated, and the moment was lost. Kate and June simply stared at each other in great discomfort until the copier finished its job. She scooped up her phonics worksheets and hurried out without saying anything.

Kate received another unpleasant surprise seconds later when she delivered the book and the worksheets. She saw her uncle George, looking eager to please, sitting at the desk with Heidi.

Heidi was explaining, "I will only select one or two students to be my research assistants, the crème de la crème as it were. I'll let you know if you qualify."

George thanked her politely and got up. He locked eyes with Kate and instantly flushed red with shame. Kate set down the *Brown Bear* book and the phonics worksheets. She stared at her uncle, for the first time ever, with deep disappointment.

———

Over in a cleared-out area of the lobby, parents and children were gathering for Heidi's performance.

Kate's preliminary duties were over, so she sat on a chair in the back. George approached, sheepishly, and sat down. He stammered, "Kate, that thing back there with Heidi? It wasn't what you think."

"Since when do you care what I think?"

"Since always."

Kate snorted. "Don't say anything more about it. And I won't, either."

They sat in silence for two minutes. Kate tried to remain angry, but when Heidi took her place before the crowd, she could no longer contain herself. "Uncle George, why is she dressed all in white, like a Swiss milkmaid, to read *Brown Bear, Brown Bear*?"

George, eager to be forgiven, answered slowly and comically, "I do not know."

"Shouldn't she be dressed in brown? Or like a bear? You know? Maybe even a brown bear?"

"That's the outfit she wore today. That's what she wears every day. She's just weird."

"Maybe. But maybe not. Maybe today is National Swiss Milkmaid Day, and the rest of us forgot to dress for it."

"Yeah, maybe."

Dr. Austin entered and raised his arms for silence.

"Welcome, all, to a Story Time in the lobby. We all hope our next one will be a Story Time on the roof." He pointed straight up. "On our newly renovated wooden stage."

Dr. Austin extended both arms magnanimously. "We are all here because we love and value reading."

He paused and looked around the lobby until he spotted June. He gave her the prearranged signal to step forward. But, although she visibly tried to do so, June could not move her feet. Instead, her head rolled back on her shoulders until she was looking straight up. Her gaze fixated on one of the four chandeliers that hung on seventy-foot steel chains from the ceiling.

Cornelia came up behind her and gave her a shove, starting her on her way. June managed to move through the crowd with her head down until she reached the front. Then she handed over the envelope and turned to go.

But Dr. Austin held her there by the wrist as he informed the crowd, "The results for today's tests are just in. They are right here in this envelope. I have not yet seen them." He looked to June to verify that fact. "Have I?"

June shook her hanging head, whereupon Dr. Austin released her wrist. June retreated in a panic as Dr. Austin continued, "I will share them with you now."

He muttered to himself, "I see. I see." Then he proclaimed, "Our King's County students have outscored their counterparts in Connecticut on *The Connecticut Assessment of Student Skills*, and they have outscored their counterparts in New Mexico on *The New Mexico Test of Mathematical Concepts*. Congratulations to all."

Cornelia stepped forward and gave the applause sign. The parents all recognized it and responded.

Dr. Austin waved to them. "Now we have a very special treat for you. Our students in grades one and two, aka the Juku Warriors, would like to show you how they have been spending their time at the Whittaker After-School Preparatory."

Dr. Austin signaled the new Math 6, a heavyset woman sitting uncomfortably in a tight *gi*. The Juku Warriors ran out and lined up. "A lot of American schoolchildren can name the fifty states in the United States," Dr. Austin told the crowd. "But how many can name the forty-seven states in Japan?"

A little girl in a *gi* raised her hand.

George whispered to Kate, "I rehearsed this part with them."

The little girl shouted, "They're not called states!"

Dr. Austin feigned surprise. "No? What are they called, then?"

"Prefectures!"

The parents in the audience laughed.

"I see. Can you name them?"

The little girl shouted, "Sure!" and all seven Juku Warriors broke into a loud recitation: "Aichi, Akita, Aomori—"

The recitation went on, but Dr. Austin talked over them, explaining how students in grades three to five, the Cram Crew, work with their Japanese counterparts.

"Fukui, Fukuoka, Fukushima . . ."

The audience waited patiently while the children named all forty-seven. Then Dr. Austin asked, "By the way, can any of you count to ten?"

The children started to count in English, but then they quickly switched to Spanish, then French, then something indecipherable. When they finished, Dr. Austin explained to the crowd, "Cambodian, ladies and gentlemen."

Cornelia stepped forward again to lead the applause. Then Dr. Austin sat down and let his wife take over the show.

Cornelia beamed a smile at Heidi, standing off to the side, book in hand. She declared, "How rare it is to be named after your mother's favorite book and to come to embody the spirit of that book."

Kate leaned over to George. "What? Her favorite book was *The Gross, Disgusting, Nasty Girl*?"

Kate then watched, thoroughly unimpressed, as Heidi Whittaker Austin delivered a sickly sweet performance of *Brown Bear, Brown Bear, What Do You See?* At the end Heidi bowed and curtsied to the crowd. It was Kate's cue to get up and distribute the worksheets.

Dr. Austin got up, too. After another quick pitch to the parents for the Whittaker After-School Preparatory, he read aloud the directions. Kate retreated to a distant table and watched as the children, somberly and diligently, began looking for the *b* sound in words.

17

Singing at
an Inappropriate Time and
in an Inappropriate Place

After the last of the audience members had departed, Heidi stomped over to Kate. "I hope you're not thinking of going to the audition today, because you don't have a chance!"

"Calm down," Kate responded, as if to an escaped mental patient. "Now what are you talking about?"

Heidi hissed, "You *are* going to the audition today, aren't you?"

Kate was startled to realize that, until that moment, she had totally forgotten about the *Orchid the Orca* audition.

"Fortunately," Heidi said, "you won't have to embarrass yourself. I have work for you to do." She pointed toward a large stack of books and papers on her desk. "Take those into the office and type them up. Neatly. Put my name at the top." Heidi then flounced away.

Kate took a deep breath and exhaled slowly. She pronounced the word "Whatever" softly to herself. Then she walked to Heidi's desk, picked up the pile of materials, and carried them into the office.

Kate sat down and prepared to type, but she felt a sudden chill and spun around.

Whit was standing in the doorway staring at her. "You're my sister's assistant," he said. "Bad luck for you."

Kate had no intention of conversing with him, but she did answer civilly, "Yeah."

Whit raised his eyebrows. "Shall I put in a word with Mother and have you transferred to me?"

Kate racked her brain for just the right insult, something to crush him like a cockroach. But she lacked the energy to reply at all.

Whit took a step closer, so close that Kate could smell his aftershave. Her nose wrinkled in distaste as he lowered his voice, "You improve the scenery here. You increase the number of hot girls, from none to one."

Kate redoubled her efforts to find the perfect cockroach-crushing remark, but before she could think of it, Cornelia entered the office.

"Whit, honey, we have an engineer from Technon to help you set up your science project."

"Aw! Does he really need me to be there?" Whit complained.

"Oh, Whit!" Cornelia laughed. "You are so funny! You come on now." Cornelia headed out; Whit followed, sighing theatrically.

Kate again prepared to type. But she hadn't made a keystroke before she heard George's voice behind her. "Hey, I figured you were going to audition for that *Orchid the Orca* part."

Kate managed to grunt, "Hey, you figured wrong."

"Come on, Kate. Do you mean you really don't want to do it?"

"No. I'd rather work at my personal assistant job to keep you in your dream school."

George stepped up to the desk. "You know, Kate, aside from my uncanny ability to spot redundancy, repetition, and repetitiveness at any distance, I have an even more valuable skill. Did you know that I can type eighty words per minute? With no mistakes? Not even stupid ones?"

Kate finally looked at him. "You're that fast?"

"Come on. Vacate the chair."

George sat down in her place. He shuffled some papers. Then his fingers started to fly.

Kate didn't want to distract him, but she had to know something. "Uncle George, why is there an essay in your handwriting in that pile?"

George kept typing, but he answered, "I was hoping you wouldn't notice."

"It was right on top."

"Naturally." He did stop. "I thought...if I was nice to Heidi, then she'd be nice to you."

Kate rolled her eyes. "Well, that didn't work!"

George told her, with utter sincerity, "I'm really sorry I got you into this, Kate."

Kate pointed at the keyboard, so George resumed his manic typing. "I'm not sure who got me into this. Ma and Pa? June? Anyway, it wasn't you. You're a kid. I'm a kid. They're the grown-ups."

"But I could have taken your side, right from the beginning. If I had said no, then our house wouldn't have gotten lassoed into the Whittaker district. But I was only thinking about me."

Kate shook her head. "Don't feel bad about that. I only think about me. All I cared about was being the star of *Peter Pan*. I never thought about what you wanted for a minute."

George paused. "I guess I wanted to be a star, too. A test-taking star, since I'll never be any other kind."

George resumed his furious typing. Kate turned away in time to spot someone running past the door. She leaned out and saw Bud Wright cramming into Elevator #1 with a black-and-white fish costume. She asked George, "Hey, did you ever go to Bud Wright's Swim-with-a-Dolphin Aquatic Park?"

"Yeah. It's a county science requirement. Every fifth grader has to go or they can't graduate to middle school."

Kate sneered. "Some science lesson, right? You watch a big, extremely depressed fish swim around in a circle all day."

"Actually, orcas are not fish. They're aquatic mammals. Like dolphins."

"And Mr. Bud Wright was standing there at the door with these stupid I LOVE ORCHID THE ORCA T-shirts. God, that poor fish."

"Aquatic mammal."

"Yeah. I hate to even say her name. It's such an insult. She's a wild creature, Uncle George. She's, like, the Amazon queen of the ocean. She's not some cute little character in a fairy tale."

George reached over dramatically and pressed the print button. "That's it. Six five-paragraph essays, all neatly plagiarized by Heidi the Milkmaid. Let's go."

Kate smiled for the first time all day. "Okay. Let's go."

Kate and George hurried into Elevator #3 and rode up to the County Commission Room. They burst through the door just as Heidi was finishing her audition.

Cornelia turned and stared at Kate quizzically.

Susan Singer-Wright announced, "Oh, good! Here's another auditioner. Go ahead, honey. You're next."

Heidi sniggered and tossed a copy of *Orchid the Orca* in Kate's general direction. It landed on the floor, and that's where it stayed.

Kate pointed George to a seat; then she walked in front of the dais. She looked over the panel of judges seated before her. There was Susan Singer-Wright, looking distracted; the new Reading 8, looking nervous; and Walter Barnes, looking asleep. Kate woke him by announcing loudly, "Ladies and gentleman! I am Kate Peters. And, as you shall soon see, I am also *your* choice to play Orchid the Orca!"

Then to everyone's surprise, and George's delight, Kate broke into a song from *Peter Pan*. She visualized her backyard and the big tree and the flying harness. She glided gracefully in place, forward and back, and let the words of "Never Never Land" pour out.

She sang with all the longing inside her for Lincoln and her old way of life. Kate would have continued to belt out the song, but Cornelia leaped to her feet.

"That's enough of that! There is no singing in this role. And no dancing! This is completely inappropriate. If it were a singing role, Heidi would have sung, and sung beautifully. The girl is not even reading from my book."

Cornelia looked pointedly at Susan Singer-Wright. Susan shrugged, banged her gavel, and asked the other judges, "Who votes for Heidi to play Orchid the Orca?" All three dutifully raised their hands. "Who votes for the other girl?" No one moved, so Susan stated the obvious. "Heidi wins."

George walked over to Kate, deliberately stepping on Heidi's copy of *Orchid the Orca* along the way. Kate laughed, bowed deeply to the judges, and started out with him. But before they could leave, the new Reading 8 spoke up. "I think Heidi should have an understudy, though. I vote for Kate Peters for that."

Kate looked back at her, stunned.

So did Cornelia. Her jaws ground violently. But then she smiled. "Yes. Why not? What a good idea. All Broadway stars have understudies. Heidi Whittaker Austin should have what all stars have."

Kate made a slight curtsy to acknowledge the news. Then she and George backed out through the door. As soon as they got into the hallway, Kate grabbed George under the elbow, the way Pogo had grabbed her. She whispered, "No talking! I don't want to talk about what just happened. Ever. I just want to show you something. Something secret."

18

A Language That May
or May Not Be Gibberish

An evening thunderstorm was approaching when Kate and George emerged on the roof. She led him to the mushroom cap and showed him how it bent back on a hinge.

The electricity in the air made the hairs on George's head tingle. He smiled at Kate, very curiously, and then followed her down the iron ladder.

At the bottom, Kate fumbled until she found the green lantern. Only then did she break her silence. "Pogo took me here today."

"Pogo? The mute librarian?"

"Yes. Ever since that business with Whit and the book, it's like she wants to tell me something, but she can't. So she's trying to show me, instead."

"Okay. So what did she show you?"

"A secret room. I think it was built behind one of the Whittakers' offices."

George pictured the building plans from the King's County website. He calculated the distance and direction they had traveled and concluded, "It must be behind Cornell Number Two's."

Kate nodded in the dim light. "That would make sense. Some of his stuff is in there."

She took George's hand in hers and reached forward, whispering, "Behold." They pushed the wall and felt it rotate inward. George gasped. Kate confirmed his thought. "That's right. A secret passage."

George held on tightly to Kate's hand as they slipped into the narrow space behind the bookcase. Kate held up the lantern to let him take in the room and its objects. George turned his head slowly, following the glow of the lantern.

Suddenly, Kate's eyes snapped wide open, and she stifled a scream. George whirled around to see why. He fell back against Kate, horrified, because a black figure was now blocking the secret passage. Then the figure spoke:

"Jack and Jill went up the hill."

"Pogo!" Kate exhaled. "You nearly gave me a heart attack."

In a trembling voice, George marveled, "She speaks?"

Kate thought about that. "Sort of."

"Well, can I ask her questions?"

"You can try."

George straightened himself up and asked, "Whose room is this? What is it used for?"

Pogo replied:

> "For many a stormy wind shall blow
>   E'er Jack comes home again."

"I thought so," Kate explained. "You can ask her questions, but her answers won't match them."

Lightning flashed on the roof. It was dimly visible through the rotating door. Pogo took the lantern from Kate and led them around the bookcase into the center of the room.

She held the light high to illuminate a portrait hanging on the left wall. It was a likeness of Cornell Whittaker Number Two, like the one in the lobby, except that he was wearing a black robe and a black floppy hat.

"Why is he dressed like Mickey Mouse in *The Sorcerer's Apprentice*?" George asked.

Pogo didn't answer.

Kate approached the floor-to-ceiling bookcase, rose

up on her tiptoes, and pulled out a leather-bound book. "Check this out, Uncle George."

Kate pointed back to the portrait. "It's his. He wrote down everything. All of his weird doings."

George commented, "I wish we could check it out. We could take it home and read it."

Kate looked hopefully at Pogo. "Could we?"

But Pogo, by way of reply, took the book away from Kate, hopped up, and popped it back onto the shelf.

Pogo then moved the lantern to shine on the Holographic Scanner. George bent to look closer at its glass top. He ran his fingers over the bronze plaque and read aloud, "'Ashley-Nicole Singer-Wright.' You hear that name a lot around here. She's all over the school's website, too. She invented some type of amazing holographic tape. One piece of it can store more information than all the computers in the Pentagon."

"What good is that in a library?"

"It's extreme overkill for a library. But for the Pentagon, it's cutting-edge technology."

George pressed his fingers down on the glass top. "This must be it. This must be the scanner that she used for her experiments." George leaned over and picked up the electric plug. "I wonder if it still works."

Pogo moved her hand, as if to stop him. She whispered:

"Will you wake him? No, not I,
For if I do, he's sure to cry."

George said, "I'm sorry. What was that one?"

But Pogo would not repeat it.

The lightning flashed again, followed closely by a clap of thunder.

"Uncle George, she seems to want to communicate with us. So why does she keep talking gibberish like that?"

George replied in his knowing voice. "That's not gibberish, Kate. Everything she's said is from Mother Goose. She's speaking in Mother Goose rhymes."

Kate grabbed her own hair and pulled it. "But why?"

"Because of what you said. She's grateful to you. She's trying to warn you about something, in the only way she can."

Pogo turned away with the lantern, leaving them in darkness. They hurried to follow her back through the secret passage. One by one, they took hold of the iron rungs of the ladder and climbed up into the brighter and brighter flashes of lightning.

Once Pogo closed the mushroom cap on the roof, the secret room below should have turned as black as a tomb. But it did not.

Over by the wall, the unplugged Holographic Scanner began to glow red under its glass pane, a hot and frightening red, like the fires of Andrew Carnegie's hell. Then, from deep within, a cloud of wispy white lines rose up and swirled beneath the glass. The lines formed, disintegrated, and then formed again, casting ghostly shadows on the ceiling and walls of the secret room.

19

A Guided Tour
through an Old Scrapbook

After school on Friday, Kate pulled out a set of six photographs and spread them across her bed. They were photos of Charley Peters, her absent father. She examined each one meticulously, asking herself: *What brand of shoes is he wearing? What shirt logo is that? What type of sunglasses is he wearing in that sports car?* She answered herself aloud, "The best. The absolute best."

Kate looked down at the floorboards, as if she had X-ray vision. She looked for June, her invalid mother, rummaging around somewhere for her lost keys. She pronounced her, "The worst. The absolute worst." She scooped up the photos of the dapper Charley Peters and whispered to him, "I don't blame you for leaving. I'd have left her, too."

Kate stacked the photos into a shoe box, slid it under her bed, and went downstairs. She waited silently in the vestibule until June emerged, wearing a faded housedress, with the long-lost keys now clutched in her hand.

June then drove Kate to Molly's for dinner. On the way, Kate halfheartedly asked, "Tell me why I can't sleep over again."

"You need to be at home, Kate, every night. I need to know that you are safe."

"I'll be safe at Molly's. Her grandmother is there."

"But I won't be there, so it's no."

"So this is all about you?"

"Yes, I suppose it is," June admitted.

Kate gave up quicker than usual. She wasn't really interested in making June feel bad tonight. She was much more interested in speaking to Mrs. Brennan.

Molly let Kate in and started upstairs, as if they would hole up in her room as usual. But Kate told her right away, "No. I need to talk to your grandmother tonight about the Whittaker Library. Is that okay with you?"

"Will it be creepy?"

"Very creepy."

"Cool. She's in the kitchen, making dinner."

Upon seeing Kate, Mrs. Brennan set down her stirring spoon and gave her a hug.

Molly said, "Kate actually wants to talk to you tonight, Grandmom."

Mrs. Brennan laughed. "Oh? I'm flattered. Come sit at the table, both of you, while I finish this sauce."

Kate got right to the subject. "Mrs. Brennan, what did you do at the Whittaker Library?"

Mrs. Brennan handed a short stack of plates to Molly. She answered with a tinge of surprise, as if Kate should have known. "I was the director of Library Services for King's County, my dear, for many years."

"And, if I may ask, what do you do now?"

"Of course you may ask. I don't think that's being nosy." Mrs. Brennan shot a withering glance at Molly. "I am the curator of the King's County Historical Society."

"Is that like your old library job?"

"No, dear. Not at all. It's a much smaller job. It's a nonprofit organization. I'm the only paid employee."

Kate bit her lip. "Well, then, if your library job was bigger and you were the boss and everything, why did you leave?"

"That's a long story."

"I would like to hear it. I would like to hear anything that you would like to say about the Whittaker Library."

Mrs. Brennan grew quiet, so Kate did, too.

Once they were seated at the table and eating,

though, Mrs. Brennan started talking. "I assume you have met Mrs. Hodges."

Kate gagged involuntarily.

"I see that you have. Well, when I was there, I suspected she was using a razor to cut pages out of the children's books."

Molly laughed. "Why would she do that? Was she, like, into vandalism or something?"

"No, quite the opposite. She believed she was protecting the children from demonic influences."

This sent a shudder down Kate's spine. "Wow. And is there a Mr. Hodges?"

"There was one. He died. Right there in the library."

Kate and Molly both leaned forward. "How?"

Mrs. Brennan leaned forward, too. "No one knows for sure. The coroner claimed that he electrocuted himself."

"But you have doubts?" Kate said.

"Everyone but the coroner had doubts."

"Was this Mr. Hodges a librarian?"

"No, dear, he was a minister, from a church that no one had ever heard of. He was hired to investigate some incidents in the library about ten years ago."

"So the weird things began with him? With Mr. Hodges, about ten years ago?"

"Oh, heavens no! I believe he was brought in, by

Cornell Whittaker Number Two, to deal with weird things that were already happening." Mrs. Brennan's voice grew softer, as if drifting into the past. "No, if you really want to know about the origins of it, we have to go back much further than that."

Kate looked at Molly. "We really want to know about it."

"Then we have to go back to the middle of the nineteenth century, when Cornell Whittaker Number One was a young man. He became very interested in the occult. He became a practicing spiritualist."

Molly giggled. "You mean, like, séances, Ouija boards? All that stuff?"

"Yes. All that stuff."

"He was crazy?"

"Perhaps. But it wasn't considered crazy back then. Did you know that even President Lincoln and his wife held séances in the White House, trying to contact their dead son?"

Kate and Molly shook their heads.

"Cornell Whittaker Number One was a founding member of the Society for Psychic Research. He raised his son to believe in the society's principles, too. His son took it one step further, though, becoming a bit of a fanatic. Cornell Whittaker Number Two spent a fortune collecting occult books from all over Europe."

"I saw some of them!" Kate said. "He had a lot of

creepy books in a huge bookcase. He also had a really old copy of *Mother Goose*."

Mrs. Brennan nodded. "Indeed, he did. By Perrault, the original compiler of the stories. Yes, I remember when Mr. Whittaker brought that book back from London. Good heavens, that must have been thirty years ago. He was quite proud of it."

"So, you knew this occult, spiritualist guy?"

"Oh, yes."

Kate tried to sound casual. "Did he, like, walk around in wizard robes?"

Mrs. Brennan smiled. "No, dear. He walked around in a business suit." Her smile faded. "And yet, I must say, Cornell Whittaker Number Two was very odd. For one thing, he always smelled like smoke, like fire and brimstone. We knew he smoked up in that office of his, but we could never catch him at it."

They finished eating dinner. While Molly and Kate cleaned up, Mrs. Brennan said, "I have an old scrapbook from my days at the Whittaker Library."

Molly whispered, "She has an old scrapbook from her days *everywhere*."

"Molly?"

"Sorry."

"Would you like to look through it, Kate?"

Kate nodded so enthusiastically that Mrs. Brennan laughed and hurried off to find it. She returned five minutes later and squeezed into a chair on the girls' side of the table.

Mrs. Brennan opened the rectangular book and spread it before them.

She asked Kate, "Have you met Pogo?"

Kate nodded cautiously, trying to gauge Mrs. Brennan's opinion. "Oh, yes. I've met her. She's very nice."

"She is. She's a darling. But quiet."

"Very."

Mrs. Brennan turned pages until she found a photo. "Here is Miss Pogorzelski as a little girl. She's posing with her father in his workshop."

Kate studied the picture. It showed a miniature version of Pogo standing next to a very old man. She was holding a book; he was holding a power saw. "What was Pogo like then?" Kate asked.

"She was, as you might imagine, a very quiet child. She was keen to read nursery rhymes, as I recall."

"Did she have any friends?"

"No. Not that I ever saw. She had Cornelia, but you would never call her a friend."

"Who's that?" Molly asked.

Kate answered, "She's Cornell Number Two's daughter."

Mrs. Brennan turned to a newspaper clipping. "Cornelia managed to get in the newspaper quite often." The clipping showed a color photo of a young Cornelia in front of a display of *Heidi* books. She was dressed in a white frilly outfit, and she held a staff with purple-and-yellow ribbons, but she looked miserable.

"Unlike Pogo, Cornelia could never keep her mouth shut. She was not born with a library voice. She used to bellow like a moose whenever she talked. That's what her father called her, in fact: 'the Moose.' It was sad really. I think Mr. Whittaker truly disliked Cornelia. And he truly hated Jimmy Austin. I can tell you that."

It was Kate's turn to ask, "Who's that?"

"You would know him now as the eminent Dr. J. Kendall Austin."

Mrs. Brennan pointed to a photo of herself standing next to a short, skinny teenager with long hair and big square teeth. "Jimmy Austin was a kid from the community college. He used to shelve books, like Pogo; he used to work the checkout desk, like Walter Barnes. He was always scooting around the stacks. And he was always writing term papers for some mail-order college that nobody had heard of. Mr. Whittaker used to call him 'the Mouse.'"

Next was a black-and-white newspaper clipping with a large wedding photo. It showed a young Dr. Austin, now with short hair and a dark beard, standing next to Cornelia. She was seated, wearing a flowing, expensive-looking white gown, but she still looked miserable. Mrs. Brennan commented dryly, "So the little mouse married the big moose."

Mrs. Brennan closed the book. Her tone turned cold. "Jimmy was always ambitious. He got his master's degree by mail; then he got his doctorate online. He chased after whoever could forward his ambitions, like those Technon people. The day he married Cornelia, Mr. Whittaker got him appointed deputy director of Library Services.

"Soon after, don't ask me why, strange things began to happen in the library. Otherwise well-behaved children would act like wild creatures. People assumed that the children were just acting out. Then it happened to an adult, and that was another matter.

"Rumors started flying. People said the library was haunted by a ghost or a demon of some sort. The Reverend Mr. Hodges arrived on the scene, claiming expertise in all things demonic. He announced that there was indeed an evil presence in the Whittaker Library Building. And that evil presence was . . . me."

Kate and Molly gasped together. "I had always opposed the partnership with Technon," Mrs. Brennan explained. "And I had always seen through little Jimmy and the scheming moose.

"Jimmy found an old photo of me doing a Story

Time, dressed like a funny witch for *The Little Witch's Halloween Book*. He went before the County Commission and denounced me as a corrupter of youth. The commission was then, as it is now, composed mostly of Technon people. They were eager to pin the blame on someone. They forced me to resign from my job."

"Why didn't you tell them to go to hell?" Molly asked indignantly.

"Don't talk like that, Molly."

"Sorry."

"The reason I spoke no such vulgarity was that they threatened to go public with the photo and to fill the newspapers with lies about me and my family. I knew they were capable of doing just that, so I left. I don't know. Looking back on it, perhaps I should have had a stronger backbone."

Mrs. Brennan shuddered and closed her eyes. Then she stood up. "Anyway, I'm sure you girls have more important things to talk about than the Whittaker Library. Good night to you both." She went upstairs, leaving Kate and Molly sitting in front of the scrapbook.

Molly held up one finger. "Okay, here it is. You just need to do something to get kicked out of that place. Come down with some weird sociopathic disease or something."

"Please!" Kate waved the idea off. "They'd love to kick me out. Tomorrow morning. It's Uncle George they want. But as long as we live at the same address, Whittaker is my school district."

"Okay, then. George needs to get kicked out."

"How? He's their model student."

"He needs to come down with a bad case of the stupids."

"No. When George tries to act stupid, he's still smarter than most people." Kate shook her head. "Whittaker is George's place to shine. Before this, I'd always been the star and he'd always been the one behind the scenes. Now it's reversed."

Molly looked away, unable to think of anything else to say. The doorbell rang five seconds later. Molly opened the door to George. "June's in the driveway for Kate," he announced. "She asked me to come up and get her."

Kate called over to him, "Yeah. Come in. I'm almost ready."

George waited while Kate poked her head up the stairway and called a final "Good night" to Mrs. Brennan, who called back the same.

Molly hugged Kate good-bye for several seconds. "You'll get back to Lincoln soon," she told her. "I just know it."

Kate did not reply.

"And you'll get the part of Peter Pan. You just have

to wish for it with all your might. If you do that, your wish will come true. Right, George?"

George thought for a moment and then answered, "No, I don't think wishing has anything to do with it. I think events tend to follow in a logical progression."

Molly rolled her eyes. "Whatever. Good night, Kate."

George spoke past Molly to Kate, "You wish to be Peter Pan, don't you?"

Kate answered seriously, "You know I do."

"Think about what you did to make that 'wish' come true. You worked hard to make yourself a singer and a dancer. You went to all the rehearsals; you performed small parts for two years.

"If you get back to Lincoln, Kate, and you audition for Peter Pan, the directors will see that you are clearly the most talented and the most experienced candidate. They will give you the part."

George paused to look at Molly. "If, the night before they announce the roles, you close your eyes and make a wish, you may spend the rest of your life believing that your wish had come true." He turned back to Kate. "But the fact is, if you had gone to sleep without making that wish, you would have gotten the part anyway."

June honked the car horn. George said, "We'd better go." He walked ahead of the girls out to the car.

Molly spoke to Kate in a low voice. "I don't care what he says. I believe that wishes come true. And you should, too."

"All I know is this," Kate told her brusquely. "I'm not going to Lincoln with you on Monday morning, I'm going to Whittaker. And I'm not going home with my mother and father tonight, I'm going home with just my mother. So I guess I don't believe in wishes coming true, either. If I really want good things to happen, and bad things to stop happening, it'll take more than wishing. I have to act. And I have to act now."

20

The Technon Industries Science Fair

Kate's entire family arrived earlier than normal on Monday morning. Ma and Pa Melvil were there to begin their janitorial duties. Kate, George, and June were there to set up George's science fair exhibit in the library lobby. This time, George would attach his pulley system—designed to illustrate maximum lift with minimum resistance—to a second-floor railing instead of to an oak tree.

Kate carried in the Velcro bodice, while George dragged in the pulleys. June took charge of the long rope, laying it in loose circles outside the library office.

Pogo bounced around the edges of their group, eager to help in any way she could. She produced several tools from beneath her dress for George to use.

Kate could not have been less eager. "Why are you doing this?" she asked George. "You know they're going to give it to Whit."

"Why did you audition for *Orchid the Orca*? You knew they were going to give it to Heidi, but you tried anyway."

Kate shrugged.

George's bespectacled eyes twinkled. "That's why I'm doing it."

When the flying machine was fully operational, George and Kate left the pieces in place and started their school day.

Just before third period began, Cornelia entered Kate's reading class and stood in the back. She told Reading 8, "Don't mind me. I'm just here as an observer. I won't be doing anything. I'm kind of like an understudy in a Broadway musical."

Dr. Austin entered right after, accompanied by another new teacher. Reading 8 understood immediately what was happening. She packed up her few belongings as Dr. Austin approached to make her firing official.

He walked over to the list of test scores on the bulletin board, studied them, and told her, "You have been given the finest materials, the most expert guidance, and the highest salary in education. Yet you have not been able to raise the reading scores of your lowest student by even one point. In fact, they continue to sink, as if this student, this Kate Peters, were enrolled in some free public school and not paying an additional ten thousand dollars per year for her education. I suggest that you go back to a school where the students pay nothing and get nothing, for that is precisely what they will get from you. You are—"

Dr. Austin had been so caught up in his own rhetoric, he failed to realize that Reading 8 had already departed. He looked around, perplexed.

Dr. Austin took a moment to regain his composure. Then he informed Kate's class and its new instructor, "You will not be testing today." He looked back at Kate. "Which must be a relief for some of you. You will instead report to the lobby for the first phase of the annual Technon Industries Science Fair."

Kate walked out last in the line behind the new Reading 8. After only a few seconds in the lobby, Kate had seen enough. The Technon Industries Science Fair was more pathetic than even she had imagined. There were only two exhibits on display.

The first invention bore a sign, in George's tiny printing, THE FLYING MACHINE: A SYSTEM OF LOW-RESISTANCE PULLEYS, BY GEORGE MELVIL, GRADE 6.

The second invention sat on a custom-made concrete

block. It was a working model of Ashley-Nicole Singer-Wright's Laser Cannon. But according to its engraved bronze plaque, it had been modified. The plaque read LASER CANNON WITH TRACKER, BY CORNELL WHITTAKER AUSTIN, GRADE 8.

A half dozen people wearing JUDGE badges sat between the exhibits. The dozing Walter Barnes was one of them; so were Susan Singer-Wright, Bud Wright, Dr. Cavendar, and two men in Technon Industries windbreakers.

Kate looked at the judges and thought, *It's all over.* But George was still game to try, so she did her best to look enthusiastic. George helped Kate attach the Velcro bodice, as they had done many times before. Then he tied the rope around his own waist.

Suddenly, an earsplitting whoop sounded across the cavernous lobby and echoed around the bookcases. Kate and George turned to face the source of the noise.

Ma and Pa Melvil were standing together by the lobby office. They were dressed alike, in purple pants and work shirts with WHITTAKER MAGNET SCHOOL stitched in yellow on the pockets. Ma was carrying a long-handled mop, while Pa pushed a tall metal bucket filled with soapy water.

"You go get 'em, Georgie!" Ma shouted.

Pa began, "Yeah, Georgie—" but he never got any further.

Cornelia bolted out from the office and confronted them. "That does it! You two. Get in here. Now!"

Ma and Pa looked at the floor. Then they shuffled into the office and out of sight.

George and Kate exchanged one quick, anguished look. But then they refocused and prepared again to demonstrate the flying machine.

Kate stepped back to gain some takeoff room. While she did, George took a quick look around for June. He spotted her cowering behind a nearby bookcase. He gave her a thumbs-up sign, which she could not return. He gave the same sign to Kate, who did return it. Then he took a giant step toward the judges, causing Kate to rise, magically, six feet into the air.

Kate struck a pose, like Mary Martin in *Peter Pan*. George coughed and cleared his throat, but none of the judges looked his way.

Suddenly, Kate felt a tickling sensation on her thigh. She looked down, expecting to see a fly or a mosquito. Instead, she saw Whit directly below. He had just touched her, and he was preparing to touch her again. She snarled, "Get your hand off me!"

Whit smiled slyly. He moved his hand upward again as if he hadn't heard her.

Kate twisted herself and looked around. She spotted June, standing only ten feet away. June was watching the whole thing. Her mouth was moving slightly, like she was trying to speak, but the rest of her body was paralyzed with fear.

Whit's hand gripped Kate's knee and started to rub its way upward, but it didn't get very far. With one great heave, June pushed her body forward, like a hiker in a snowstorm, staggering in an unsteady line, forcing one foot in front of the other across ten feet of lobby carpeting, until she crashed headfirst into Whit, striking him with enough force to drive him backward.

Whit looked astonished. He stared at June, openmouthed. He continued to back away, in the direction in which she had knocked him, until he disappeared among the bookcases.

Kate twisted again to get a better view. She saw June beneath her now, apparently frozen in the place where she had struck Whit.

Then, out of the corner of her eye, she saw Pogo dart into the picture. Pogo bounced up and down in front of June, just inches from her face. Then she spoke:

> "A diller, a dollar,
> A ten o'clock scholar."

June managed to move slightly, and unnervingly, like a museum statue coming to life. Pogo seemed delighted. She added:

"Mademoiselle
Went down to the well,
Combed her hair,
And brushed it well.
Then picked up her basket and
Vanished!"

June and Pogo remained in their positions for another moment. Then June turned and retraced her steps into the stacks.

George had been so determined to show his invention that he was oblivious to all of this. He finally got Susan Singer-Wright's attention. She looked at the rope around his waist, the pulleys, and the girl hanging over his head, and asked, "Did you want something, sweetie?"

"Yes! I want the judges to look at my exhibit."

"Your exhibit for what?"

"The science fair!"

"Oh, sweetie, the judging is all over for that."

"It is? Who won?"

Susan wagged a finger at him like he was being naughty. "Now, now. You'll just have to wait until fourth period to find that out like everybody else."

George turned and walked back, lowering Kate to the ground in the process. Kate ripped off the bodice, cast it aside, and started looking around for Whit. "I'll punch his lights out. I'll kick his scrawny butt into next week. I swear to god I will!"

George looked around with her. "Who?"

"Whit!"

"Did I miss something?"

Kate shook her head furiously, long and hard, left and right, up and down. She finally calmed down enough to say, "Never mind. It's taken care of." She took a quick look around the stacks to find the person who had taken care of it, but June was nowhere to be seen.

After stashing their equipment, Kate and George walked back toward the judges' chairs. Kate continued to look around for Whit. And for June.

A large boy turned and whispered, "Hey, you guys, that flying machine looked awesome."

Kate answered for both of them. "Thank you, William."

Susan Singer-Wright stood before the judges, guests, and students. Her hand gestured and clanked at an assortment of past Technon Science Fair winners. Among them, Kate recognized the Holographic Scanner from the secret room.

Susan Singer-Wright said, "Our visitors from Caltech have had the privilege today of seeing this library's historic collection of superweapons of mass destruction, beginning with Cornell Whittaker Number One's own inventions. These masterpieces of design, materials, and imagination raised combat casualty levels around the world to previously unrecorded heights.

"Just before his death, Cornell Whittaker Number Two decided to add one invention to his father's collection. That invention, I am proud to say, was by our own little daughter, Ashley-Nicole Singer-Wright."

Susan paused. The Technon Industries judges applauded, followed by the other judges and the guests from Caltech. Susan pointed out the Holographic Scanner.

"Ashley-Nicole's idea for her sixth-grade science project was to expand the capacity of the holographic tape used on library books. Back then, the tape only had enough capacity to hold a book's title, author, and ISBN number."

George whispered to Kate, "That's redundant."

Kate was not in the mood. "So what?"

"So she said International Standard Book Number *number.*"

"Right. She did. And the roof did not fall in."

Susan held up a small piece of tape. "By the time she had finished, Ashley-Nicole had expanded the tape's storage capacity by so much, that each one-inch strip could hold the entire contents of the *Encyclopaedia Britannica* and the *OED* dictionary."

"That would be the *Oxford English Dictionary dictionary*," George muttered.

"The science fair judges from Technon Industries were so impressed that they purchased the invention from her on the spot."

Susan pointed to a long tubular invention. "In seventh grade, Ashley-Nicole turned her attention to infrared motion detection. The story has it that she wanted to know when her parents were hanging around spying on her." At this, Bud Wright guffawed from his folding chair. "So she invented a little old device called the BioSensor. It uses laser technology and infrared cells to detect when a warm-blooded human is trying to hide in an area."

Susan moved to the next invention. "In eighth grade, she outdid herself. She combined a little history and a little science. She created a titanium model of Cornell Whittaker Number One's most successful cannon and affixed it to the most powerful laser yet invented, producing the Laser Cannon.

"It superheated the molecules in targeted objects until they combusted and just exploded! She demonstrated it by aiming it at a book right here in the library and blasting it to kingdom come. This brought our little Ashley-Nicole to the attention of the big boys, the DoD Department in Washington."

George's lips barely moved. "That's the Department of Defense *department*."

Susan pointed her hand at the final invention. "The United States Armed Services have since invested heavily in the Laser Cannon."

Susan kept on pointing until Kate, George, and everyone else could not help but see that Ashley-Nicole's Laser Cannon and Whit's current invention were exactly the same thing.

Cornelia jumped up to explain. "Whit has continued the great tradition this year. He has taken all of these inventions a step further—and not a *little old* step, either—a big new step, by adding a sophisticated electronic tracker to the Laser Cannon. It can now detect an enemy on its own, focus in on it, and destroy it. Technon Industries is more excited about its prospects than anything they have ever seen."

It was Kate's turn to mutter to George. "He doesn't even show up for science class. I bet he doesn't even know what *laser* stands for. But Science Eight is too scared to report him."

"The judges will now do their work," Cornelia said. "They will decide between Whit's invention and the other invention, that one with the girl swinging from the rope. They did a nice job on that, didn't they? Let's give them a hand, too."

Cornelia paused. A few Mushroom Children, led by William Anderson, applauded. "Now, some of you are scheduled to report to the County Commission Room. The rest of you should report to your regular classes. We will all meet back here at the end of fourth period to see a demonstration of the winning project. Whichever one that may be."

George whispered, "Can you stand the suspense?" He pointed to Elevator #1. "I have to go up and watch democracy in action."

"I'm going, too," Kate told him. "Molly's grandmother is speaking today. I want to hear her."

"You're cutting class? What if you get caught?"

"Are you kidding? Science Eight will be happy I'm not there. I bring his class average down."

21

A Spirited Defense
of a Local Landmark

Kate crowded into the elevator with George's class, standing a foot taller than most of them. They all filed into the County Commission Room past a sign that read THIS WEEK'S ESSAY TOPIC: WHY THE FEDERAL GOVERNMENT SHOULD NOT INTERFERE WITH THE REPURPOSING OF OBSOLETE BUILDINGS.

George sat with his classmates, but Kate slipped into the visitors' section and waited. A big uniformed officer plopped down in the chair next to her. Kate tilted her head to look at his badge. It read SHERIFF WRIGHT.

When Bud Wright entered, he took the seat on the other side of the officer and said, "Good morning there, Bubba."

The sheriff replied, "Mornin', Bud."

Mrs. Brennan entered the room and spotted Kate right away. She worked her way over and sat down just as Susan Singer-Wright banged the gavel.

"This is a special session of the County Commission. Mr. Bud Wright has a very exciting new proposal for the county. Here is Mr. Wright."

Bud rose and approached the dais. "Thank you, darlin'. As you know, I recently purchased the old Palace Theatre. That thing's been sitting empty on Main Street for ten months now. The last play they had in there was god-awful. I never took my family there; I bet most of you never did, either. If you did, I wouldn't have been able to pick it up so cheap in foreclosure."

Bud paused to guffaw. "That's why I'm proposing County Bill 52986. It would grant me permission to re-purpose this old building into a place that the families of King's County will love to visit."

Bud reached into his plaid sports coat and pulled out what looked like a large handgun. "Don't worry now, Bubba. I know what you're thinkin'. 'Uh-oh. Old Bud's gone postal.' But that's not it at all."

It was the sheriff's turn to guffaw.

He held up the weapon for the commissioners to examine. "Now, on Ashley-Nicole's last trip back here from MIT, me and Susan and her decided to have us a family night out. Where did we go? A place I heard about up in Riverton called the Paintball Emporium.

"Let me tell you, we had a wingding of a time. We put on helmets and slickers and shot wads of paint at each other, and at everybody else there, for an hour. It was pure, flat-out fun. It's high time we had something like that here. That's why I am proposing today to convert the useless old Palace Theatre into Bud Wright's Paintball Palace." Bud smiled at the commissioners and returned to his seat.

"Thank you, Mr. Wright," Susan said. "That is an exciting idea." She scanned the crowd until she saw Mrs. Brennan. She announced, "Now we have another special treat, our old friend Mrs. Brennan."

Mrs. Brennan walked to the center of the dais. "I am here as the official representative of the King's County Historical Society."

"I didn't know we had one of them," Bud commented loudly.

Mrs. Brennan answered without looking at him. "We do. It is a nonprofit organization concerned with preserving our heritage."

Bud stage-whispered to his brother. "Concerned with protecting chipmunks, too, I bet."

Mrs. Brennan collected her thoughts. Then she spoke, distinctly and eloquently. "Before you vote to 'repurpose' this wonderful building, please consider some moments from its history. Abraham Lincoln delivered a speech from the stage of what was then the *new* Palace Theatre, on the day that it was dedicated in eighteen forty-one. Stephen Douglas, Woodrow Wilson, and both Theodore and Franklin Roosevelt have spoken either from its stage or from its front steps.

"Charles Dickens read from *The Old Curiosity Shop* at the Palace Theatre in eighteen forty-two. Oscar Wilde lectured there on aesthetics in eighteen eighty-two. The great actress Sarah Bernhardt graced its stage in *Camille* in eighteen eighty-nine.

"The Palace Theatre is not just a part of King's County history; it is a part of American history. It has hosted the proudest and most significant events to occur here in King's County. Let us honor that history today and request that it be preserved as a national historical site."

Susan banged the gavel. "All in favor of County Bill number 52986."

The commissioners raised their hands as one and said, "Aye!"

Susan banged the gavel again. "It is so passed."

Mrs. Brennan turned and started back to her seat, but Cornelia Whittaker-Austin stopped her on the way.

"There's only one historical building in this county," she informed her. "And you're in it."

Mrs. Brennan had planned on sitting down again, but Kate met her in the aisle. "Come on, Mrs. Brennan. Let's get out of here. These people make me sick."

Mrs. Brennan smiled. "I'll leave with you, Kate. But please promise me you won't let people like this make you sick. They're not to be empowered that way."

The two ducked into a waiting elevator. "But they *do* make me sick. And they were so mean to you."

"It's all right, dear. They don't know any better. Someone has to stand up to them, though, or they'll take over the world."

Kate looked down as the elevator descended to the lobby. She spotted June walking with a pair of folding chairs. She felt her usual surge of anger and said, "Some people won't stand up for anything." But then she remembered June's confrontation with Whit and had a change of heart. She pointed through the glass and told Mrs. Brennan, "That's my mother down there. She works here now, to help pay for my herbal protein shakes."

Mrs. Brennan seemed very surprised. "That's your mother?"

"Uh-huh."

"I guess I've never really gotten a good look at her.

Her face looks familiar." Mrs. Brennan pursed her lips and thought for a moment. But when the elevator doors opened, all she said was, "Well, thank you for coming, Kate. I do appreciate it. And I hope to see you soon."

22

Honorable Mention

Kate spotted her fourth-period class walking up in single file from the basement. She slipped into line with them and helped fill in a large cluster of folding chairs.

After a few moments of dead time, Susan Singer-Wright hurried in from the entranceway with cigarette smoke still seeping out of her nose. She began breathlessly, "Hello again, boys and girls. Now, I believe we are going to pick up where we left off with a demonstration of Whit Austin's invention."

Two men in Technon Industries windbreakers entered from the east stairwell carrying a book and a steel vise. Ma and Pa Melvil followed, carrying a wooden sawhorse between them. Ma and Pa set their burden down, bolted the vise to it, and took off. One of the

Technon men then steadied the sawhorse while the other positioned the book, a small, thick children's book entitled *Pat the Bunny*, in the grip of the vise.

The men joined Cornelia and Whit behind the Laser Cannon. Whit did not move. One of the men then flipped up a metal safety catch, exposing a thick red button. After a moment, he pointed at the button. Whit finally understood him and pressed it.

The Laser Cannon hummed quietly to life. After ten seconds, a thin red ray emanated from its muzzle. The ray shot across the expanse of the lobby, struck its target, and burned a small, smoky hole into *Pat the Bunny*.

Kate broke into short, sarcastic applause. The rest of the audience continued to stare silently.

In harsh whispers, Cornelia conferred with the Technon Industries men, waving her arms and pointing her large finger from one to the other. Finally, she addressed the audience. "I am told by the professional weapons developers at Technon Industries that Whit's invention is far too destructive to demonstrate here today. But they want me to tell you that he *is* the winner, by unanimous vote, of the Technon Industries Science Fair."

Cornelia gave the two-handed applause sign.

"By the way," Susan then added, "little George

Melvil gets the Honorable Mention ribbon, which was awarded to him a few minutes ago in his classroom."

George caught Kate's eye across the lobby and dangled a small ribbon for her to see.

Cornelia smiled proudly. "Now comes the moment we have been waiting for: your Technon Industries Science Fair winner, Whit Austin."

Whit stepped forward and launched into another speech about his grandfather and his great-grandfather.

Kate walked over to George, who was seated with his science 6 teacher and classmates. She said, "George Melvil? You're wanted in the office for a picture with your Honorable Mention ribbon."

Science 6 smiled nervously, but he made no objection. George hopped up and followed Kate. He whispered, "What was that about?"

"Do you really want to hear this speech?"

"I'd rather have slivers of bamboo shoved under my fingernails."

"Me, too. Let's get the flying machine and get out of here."

June was waiting outside the office with the rope already coiled up and ready. Kate and George grabbed the rest of the equipment, and the three of them hurried out. Kate waited for June to say something about the incident with Whit.

June did not.

Kate decided that she would not, either.

When the Geo Metro pulled into the driveway, the right side of the duplex was shaking noisily.

George turned to Kate, puzzled. "What are Ma and Pa doing here now?"

The noise stopped as soon as Kate, George, and June got out of the car. Ma and Pa stepped out onto the front porch in their clogging gear. Pa pointed at George, and Ma called out, "How'd you do at that genius science fair, Georgie? Did you win again? I bet you did."

George walked over to them while Kate and June unloaded the car. He reached up through the porch railing and handed his mother the ribbon. "I won this."

Ma and Pa started to whoop.

George interrupted them. "Wait a minute. Why are you home so early?"

Pa raised up his shoulders sheepishly. "That big lady, that Mrs. Whittaker-Austin, she told us to get out."

Ma picked up the story. "She said we was bothering you kids too much, so she changed our hours."

"She switched us to the graveyard shift," Pa said. "Midnight to six. I guess there ain't nobody to bother then."

"That's right," Ma cackled. "There ain't nobody to bother in a graveyard! Except the ghosts!"

George's eyes suddenly filled with tears. "Listen: I don't want you two working as janitors, on a graveyard shift, just so I can go to that place. I don't want that."

Ma waved his objections away. "Go on, Georgie! It don't matter to us. And it's only three nights a week."

Pa agreed. "It's not gonna interfere with our clogging at all."

"No. This is not right. I don't want this."

Ma and Pa both laughed through his protests. As they went back inside, Ma said, "You just keep winning those ribbons and passing those big tests, Georgie."

"You'll be in a genius college soon," Pa added.

All George could do was repeat, "This is not right."

George spent that night brooding. He thought about Kate's treatment at the *Orchid the Orca* auditions. He thought about his own treatment at the science fair. He thought about how shabbily Ma and Pa and June were treated all the time. Just before the stroke of midnight, he came to a decision.

Starting the next day, George stopped doing well on his standardized tests. He stopped writing good five-paragraph essays. George's seat slowly but surely began to slide downward through the rows in his classrooms.

George had made up his mind. He wanted out.

23

The First-Ever
Story Time on the Roof

Early Friday morning, during the first part of *The Montana Math Assessment*, Kate received a note telling her to report to Cornelia on the roof.

As soon as Kate stepped off the service elevator, Cornelia cornered her. "Today is the first-ever Story Time on the Roof. Everything must go perfectly for Heidi. You will make sure that it does. You can start by getting the cart of books from Walter Barnes. Do you understand?"

Kate assured her, with calm detachment, that she understood. She went down to the first floor, where she found Walter Barnes asleep. She wheeled his cart away quietly and brought it upstairs.

When Kate returned, Cornelia studied the contents

of the cart and exploded. "That narcoleptic old fool! Where is it? Where is *The Three Billy Goats Gruff*? That's the one book that Heidi is reading, and it's the one book that is not on the cart! What is the matter with him? What is the matter with you? Now get out of here, and don't come back without it!"

Kate descended again to the first floor. She checked the shelves for *The Three Billy Goats Gruff*. Then she checked the computer catalog. No luck. Her detachment soon gave way to fear of Cornelia's wrath.

Then she remembered where she had seen a copy of the book. It was in the secret room, on the Holographic Scanner.

She took Elevator #2 to the eighth floor. Then she crept up the stairs to the roof. She peeked out and saw that Heidi and Cornelia were far away, so she crept to the mushroom cap and bent it back. She slipped inside, closed it behind her, and climbed down to the bottom.

Kate was alarmed to find the door to the secret room open and the glow of a lantern seeping out from it. She stepped inside, not daring to breathe, but she relaxed when she saw Pogo.

Pogo was leaning over the face of the Holographic Scanner with a large envelope in her hand. Kate watched her slide a book across the glass and then pop it quickly, like a hot potato, into the envelope.

Pogo picked up the lantern and started out. But she

pulled up in an openmouthed, silent shriek upon seeing Kate.

Kate whispered, "It's just me, Pogo. I'm sorry to startle you."

In reply, Pogo held up the manila envelope.

"I need to ask you a favor," Kate said. "I need to find a copy of *The Three Billy Goats Gruff* or Mrs. Whittaker-Austin might kill me. She's really on a rampage."

Pogo held the envelope higher. Then she spoke:

> "Will you wake him? No, not I,
> For if I do, he's sure to cry."

Kate struggled to understand. "What are you saying? Do you have the book?"

Pogo nodded yes.

"What? Is it in that envelope?"

Pogo bobbed and nodded some more.

"Okay, then, can I have it?"

Pogo shook her head no, vehemently. She pointed to herself, and then to the envelope, and then to herself again.

"You?" Kate interpreted. "You will give her the copy of *The Three Billy Goats Gruff*?"

Pogo nodded yes with bone-jarring enthusiasm. Then she pointed to the exit, indicating that Kate should leave.

Kate whispered, "Thank you," and slipped out. She moved swiftly and silently, retracing her steps back to the lobby.

Later, when she arrived back on the roof, she saw that Walter Barnes had relocated there. He was now sitting by the stairwell wall with his head leaning heavily against the white cement blocks. He held the remains of a peanut butter and jelly sandwich in one hand. Kate placed a set of *t*-sound phonics worksheets on the cart next to him. As she did, she noticed a large manila envelope sitting there, too.

At five o'clock, parents and children started arriving for the first-ever Story Time on the Roof. They exited the service elevator to find a semicircle of folding chairs awaiting them, a cozy island of safety among the boards, nails, and tarps strewn near the still-unfinished stage. The adults took seats and pulled the smaller children onto their laps.

At precisely 5:15, the door to the stairwell opened. George walked out followed by a giggling line of Juku Warriors. As soon as the line halted, George announced, "We were supposed to spell a very large word for you today, but we decided that we would sing it for you instead. So here is how it goes."

George gathered the boys and girls on either side of him. Then, in a surprisingly confident voice, he led them in a spirited rendition of "Supercalifragilistic-expialidocious."

George and the children bowed at the end, and the parents all laughed, whistled, and clapped.

Just after the noise died down, Dr. Austin, Cornelia, and Heidi emerged from the service elevator. Dr. Austin waved to the children and welcomed certain parents by name.

George took a seat in the audience as Dr. Austin joined the Juku Warriors. They began by reciting the forty-seven prefectures of Japan. When they reached, "Yamagata, Yamaguchi, Yamanashi," Dr. Austin began his pitch for the Whittaker After-School Preparatory.

He apologized for the construction debris, saying, "This rooftop project has disturbed things around here. That's for sure. But it will all be worth it. We will be hosting many more Story Times on the Roof, including one for the First Lady of the United States next month."

The parents broke into spontaneous applause.

"And, we hope, one for her husband after that," Dr. Austin added.

They clapped again.

Cornelia then stepped forward to take over the proceedings. Dr. Austin made his way toward the back. In order to do so, however, he had to pass the sleeping figure of Walter Barnes. Hoping no one would see him, Dr. Austin nudged the book cart into Walter Barnes's leg, waking him up and, in the process, causing the manila envelope to fall to the ground. "Pick that up, Walter!" he hissed. "And for heaven's sake, stay awake."

Kate watched from ten yards away, leaning against the four-foot-high roof wall. She was planning on looking down at the river during Heidi's performance, but Pogo suddenly appeared beside her. Pogo was holding a second manila envelope under her arm. There was obviously a book inside this one, too, and she showed it to Kate. It was the antique *Perrault's Mother Goose*.

Cornelia introduced Heidi loudly as "the winner of the very competitive *Orchid the Orca* contest. Heidi will soon play the part of Orchid the Orca for the First Lady of the United States. Ladies and gentlemen, boys and girls, with no further ado, here is Heidi Whittaker Austin."

Heidi skipped out from behind the stairwell wall dressed as usual in her white crinoline. She waved to the children and called, "Who's ready for a story?"

The parents smiled and waved the children's hands for them.

"Today's story is called *The Three Billy Goats Gruff*! Do any of you know this story?"

Some of the children responded with bashful nods.

Heidi turned to select the book from the cart. Even from Kate's distant vantage point, she could see the look of exasperation on Heidi's face when she could not locate it. Heidi looked around for her mother, who, in turn, looked around for Kate.

Kate suddenly felt ill. She considered running for her life across the crowded roof. She considered a wild leap into the river. But she was spared having to make either choice by a sudden commotion.

Kate looked in the same direction as everyone else. Then she saw what they all saw.

There, posed in the stairwell doorway with *The Three Billy Goats Gruff*, was Walter Barnes. His jacket was now off, and his shirt was open, revealing a sallow, sunken chest. His tie was loosened and turned around, hanging behind him. He had drawn two large circles, apparently with strawberry jelly, on his cheeks. His eyes blazed maniacally behind his thick glasses and seemed to give off a red glare.

Kate looked at the adults in the audience. Most of them seemed surprised, but amused. Dr. Austin's eyes, however, opened wide in shock, while Cornelia's narrowed in anger.

The children drifted closer to their parents, their eyes still on the doorway, when, in a booming voice, Walter Barnes dropped the book onto the cinders and intoned, "Trip, trap! Trip, trap! Trip, trap! Who's that tripping over my bridge?"

The children all stopped moving and listened, instantly entranced by the sight of the character and the sound of his voice. Walter Barnes broke away from the doorway and strode among them—strutting, fretting, emoting every ounce of drama from the tale of the three billy goats and the ugly troll.

Kate watched Heidi walk off petulantly, sit next to her mother, and stare down at her feet. But everyone else on the roof watched Walter Barnes delightedly, totally absorbed in his virtuoso performance.

Walter Barnes finished with a great flourish, posing ramrod straight, like a comical statue. The audience, young and old alike, burst into enthusiastic applause.

He responded to the crowd's adulation with a brief encore, articulating slowly and deliberately, "Jack and Jill went up the hill."

Upon hearing those words, Pogo took off from her spot next to Kate. She scooted along the perimeter and disappeared behind the stairwell wall. Only Kate saw Pogo's hand reach out from behind the wall to deposit a book on the cart. An antique book, opened to a certain page.

Walter Barnes took a final bow. Then, as if it were part of the act, he leaned over and started to shuffle sideways, like a baggy-pants vaudeville dancer, toward the book cart. He moved in an unwavering line, as if the cart were an electromagnet and his head a metal ball. His head clanged into the cart, cushioned slightly by the opened book lying atop it. Then he collapsed into his seat, seemingly as deeply asleep as he had been before.

Kate looked around at the people on the roof. Clearly, no one had any idea what to do next. Dr. Austin continued to stare at Walter Barnes with his mouth open. Cornelia and Heidi continued to fume. Kate stepped away from the wall. She held her hands up high over her head and started to applaud. Immediately, all the kids and parents did so, too.

The ovation seemed to snap Dr. Austin out of his trance. He waited until the wave of clapping had subsided and then walked before the crowd with his own hands raised high. He shouted to them, like a master of ceremonies, "One of King's County's finest librarians, ladies and gentlemen. A fixture here at the Whittaker Magnet School, Mr. Walter Barnes."

Cornelia recovered, too, but not in a happy way. She stormed over to Walter Barnes and, as discreetly as she could, started berating him for interrupting Heidi. Then she berated him for not listening to her. Then she poked him, and she discovered why he wasn't listening.

Walter Barnes was dead.

Cornelia started screaming. She ran toward Dr. Austin in hysterics, pounding clumsily across the roof.

Pogo approached the book cart on tiptoes. She scooped up *The Three Billy Goats Gruff* and *Perrault's Mother Goose*. She slid both into a large envelope; then she tiptoed back.

At her husband's side, Cornelia was bellowing, "He's dead! Oh my god, I touched him. I touched him and he's dead!"

Dr. Austin pushed and pulled Cornelia as best he could toward the service elevator. He motioned frantically for Heidi to get in, and they all disappeared.

Kate watched them go and then turned back to the audience. After a series of hushed exchanges and anxious looks, the parents and children funneled quietly toward the stairwell. The first-ever Story Time on the Roof had come to an inglorious end.

Kate stared at the supine figure of Walter Barnes. She felt a pang of sympathy for the old librarian. But that pang was quickly replaced by another feeling, a feeling that something big had just happened. She didn't know what it was exactly, but she did know this: It was something that the Whittaker-Austins, with all their money and all their power, could not control. It was a first chink in their armor. Perhaps it was a door to a door to a door that would lead her out of there.

24

The Weirdness Is Rising

On Saturday afternoon, June signed for a FedEx delivery addressed to Kate Peters. She carried the package up the front stairs and knocked on the bedroom door.

Kate opened the door sullenly, but upon recognizing the FedEx logo, she quickly brightened. "What's that?"

"I don't know. I don't have my glasses on. What's the return address?"

Kate took the package. She read her own name. Then she read "King's County Library System" as the return address.

June blinked in surprise. "Oh? I thought that it might be from your father."

That had not occurred to Kate. But now that June had said it, and now that it was obviously *not* from him, Kate filled up with resentment. She snarled, "I guess you're wrong," and slammed the door.

She heard June's voice from the other side. "Kate? I didn't mean it like that. I really thought it might be from...him. That's why I said it. It was stupid of me."

Kate leaned her back against the door and exhaled. Then she mumbled, just loud enough for June to hear, "All right. Don't worry about it. Forget it."

When the sound of June's footsteps faded from the landing, Kate ripped the tab on the package and opened it. She reached in, pulled out a leather-bound book, and held it up wonderingly in her hand. She whispered, "Cornell Whittaker Number Two's diary. Pogo? You sent this to me?"

Kate flopped forward onto her bed, opened the diary, and started to read. She pored over the pages of neat handwriting for an hour, punctuating the silence in her room with occasional utterings, such as "Oh my god" and "I don't believe this."

Finally, at 4:00 P.M., she picked up the phone and called Molly. "Listen: Can you come over here tonight? And can you bring your grandmother's scrapbook? The one about the Whittaker Library?"

"Sure. I guess so. Why do you want the scrapbook?"

"I just got a FedEx package delivered to me with Cornell Whittaker's diary inside."

"No way!"

"Yeah. I'm telling you, the weirdness is rising."

Molly's parents dropped her off right after dinner. Kate was sitting out front, driven there by the syncopated pounding of the Tri-County Cloggers on the back porch. But tonight she welcomed the noise. She hoped to talk to Molly about things that no one else should hear.

Molly sat down on the stoop next to Kate and pulled two items from a canvas bag: her flute and her grandmother's scrapbook.

Kate held up the diary. "Check it out. You're not going to believe some of the stuff in here."

But she had no sooner opened the leather-bound book when she heard a door open and felt a light tread on the porch boards. George leaned over the railing and asked casually, "Hey, what are you guys doing?"

He stared at the odd pair of books on the girls' laps while Kate fashioned a reply. "It's, like, girl talk, Uncle George. Please excuse us."

George nodded thoughtfully. "I see. Girl talk about the Whittaker Library? And whatever that other book is about?"

After a long pause, Kate offered a compromise. "If I

let you stay, will you promise not to be a know-it-all? Not to talk ninety percent of the time and insist that you are right one hundred percent of the time?"

George took offense at that. "I won't talk at all if you don't want me to. And you two can be as wrong as you like. I don't care."

"Okay, then. You can join us."

George remained where he was, leaning on the railing. Kate opened the diary to a page that she had bookmarked. She asked him, "Remember this? This is the diary of Cornell Whittaker Number Two."

George sputtered. "How did you get that out of the secret room?"

"Pogo sent it to me FedEx."

Molly asked, "Who is Pogo again?"

"She's a librarian. A very strange librarian who... likes me."

Molly raised her eyebrows. "She *likes you* likes you?"

"No. She just likes me. I don't know why."

George interrupted. "You know why. You stood up to her enemies—Mrs. Hodges, Mrs. Whittaker-Austin. And you helped her friend, the can man. I'll bet nobody's ever done anything like that before."

"Do you think so?"

"I know so." George caught himself. "Of course, I could be wrong a certain percentage of the time."

Kate pointed at the scrapbook. "Look through there," she told Molly. "I saw an article about Cornell Number Two coming back from London with a rare book collection."

Molly heaved open the cover and turned to the middle of the book. "Yeah. I saw that, too."

While Molly turned pages, George pointed out, "Rare books are very big on the Internet. So is spiritualism. If you want, I can check out the prices of—"

Molly interrupted him. "Here it is! He's posing next to a shelf full of old books."

Kate asked, "What's the date of that clipping?" Molly read off the date, and Kate flipped quickly through the diary pages. But, just as she found her place, the other door of the duplex opened. Kate's shoulders tightened.

June walked out holding a black phone in front of her. "Kate, it's for you."

"Who is it?"

"I don't know. It's a boy."

Kate's tone changed abruptly. "Derek Arroyo?"

June stared futilely at the caller ID readout. "I don't know. I don't have my glasses."

Molly asked, "Does he sound real cool?"

"No. He sounds real nervous."

Kate and Molly exchanged a blank stare. Then Kate took the phone and turned it on. "Hello." She listened for only a few seconds before her mouth fell open.

Then her eyes shot over to Molly's. She answered the caller, "Yes, William. I do know who you are."

Molly extended her arms in a gesture that asked, "Who?"

Kate said, "Well, that's nice. I hope you enjoy your new place. But listen, I am really busy now." For Molly's benefit, Kate pantomimed sticking a finger down her own throat. "Okay. Yeah. Good-bye."

Kate turned the phone off and snapped her head backward, like she had just been released from a force field. She handed the phone up to June, who carried it back inside.

Molly asked the obvious question. "Who was it?"

"It was William. William Anderson. He sits next to me in all of my classes." Kate looked up at George. "That should tell you how smart he is."

"Why did he call?" Molly asked. "Does he like you?"

George said, "Does he *like you* like you?"

"Shut up, both of you. He called to say he just moved onto our block." Kate suddenly looked around in a panic. "My god! He could be right across the street. He could be looking at us now, through big binoculars, or night-vision goggles."

Molly looked around, too. "That is really creepy."

Kate shook her head, like a wet dog. Then she pointed emphatically to the books sitting on their laps. "Forget it. Come on, you guys. No more interruptions.

I found three entries from the day when Cornell Number Two returned from London with those books. Here they are. Listen, listen, listen: Entry one: 'They once lived in our astral plane. Now they move from plane to plane.' Entry two: 'I will be greater than Father in this one regard. He was confined to one plane his entire life. I shall know a second plane.' And entry three: 'Something that Father only talked about, I shall do, and I shall do it soon.'"

Kate looked up. She and Molly stared at each other for a long moment. Then they turned, together, and looked at George.

George took the opportunity to say, "Oh? Are you asking Mr. Know-It-All?"

Kate clenched her teeth. "Yes. In this case, in this one specific case, we would like to hear what you know about the topic. Please."

"Okay. Here's what I know. Spiritualists, people who believe in ghosts and that sort of thing, believe that there is another level to the world, another 'plane,' where they can talk to the dead."

George stopped there, so Kate tried to paraphrase him. "Cornell Whittaker Number Two talked to the dead?"

George shrugged. "I seriously doubt it. At that point in his diary, however, he believed he was about to."

Molly pointed at the scrapbook on her lap. "So... What does that have to do with the old books?"

George smiled innocently. "I have no idea." He watched Kate's eyes narrow in on him in anger. But then her eyes darted to the right, to the sidewalk, and grew wide. George turned and saw three people approaching—a well-dressed man and woman, and a tall, pasty boy.

The boy called out, "Hey, Kate! Can you believe this?"

Kate muttered, "No. I cannot."

The boy explained to his parents, "Mom, Dad, this is Kate Peters. I sit next to her in all of my classes."

The man and woman smiled. The woman said, "Hello, Kate. We're Mr. and Mrs. Anderson, your new neighbors. Who are your friends here?"

Kate managed to reply, "This is my friend Molly and my uncle George."

"I'll tell you what, William," the man suggested. "Why don't you hang out with your friends here while your mom and I walk up to the store."

William replied, "Okay, Dad," climbed up the three porch steps, and stood next to George. His parents continued on their way, leaving four silent kids in their wake.

With as much self-control as she could muster, Kate asked, "William? What are you doing here?"

"Like I said on the phone, we live here now."

"But you don't live in this house, do you? So what are you doing here?"

William pointed behind him. "Actually, I live five duplexes down. We're renting a left side. The owners are on the right." No one replied, so he added, "Did you know that this block is now inside the Whittaker Magnet School District?"

"Yes," Kate told him icily. "We did know that."

"Well, my block used to be in that district, too. But the lines got changed, so my mom and dad decided we'd better move over to this block."

George interrupted him. "Wait a minute. They moved your block out of the Whittaker district when they moved this block in?"

"Yeah. That's happened to me a couple of times now. I've lived all over the city."

George suggested, "Is Dr. Austin trying to get rid of you?"

"Oh yeah. Big-time. But my mom and dad won't let him."

Molly muttered so that only Kate could hear, "Guess what. We're trying to get rid of you, too."

William smiled nervously, and the four of them reverted to their silent state.

After a long pause, Kate took charge. "Listen, William. We're talking about something very important here. It's about Cornell Whittaker Number Two and his diary and the Whittaker Library. You either have to leave right now, or you have to swear you can keep your big mouth shut."

"Oh, absolutely!" William swore. "I can keep my big mouth shut. I keep my mouth shut all the time, about all sorts of—"

Molly cut him off. "This is not a good example of keeping your mouth shut."

William shriveled in contrition. "Oh. Sorry. I'm really sorry."

"He's sorry," Molly muttered to Kate. "I'll say that for him."

But William seemed impervious to insult. "Yes, I am. And I'll show you. I know a lot about Whittaker. I used to be a Juku Warrior. Then I was on the Cram Crew. Now I'm actually a student there."

"How do you feel about that?" Kate asked.

William shrugged.

Kate leveled an intense stare directly into his eyes. "Let's try that again. How do you feel about that?"

William's smile faded away. He blinked for several seconds. Then he wiped his eyes on his sleeve. "I hate it," he said at last.

Kate favored him with a kind look. "I know what you mean. We hate it, too." She stopped to look at George. "Or at least I do."

George protested, "Wait a minute! I hate it, too. I want out of there."

Molly added, "I hate it, and I don't even go there."

"I'm going to find us a way out," Kate said. "I don't know how yet, but I believe a door will open and we will be able to escape through it. Are you with us, William? Do you want out, too?"

William was now openly in tears. He assured Kate, from the bottom of his heart, "Yes, I want out. I'd have quit long ago, if my parents woulda let me."

"We all need to keep our eyes and ears open, every day at Whittaker, for every weird thing that happens. We need to be prepared to act."

William dried his eyes. He sniffled. "Be prepared. That could be our motto. You know? That was our motto in Scouts: *Semper Paratus*. Be Prepared."

"Actually," George said, "that would translate as 'Always Prepared.'"

William got flustered. "Would it? I had to quit Scouts to be on the Cram Crew. I might have got it wrong."

"Don't worry about it. Heads up though, William. Here come your parents."

The four kids watched Mr. and Mrs. Anderson come back down the street. Mrs. Anderson called out, "Kate Peters? We've been talking about you since we left. Are you any relation to June and Charley Peters?"

Kate gulped. "Yes, I am. They're my parents."

Mrs. Anderson turned to her husband with an "I told you so" look. "We were just saying, 'What ever happened to June and Charley Peters?' They used to be involved in everything."

Kate felt like she wanted to run. Or burst into tears.

Then George spoke up. "They are now divorced. Charley's gone. He's in Asia. And June is not feeling too well."

Mr. and Mrs. Anderson squirmed on the sidewalk. Neither said a thing until Mr. Anderson called over to his son, "Come on, William. We have to get home and unpack."

William left the porch obediently, and the three Andersons retreated down the street.

Molly's parents pulled up to the curb one minute later. Molly stuffed her flute case and the scrapbook into her canvas bag. She pointed to the diary and told Kate, "We have to do this again. Soon."

Kate swallowed hard, still unable to speak. She did manage to nod.

Molly got up. "Okay, you guys. *Semper Apparatus* ... Or whatever it was."

George supplied the right word: *"Paratus."*

"Yeah. Whatever. Bye."

Molly drove away with her parents. George waited five minutes before he asked, "Kate? Are you okay?"

"Yeah, sure. Why wouldn't I be?" she told him, defiantly.

George waited. The night grew darker and colder before he said, "We didn't get to talk about the real cool stuff, you know? What with the interruptions." Kate didn't reply. "Do you want to talk about what happened yesterday?"

Kate leaned back against the porch railing. "Yeah. Sure. Why wouldn't I?"

George straddled the center railing. "What do you think happened to Walter Barnes?"

Kate finally looked at him. "I don't think that was Walter Barnes. I believe something else took over his body. Something that wasn't human."

George raised one eyebrow. "Come on, Kate. Be logical."

"I believe Walter Barnes was possessed. By a demon."

"That's impossible."

"No, it's not. Lots of people believe in demons."

"Lots of people are stupid."

"What's so stupid about it? There are things in life that you do not understand, Uncle George. If you don't know that, then you're not as smart as you think."

George accepted the rebuke. "Okay. I do know that. But I know this, too: Scientists are able to prove the existence of human-type beings going back more than one hundred and sixty thousand years. They can prove the existence of subatomic particles that only appear for a fraction of a fraction of a millisecond. They can prove that nitrogen is the dominant gas in the atmosphere of Pluto. But all the scientists who ever lived, with all the equipment that was ever invented, still have not been able to prove the existence of one Bigfoot or one Loch Ness Monster, or one supernatural demon anywhere in the world at any time."

George looked at Kate. She seemed checkmated into silence by his cold, scientific analysis. So he added, "Still, that clearly was not the Walter Barnes that we all knew and loved."

The low thrum of clogging on the back porch stopped abruptly. Kate got up and started inside. She told George wearily, "Whatever. You can think what you want. Good night."

George hopped over the railing and followed Kate in through the vestibule. "Okay. Okay. Even though it's impossible, let's say that he was . . . that he was possessed by some supernatural demonlike creature. That raises some new questions, like: How did this demon thing enter the body of Walter Barnes? And, did it leave Walter Barnes when he died? And, if it did leave, where did it go?"

Kate smiled devilishly. "Why don't you go back to your room and sleep on that?"

George looked terrified. "I'd rather not." He followed Kate into the kitchen. She rummaged through a cabinet until she found an old metal thermos with a blue top. She held it up. "I'm bringing an empty thermos, every day, hidden in my backpack. From now on, my Mrs. Hodges protein shakes get dumped right in here."

"Good idea."

George followed Kate up to the landing. There, he hung around surfing the Internet while Kate got ready for bed. He clicked through websites devoted to nineteenth-century London, spiritualism, and antiquarian books. When he heard Kate behind him, he asked, "Would you mind if I slept over here? The floor would be fine."

"Why? Are you afraid of Bigfoot? Or the Loch Ness Monster? Or, maybe, demons?"

George gulped. "I'm not afraid of the first two. And I don't believe in demons. Not at all. But," he finally admitted, "I am a little afraid of the *possibility* of demons. But only a little. And only at night."

He turned around to see that Kate was already standing in the doorway holding out a sleeping bag and an extra pillow.

25

Putting Some Crazy Rumors to Rest

On the Monday morning following Walter Barnes's bizarre performance, Dr. Austin called all students, teachers, and staff of the Whittaker Magnet School to an assembly in the lobby. Kate slipped away from her classmates and found George. They sat together in the back row, staring around curiously, as Dr. Austin emerged from the elevator.

Kate whispered, "Do you think this is about Walter Barnes?"

"It has to be. Parents were there and saw it, right? He can't just say that it never happened."

Dr. Austin stood at attention before the student body, examining faces at random. "Just as our cherished

Whittaker Magnet School is preparing to fulfill its destiny and to step onto the national stage, this happens." He shook his head sadly. "A terrible tragedy. One of our staff, and a trusted member of the Whittaker team, has, unfortunately, let that team down. I'm sure that some of you have heard crazy rumors about Walter Barnes during Friday's Story Time. I am here to assure you that they are nothing more than that. Crazy rumors.

"There is even a rumor that Mr. Barnes is dead. Well, let me assure you, I just spoke to him moments ago. I inquired about his health; he told me he was fine. Then I informed him that he was fired.

"Walter Barnes is not dead. Walter Barnes, I am sorry to say, was merely dead drunk. That is what caused his erratic behavior. We hope that your parents will rest assured that he has been removed permanently and that nothing of this kind shall ever happen again. They have my solemn promise on that."

Dr. Austin raised one hand like he was being sworn in. "To keep that solemn promise, I must have your help. I cannot do this alone. I want you to report anything out of the ordinary directly to me. In fact, for every report of unusual, abnormal, or aberrant behavior, you will receive ten additional bonus points on any test of your choosing. Now, you may all go back to your classes."

———

William Anderson caught up to Kate on the stairwell. He whispered to her, "So... what did you think of that?"

She answered for anyone to hear, "I didn't believe a word of it. It was a Story Time. Without phonics."

"Huh?"

"It was a story, William. Now Dr. Austin expects us to go home and repeat that story to our parents. But don't you do it."

William's face reflected his struggle to understand. He whispered, "Okay, Kate. I won't tell my parents. Not about this, not about that other stuff, not about anything."

"Good. *Semper Paratus*."

26

The Very Public Arrival
of the Secret Service

On Wednesday, while Kate and George worked their after-school jobs in the lobby, a black Lincoln Town Car pulled up to the front doors. The car was unmarked, but it carried U.S. GOVERNMENT plates on the front and back.

The first person to step out of the car wore a laminated identification badge on his suit's breast pocket. It said MCCOY, JAMES J. in large letters, followed by AGENT IN CHARGE in small letters. He walked briskly toward the Whittaker Building, looking neither left nor right.

The second person out wore a similar badge attached to the pocket of his checked sports coat. It said PFLAUM, JONATHAN P., AGENT. He struggled to drag a large weaponlike device out of the car with him. It looked like a long metal version of a Super Soaker squirt gun.

The third person to emerge wore no security badge. She was tall and muscular, a chiseled bodybuilder, with short cropped hair. She had extraordinarily healthy-looking skin, dark brown, close to the color of the silk shirt she wore beneath a two-piece ivory suit.

She did look left, right, and upward, taking in the Story Time poster, the *Id pendemus* motto, and the beginnings of the lurid *Andrew Carnegie in Hell* mosaic.

She stopped to read a memo taped to the glass doors and repeated the words aloud, in TV anchorwoman English: "'This week's essay topic: Why the President Should Appoint Dr. Austin to His Commission on Teacher Accountability.'"

She took out a small electronic device—a thin, handheld computer with advanced communications capabilities—called the WebWizard X, and scanned in the poster and the memo.

Susan Singer-Wright and Cornelia Whittaker-Austin, wearing purple name tags with yellow lettering, had positioned themselves in the lobby next to a high-piled *TBC* book display.

Kate and George had positioned themselves just behind them, on the other side of the display, where they remained effectively invisible to the women.

Cornelia called out to the agents as they approached, "Welcome to the building that my grandfather Cornell Whittaker Number One built as a monument of granite and steel, and that my father, Cornell Whittaker Number Two, built as a monument of great books. Now my husband, Dr. J. Kendall Austin, is—"

James J. McCoy, the agent in charge, interrupted her. "Excuse me, ma'am. We have specific objectives and a limited timetable today."

Cornelia finished her thought, anyway. "—building it as a monument of educational excellence."

Agent McCoy addressed his subordinate. "Agent Pflaum, get to work from the basement up. I'll work from the roof down."

Agent Pflaum nodded and lugged his large weapon with him toward the stairwell.

McCoy himself took off toward Elevator #2, unfolding a set of blueprints of the Whittaker Building as he walked.

George took a quick look at the clock and whispered, "I can't stay any longer." He hurried off to meet the Juku Warriors in the County Commission Room. But Kate had no intention of leaving. She bent lower, pretending to straighten the *TBC* book display.

Cornelia said, "I will make a brief statement to the First Lady's chief of staff. Then I will excuse myself and proceed upstairs to my husband's office. You delay her for five minutes to build up anticipation for meeting Dr. Austin."

The woman in the ivory suit approached Susan and extended her right hand. "I am Rosetta Turner, the First Lady's chief of staff."

"You sure are!" Susan gushed. "I recognize you from the TV. I am Susan Singer-Wright, the chair of the King's County Commission."

Cornelia reached out, grabbed the hand, and pumped it. "I am Cornelia Whittaker-Austin, of the King's County Whittakers, who built the building that she sits in and the chair that she sits on."

Rosetta Turner took her right hand back and massaged it with her left. "I see."

"Now you must excuse me," Cornelia told her. "I have to go upstairs to help the doctor." Rosetta and Susan watched her stomp away toward Elevator #2.

Before Susan could engage her in small talk, though, she and Rosetta heard a loud clattering. Bud Wright had entered through the glass doors and was rolling a power washer, complete with attachments, toward them.

Susan gushed again. "Oh! There's my husband!" She waited for Bud to roll up to them and park the power washer. "Bud! This is Rosetta Turner, the First Lady's chief of staff!"

Bud wiped his hands on his pants. Rosetta shook hands with him as briefly as possible.

"I am pleased to meet such a high representative of the U.S. government, ma'am. I am Bud Wright, the owner of Bud Wright's Swim-with-a-Dolphin Aquatic Park, and I need to talk to somebody about the government's regulation of orcas. The Japanese are willing to sell me an orca, so the U.S. government just needs to get out of the way."

Rosetta interrupted him. "Excuse me, but are you talking about fish?"

Bud blinked rapidly. "Yes, ma'am."

"Well, do I look like someone who is even remotely connected to the subject of fish?"

"No, ma'am."

"Then please stop." She turned to Susan. "Where's the doctor?"

Susan smiled, puzzled. "Who?"

"The one who wants to get on the presidential commission."

"Oh. That would be Dr. Austin. He can't meet with you this very minute. He can, though, meet with you in five minutes." Susan dared to take Rosetta by the elbow of her ivory suit. "In the meantime, would you like a little peek at our school?"

She guided Rosetta toward the basement stairwell,

prompting the First Lady's chief of staff to ask, "The school is down here?"

"Yes, ma'am. The Whittaker Magnet School. The number-one standardized testing school in the United States."

Bud spotted Kate by the bookcase. He said, "What are you doing there, little girl?"

Kate gulped and prepared to speak, but Bud beat her to it. "Come give me a hand. We got us a ceiling to clean. Grab that roll of plastic."

Kate followed Bud to the doorway, where she saw a fat, cylindrical roll of plastic sheeting. She hefted it onto her shoulder and set off dutifully behind him.

Rosetta Turner wrinkled her nose at the scent of protein supplements and squinted her eyes against the glare of the fluorescent lights. She stopped and peered into a classroom. "Do these kids get outside to exercise?"

"Oh, yes, ma'am," Susan lied. "We encourage a healthy diet and lots of exercise. We even have treadmills in some classrooms."

"In the classrooms?"

"Yes, ma'am."

Rosetta conceded, "That's good. The First Lady is opposed to flabby children."

Rosetta pointed a glossy fingertip at the cigarette

pack sticking out of Susan's purse. "The First Lady would not want to see that, though. The First Lady would recoil at the very prospect of tobacco in a school."

Susan smiled contritely. "Yes, ma'am."

Rosetta glanced down at her Cartier Panthère watch. "All right. It's been five minutes. Let's go meet the doctor."

Bud showed Kate how to place sheets of heavy plastic over the display tables in the lobby. He told her, "Work your way upstairs. Just cover the inside cases, near the railings. When you get all the floors covered, give me a wave, like this." He demonstrated a standard hello-type wave. "I'll be up on the eighth floor. When I see the wave, I'll start power-blasting the ceiling."

Bud had no sooner started rolling the machine toward the elevator, though, when Rosetta and Susan emerged from the stairwell. He detoured to cut them off.

Susan cried gaily, "There's Bud!"

Rosetta warned him. "You again? This had better not be about fish."

"No, ma'am. It's about housing. People need housing. Am I right? Do you see all these homeless people walking around? Do you want to do something about them?"

"You want to build affordable housing for the homeless?"

"No! No! Not for them! I want to build houses for decent hardworking Americans. Not for shiftless bums."

Rosetta reached Elevator #1 and pushed the button. "So why don't you?"

Bud threw up his hands. "Federal regulations again! All the remaining woodlands in King's County are protected by the Department of the Interior. Why is that?"

"I have no idea."

"Well, I do. They claim they got some endangered species livin' in there. Some little squirrelly thing, the woodlands chipmunk. What kind of deal is that? People can't buy affordable homes, in a good school district, because of some chipmunk? I don't think that's right."

Rosetta pounded on the elevator button. "The First Lady likes chipmunks."

"I'm sure she does! Everybody does. That's part of the problem, see? It's a public relations problem. Chip and Dale? Alvin and the Chipmunks? Everybody loves them. If it were some endangered cockroach or rat or snake, it wouldn't be protected because they've got a bad rep, like orcas."

"I warned you about the fish."

"Yes, ma'am. Sorry. But back to those roaches and rats and snakes. What would we do to them? We'd spray 'em dead from the air, and the bulldozers would roll. But, no! You can't mess with chipmunks."

The elevator doors opened, revealing Agents McCoy and Pflaum standing inside.

Rosetta said, "Excuse me."

She and Susan joined the two agents. Rosetta remained facing the back wall until the doors had closed completely. Then she leaned toward Agent McCoy's ear and whispered so that only he could hear, "If that man gets within twenty feet of the First Lady, you're to shoot him."

He answered dryly, "Yes, Miss Turner."

Agent Pflaum stared at Susan Singer-Wright's name tag with great intensity. She smiled nervously, looked away, and looked back. He was still staring. She finally asked him, "Is something wrong, Agent?"

Agent Pflaum's face reddened. "No, ma'am. I'm sorry to stare at you, but I have been thinking about your name, and I have a question."

"What is that?"

"Are you by any chance related to the inventor of the BioSensor?"

Susan favored him with her widest smile. "I surely am! That would be little Ashley-Nicole, my daughter. Yes, that would have been when she was twelve, or was it thirteen? It was right around when she got her braces."

Behind her, Agent McCoy snorted. "The BioSensor. Ha! Let me tell you something, Pflaum. If you want to know if a warm-blooded creature is hiding in a closet, you open the door and look."

Agent Pflaum answered excitedly. "Okay, but! In the very act of opening the door, whoever is inside could shoot you! Or could shoot past you at the First Lady. The BioSensor tells you whether anyone's in the closet before you open the door."

"Part of your job, Agent Pflaum, is to take a bullet for the First Lady," Agent McCoy reminded him.

When the elevator doors opened on the eighth floor, Cornelia was standing there blocking the exit. She held the door open with one outstretched hand and intoned, "Welcome to the top floor of the Whittaker Building. This floor contains the offices of my grandfather Cornell Whittaker Number One; my father, Cornell Whittaker Number Two; my husband, Dr. J. Kendall Austin; and—"

Agent McCoy cut her off again. "Dr. J. Kendall Austin, ma'am. He's the one we're here to see. The rest will have to wait."

Cornelia informed him, through clenched teeth, "The rest, sir, are deceased."

"I'm sorry to hear that, ma'am."

"Maybe some other time," Rosetta added diplomatically.

Cornelia stepped back to let the four occupants out of the elevator. She pointed to her left, where Dr. Austin stood holding a copy of *TBC: Test-Based Curriculum*.

Dr. Austin bowed.

Cornelia announced, "This is Dr. J. Kendall Austin, the director of Library Services for King's County, the founder and headmaster of the Whittaker Magnet School, and the author of the most influential book in American education, *TBC: Test-Based Curriculum*. This is Rosetta Turner, the First Lady's chief of staff. And these are two agents."

Dr. Austin smiled slowly. "It is a pleasure to meet such distinguished representatives from our nation's capital."

No one said anything else for a long moment, until Cornelia pointed down the hallway. This reminded Dr. Austin to say, "Ah, yes. We have some people for you to meet in the County Commission Room. Some very little people, with some very big brains. We call them the Juku Warriors. Shall we?"

George and June had been hard at work all this time. George, as part of his rebellion, was trying to teach the Juku Warriors another song.

June had guarded the door as George had performed one of his favorite numbers from *Peter Pan*. He sang it for them with surprising force and dramatic flair.

When Dr. Austin's smiling face appeared on the other side of the Plexiglas, June emitted a high-pitched squeak and ran toward the back. George, June, and the Juku Warriors instantly reverted to their dreary tasks, busying themselves with answer sheets and No. 2 pencils.

Rosetta Turner walked directly to the back to observe the children's activities. Agent McCoy walked to the dais and bent to examine it. He pointed Agent Pflaum toward the closet. "Check it out."

After a quiet minute, Dr. Austin clapped his hands. The Juku Warriors stood at attention and bowed. Then he held up an index finger to the visitors in a "Watch this" gesture. He called out, "GRE vocabulary words," and the children started to rattle them off: "Perspicacious, sesquipedalian, antidisestablishmentarianism..."

Rosetta held up both of her hands to stop them. "Now, what do those big words mean?" she asked a little girl in front.

The girl giggled. "I don't know."

Dr. Austin laughed heartily. Then he proceeded to do the prefectures of Japan routine for Rosetta, which she endured with barely concealed impatience.

When it was over, Dr. Austin turned to George. "This is George Melvil, one of our student assistants."

Rosetta eyed him suspiciously.

"He is one of our brightest young scholars. Come,

George, walk with us. Perhaps Miss Turner will have questions for you on what it is like to be a Whittaker student."

Kate had by now worked her way up to the seventh floor putting sheets of plastic over bookcases. From that spot, she could hear Cornelia on the hallway above telling the guests, "Pardon our construction mess. We are in the process of restoring this historic ceiling mural to its original condition. No expense is being spared.

"My grandfather Cornell Whittaker Number One was a perfectionist. He insisted that this mural depict the exact horse that our first president rode during their historic meeting."

She told Rosetta, "My grandfather chose this pose himself. Don't you think it's the perfect choice?"

Rosetta surprised everyone by asking, "I don't know. What do you think, George Melvil?"

George answered, "Washington should never be pictured on a horse with one leg in the air. It goes against the unofficial rules of military statuary."

Cornelia stopped ignoring George. She growled, "Don't you have an after-school job to go to? To earn your tuition?"

But George expanded his answer. "By tradition, two forelegs in the air means that the military man died in battle; one leg up means he died of wounds resulting from a battle; no legs up means he died of natural causes. Washington should always be shown on a horse with both forelegs on the ground."

Cornelia moved closer to George, looming over him, like she was contemplating tossing him over the railing.

George stared up at her defiantly.

One floor below, Kate secured the last plastic sheet over the last bookcase. She gave Bud Wright the wave signal, and the standoff between George and Cornelia was interrupted by the throaty sound of the power washer's motor roaring to life.

Bud was set up directly across from the group of visitors, just outside Dr. Austin's office. He waved back at Kate, raised the long rubber nozzle, and let rip with a stream of superconcentrated water. He honed in on the very area under discussion and, in the time it took for anyone to realize what was happening, power-blasted off the first president's head.

George was the only member of his group who laughed, although Kate was laughing heartily down below. Dr. Austin waved his arms frantically until Bud managed to kill the motor and reduce the destructive spray to a slow drip.

Bud's voice echoed across the expanse of the great rectangular prism. "Dang."

Dr. Austin stared fitfully at the now-headless depiction of George Washington. He assured his visitors, "We will, of course, be repainting that."

The group dispersed. The agents went off to finish their building check. Dr. Austin and Cornelia hurried back into his office to discuss the ceiling repair. Rosetta Turner, however, surprised George by placing a manicured hand on his arm and holding him still.

Once they were alone, she asked him, "George Melvil, do you like going to this school?"

George squirmed. "I don't know. It's okay, I guess."

Rosetta arched one thin eyebrow. "I hear you have to take an entrance exam to get in. Is that right?"

"We do. Yes."

"I know you do. I received a complete report on it. Guess who got the highest score in the county."

George admitted, "Me."

"That is correct. So I'm thinking you tried pretty hard to get in."

"Yes, ma'am. I suppose I did."

Rosetta leaned closer. She lowered her anchorwoman voice. "Let me play the devil's advocate for a minute, George Melvil. If you tried so hard to get in here, why can't you say something more enthusiastic than 'It's okay' now?"

George looked around, as if for help. He finally blurted out, "It's okay if you want to be here. If this is what you want to do, then it's okay. You'll probably get into whatever college you want."

Rosetta scrutinized his face closely. "But?"

"But some kids want to do other stuff, too. Like my niece." He stopped to explain. "She's older than me. She's in eighth grade."

"That happens."

"We live in the same duplex, so she got roped into the Whittaker Magnet School District. You can see it on the website. It's like a big, black, mutant octopus blob. It reaches out and—" George stopped abruptly; his eyes snapped open in fear.

Rosetta turned and saw the source of his sudden terror. Dr. Austin and Cornelia were back out in the hallway, and they were staring fiercely at George.

Dr. Austin informed Rosetta. "I am sorry, Miss Turner, but young George has an after-school job, which he is currently neglecting. Aren't you, George?"

"Yes, I am," George admitted. "That's exactly what I'm doing." He backed down the hallway and hurried into the County Commission Room.

27

For Argument's Sake, What if There Were a Demon?

On Thursday afternoon, Cornelia entered Kate's reading class halfway through their review of *The Louisiana Test of Literacy Skills*. She was holding a poster and a pink slip of paper.

The new Reading 8 stopped reviewing and froze in fear. She stammered, "I've-I've done my best. Every day. Truly I have."

Cornelia ignored her. "Many parents, for many years, have suggested that we adopt a required school uniform here at Whittaker."

She consulted the paper. "Dr. Austin has now agreed with them. Quote: 'Uniforms will remove sartorial distractions from test takers.' End of quote."

Cornelia unrolled the poster. "I have a sketch of the uniforms right here. As you can see, the boys' uniform will be based on Whit's classic blue blazer, tan slacks, white shirt, and purple-and-yellow-striped tie. The girls' uniform will be based on Heidi's white frocks. I am here today to measure the girls who do not have the money to buy their own uniforms."

She rolled the poster back up, placed it on a desk, and took out a notepad. "Now, where is Kate Peters?"

Kate ducked down in her seat, but Reading 8 was quick to point her out. "Come up here quickly," Cornelia commanded.

Kate got up and walked forward, but she didn't do it quickly. Cornelia dragged the teacher's stool to the center of the chalkboard. "Climb up on this and look straight ahead." Kate started to protest, but Cornelia and Reading 8 each took her by an elbow and lifted. Kate scrambled to keep her feet beneath her. She found herself standing three feet in the air, looking out over her classmates, most of whom averted their eyes.

Cornelia ran a yellow tape measure from Kate's hip to the top of her knee. "You're about the same size as Heidi. Perhaps Heidi has an old frock in the Goodwill bag. I'll see. Go back to your seat."

Kate looked out at her classmates again. She posed for them on one leg, her arms thrown back, like Peter Pan about to fly from the Darlings' nursery window. Then she hopped down from the stool and walked back to her seat, bowing and smiling at the stunned Mushroom Children.

Cornelia did not call up any other students from the class. She handed Reading 8 another slip of paper, growled, "Read this," and left.

Reading 8 first read the note silently. Then, exhaling relief, she read it aloud. "Everyone involved in Heidi Whittaker Austin's *Orchid the Orca* performance must attend a compulsory rehearsal on the roof. Immediately."

Kate closed her test booklet and gathered her belongings.

Cornelia ran the *Orchid the Orca* rehearsal like a cross between a Broadway show and an army boot camp. In between words of encouragement to Heidi, she shouted orders at June, Kate, and Pogo.

June had been told to set up folding chairs for the audience. She was apparently doing a bad job, as Cornelia had to stop the rehearsal twice to stomp over and show June the correct way to do it.

Kate and Pogo had been dispatched downstairs to fetch two items—a black cart to hold books and a rolling refrigerator to hold cans of soda.

When Kate and Pogo exited the service elevator in the basement, they encountered the gaunt frame and bloodless face of Dr. Cavendar. He was inside the library shipping/receiving area, standing over a rolling refrigerator and peering through its glass top.

Kate stole a glance at Pogo and then said timidly, "Mrs. Whittaker-Austin told us to bring the refrigerator up to the roof."

"This refrigerator is not currently available," Dr. Cavendar replied. "It is being defrosted. You must locate the other one and bring that upstairs."

Kate and Pogo moved away sideways, afraid to turn their backs on him. As they rounded the corner, Pogo whispered:

"Doctor Foster went to Gloucester
In a shower of rain."

Kate answered, "You can say that again."

They located the second refrigerator in the Protein Lab. Pogo started to wheel it away, so Kate suggested, "I'll look for a book cart."

Kate walked back up to the lobby and found an empty cart. She wheeled it into the service elevator and pressed the button for the roof. But before the doors could close, a hand slid in, causing them to reopen.

The hand belonged to Whit. He looked Kate up and down, and then stepped into the elevator. He stood a mere foot away from her as she again pressed the button for the roof. He said, "You know, I'd really like to press your buttons."

Kate looked at his eyes, then at his right foot. "Oh my god!" she shrieked. "A tarantula!" She stomped her heel down on his foot with the unleashed power of her accumulated rage. Whit's eyes bulged out like a cartoon frog's.

Kate smiled evilly. "Or maybe it wasn't."

The elevator doors opened onto the roof and Whit hobbled out. Kate stayed behind, struggling to get the cart moving over the black cinders of the rooftop.

Cornelia stopped rehearsal to shout, "You with the cart! Get out of the way! You're distracting Heidi."

Kate wrestled the cart toward the back wall, where Pogo stood with the refrigerator. But Cornelia again bellowed at her, "Where are you going now?"

Kate stopped completely. "I guess I don't know."

"Then don't go anywhere! Don't rattle a book cart across a roof while an artist is trying to perform. Stay put until you're told what to do."

Kate did as she was told. Shortly after, Cornelia announced that rehearsal was over.

While everyone else fled downstairs, Pogo bounced

from foot to foot in front of Kate and motioned for her to stay behind. As soon as they were alone, they ran to the mushroom cap, ducked under, and descended the ladder. Pogo turned on the lantern, opened the door, and whispered:

> "Rub-a-dub-dub
> Three men in a tub
> And who do you think they be?"

Kate whispered back, "Show me, Pogo. Show me who they be." Kate followed her into the hiding place behind the bookcase, puzzling over her latest rhyme. She figured it out as soon as three men—Dr. Austin, Bud Wright, and Dr. Cavendar—pushed open the secret door on the far wall.

Dr. Austin spoke as they entered. "Let's meet in here, gentlemen. It's possible those Secret Service agents bugged my office." He sat behind the desk and flipped open a notepad. "As you know, we have purchased four hundred eighty cans of soda for the First Lady's visit. They are currently being stored in the back of Cornelia's Hummer. Someone will need to transfer them inside."

"What about that hobo that Cornelia ran over?" Bud suggested. "The judge sentenced him to do twenty hours of community service for assault. Let's put him to work."

"An excellent idea," Dr. Cavendar said. "We will get him to bring this soda in and load it in the refrigerator. In the process, we will get his fingerprints. We may need them later."

Kate and Pogo exchanged wide-eyed looks.

"Now, let's get this next part over with," Dr. Austin told Bud. "Bring in Hodges."

Bud slipped through the passage and returned in half a minute with an obviously terrified Mrs. Hodges.

Dr. Austin tried to put her at ease. "Please do not be alarmed, Mrs. Hodges. We must meet in here for security reasons. You are perfectly safe."

Mrs. Hodges rasped at him, "How long has this room been here?"

"I do not know."

"Why didn't my husband and I know about it?"

"Because no one knows about it. It does not exist on any blueprints. It was sealed upon Cornell Whittaker Number Two's death, and his will stipulated that it never be reopened."

Mrs. Hodges arched both eyebrows. "Then why was it reopened?"

Dr. Austin thought quickly. "Because the will, obviously, referred to the general public, not to his beloved family members."

Mrs. Hodges's eyes darted from corner to corner. "There is evil in this room. I can feel it."

Dr. Austin sighed. "How is this relevant to our current problems, Mrs. Hodges? More importantly, how is it relevant to the behavior of Walter Barnes last Friday?"

"That wasn't Walter Barnes. That was a demon."

"I do not believe that."

"But you will! You will have to!"

"Surely there is a more rational explanation."

Mrs. Hodges stepped to the edge of the desk. "Need I remind you, Dr. Austin, what happened in this library ten years ago?"

Dr. Austin fidgeted. "No one is at all sure what happened back then."

"My husband was! And he lost his life for it! Let me refresh your memory, Doctor. Children—dozens of them—and at least one adult, were possessed by demons. Demons who lived in books! It happened right here. Right in this building."

Bud laughed. "Sounds like one of them horror movies at Bud Wright's Dollar-a-Carload Drive-In."

Dr. Austin waved him to silence. "Let us say, for argument's sake, that I do remember something about that. Which I do not. Not at all. But let us say that I do. What could I do to prevent it from happening again?"

Mrs. Hodges set her bony fingers on the desk. "Throughout the centuries, demons have been destroyed by fire." She raised her eyes to the bookshelves and their leather-bound contents. "You must burn every evil book in this library, beginning with the books in this room."

Dr. Austin was appalled. "No, Hodges. No! These books are priceless. You're talking about hundreds of thousands of dollars!"

"Burn them!"

"Absolutely not!"

"Then you will pay a greater price." She spun and stalked back through the passageway.

Dr. Austin walked around the desk and looked up at the bookshelves admiringly. "Antiquarian books are a great investment. This collection may even be worth millions. *And* it's something to show to visiting dignitaries, like the president of the United States." He caressed a leather-bound book on a lower shelf. Then he led the other two men out and closed the door.

Kate and Pogo stood up. Kate pointed at the door the men had used. "Did I hear them right? Children possessed by demons? Is that what they said?"

Pogo looked away.

"Please, Pogo. You have to tell me. What was that all about?"

Pogo answered:

> "It made the children laugh and play,
>   Laugh and play,
>   Laugh and play."

Kate demanded, "What did? Who did? What, or who, are you talking about?"

Pogo answered:

> "For many a stormy wind shall blow
>   E'er Jack comes home again."

Kate thought hard about the rhymes. Then she heard a sound above her, a scraping on the roof. She and Pogo hunched down. Kate whispered, "Oh my god, Pogo, they've found the ladder!"

There was a pounding of feet on the iron rungs. Kate whispered again, "They've caught us!"

George called through the door, in a stage whisper, "No, they haven't. It's just me." He slipped into the passage. "You need to work on a softer whisper, Kate."

Kate exhaled through gritted teeth. "You should talk. You came clunking down that ladder like three fat guys."

"I figured you would be in here. What happened?"

Kate's eyes glistened, and her words tumbled out. "It's just like I told you, Uncle George. This building is haunted by demons. Demons that live in books. Mrs. Hodges, Dr. Austin, Bud Wright, Dr. Cavendar, they all know about it. Whether they admit it or not, they know about it."

Kate took the lantern from Pogo and led George to the tall bookcase. "The demons may be right here, in this room! They possessed people ten years ago, and now they're starting to do it again."

George surveyed the book titles. "Why now?"

Pogo tapped him on the shoulder. She made a hammering motion with her arm, followed by a sawing motion.

George understood, and he translated for Kate. "The rooftop construction. The workers must have disturbed something, reawakened something."

Pogo jumped up and down. On one of her jumps, she snatched a book halfway off the top shelf; on her next jump, she pulled it out and down. She then laid it carefully on the glass of the Holographic Scanner.

It was an extremely old children's book, with a lavishly illustrated cover. George knew what it was right away. "That's *Perrault's Mother Goose*. First London edition. Retail value approximately fifty thousand dollars."

Kate held her hands outward like they were gripping the sides of a ladder. "Uncle George, how could you know all that?"

"I told you before. It's on the Internet. Antiquarian books are a big business. People invest in them."

Pogo bounced up and down excitedly.

George stared at the Holographic Scanner and then at the shelves, perplexed. He pressed his hands to his temples. He asked, "What's weird about these books?" Then he answered himself. "These books are all antiques, yet they all have strips of holographic tape on them. Strips of Ashley-Nicole's sixth-grade science project supertape."

"So how does that tie in to the demons? What's the connection?"

George's eyes glowed irrationally. "The connection is this: The antique books got passed over the Holographic Scanner ten years ago. So maybe those books had demons in them. And the demons got out. And they have been living inside this machine ever since."

Kate jumped back from the scanner. Pogo did not move.

Then George shook his head in embarrassment. "No. No. That's crazy. Forget it. I must be losing it."

George became so confounded that his eyes filled with tears. When Kate saw this, she walked over and put her arm around him. They stood for a long moment, just staring at the portrait of Cornell Whittaker Number Two in his black hat and robes.

Pogo stepped closer to join them.

> "One misty, moisty morning,
>   When cloudy was the weather,
>   I chanced to meet an old man
>   Clothed all in leather."

Kate whispered to George, "She's told me this one before."

George looked up at the wall. "She's talking about him, Cornell Number Two."

Pogo continued:

> "He began to compliment,
>   And I began to grin,
>   How do you do?
>   And how do you do?
>   How do you do, again?"

The three stared silently at the portrait for as long as they dared. Then they snuck back out into the evening, leaving the secret room in total darkness.

Thirty seconds later, a faint red glow began in the corner by the Holographic Scanner. Wispy white lines, dozens of them, appeared under the scanner's face, rising and falling beneath the quivering glass. They swirled together and broke back apart, in restless combinations, moving faster and faster, banging against the glass wall relentlessly, like prisoners determined to escape.

28

Items to Be Filed under *Never*

On Friday evening, Kate and Molly sat together on the back porch in the dusk. Molly was playing a mournful rendition of "Never Never Land" on her flute while Kate stared at the turning leaves of the big oak tree.

When Molly finished, she pulled apart the sections of her flute, placed them in the case, and said, "I hate to tell you this, but LoriBeth Sommers has been talking about you."

This snapped Kate out of her reverie. "What? What did she say?"

"She's telling kids that she has the lead in *Peter Pan* locked up, even if you do come back."

"Right. File that under *Never*. That girl lives in Never Never Land."

"It's so gross. She wears green tights to school every day now."

Kate simulated retching.

"It gets worse. She told Lisette that Derek Arroyo's been hitting on her."

Upon hearing that, Kate started pounding her forehead, slowly and rhythmically, against the wooden boards of the railing.

"And of course she's been bragging about singing the national anthem for the First Lady."

Kate immediately stopped fooling around. When she turned back to Molly, her face was drained of all color. "What?"

Molly explained to her, as if everybody knew it, "She's singing the national anthem for the First Lady."

"When? Where?"

"At your school! Where else? The band is playing there, too."

"Whose band?"

"Ours! The Lincoln Middle School Band." Molly added, patronizingly, "It's not like there's a Whittaker Magnet School Band, is there?"

Kate went back to pounding her head against the railing. "This just keeps getting worse."

Molly set her flute case behind her. Then she got down to business. "Listen: I did a little snooping for you yesterday."

Kate stopped pounding.

"I asked my grandmother to tell me what she knew about Mr. and Mrs. Hodges."

Kate sat up straight and paid strict attention.

"Okay," Molly said. "This Mr. Hodges guy used to crawl around the library, on his hands and knees, looking for ghosts or something. Then, one night, he went down to a workshop in the basement."

"That'd be old Mr. Pogorzelski's."

"Okay. He took some metal wire, and he wrapped himself up in it completely, like he was a mummy. Then he stuck one end of the wire into an electrical outlet." Molly pantomimed the action. "He blew out every light in the building."

Kate waited a moment and then held out her hands in exasperation. "So? Did he die? Or is this about a tragic waste of lightbulbs?"

"Oh yeah. He died. Real fast."

"That had to be on the local news! Right? This guy was alive one day, and then he was dead the next. People had to know about it."

Molly shook her head. "The public never heard a word about it."

"How can that be?"

Molly was ready with an answer. "Because Cornell Whittaker Number Two had this friend of his named as the county coroner, this creepy old doctor, Dr. Cavendar."

"Dr. Cavendar? Oh my god. He's still there!"

"Really? Then he must be like a hundred years old. Anyway, the county coroner's job is to investigate all suspicious deaths. So, like, for fifty years, there have been *no* suspicious deaths at the Whittaker Building."

"But there have been lots of deaths."

"Oh yeah."

"Did she tell you anything else? Did she say anything about, like, demonic possessions of kids?"

"I asked her about that again. But it was just what she told us last week. A bunch of kids and one adult acting like wild creatures."

"I bet it was a librarian. I bet it was Walter Barnes."

Molly thought for a moment. "No. It was a lady. She said some lady flipped out and started swinging from a chandelier with one arm, like a monkey." Molly laughed. "That part sounded pretty cool." Her smile faded. "But that's why my grandmother lost her job. Isn't it?"

Kate had hoped to talk to Mrs. Brennan that evening, but Ma and Pa got to her first. They corralled her into a conversation about their favorite subject just before the girls arrived on the porch.

Mrs. Brennan listened politely as Ma described the

differences between mountain buckdance and pitter-pat. Kate and Molly, in no mood to be polite, walked to the curb and leaned against the car.

Then Kate heard Pa mention another subject altogether, her father. She edged forward to hear. "Yeah, Charley Peters had a job over at Technon, a big sales job. That Charley was a great talker. But one day he started talking about ghosts—people seeing ghosts, or some such stuff. They fired him. You can't have no loonies running around at Technon, not with all them superweapons of mass destruction."

Kate interrupted him. "Pa! Wait a minute. What did you say about my dad?"

Pa froze, unaware that Kate had been listening. He grinned sheepishly. "You can't go by nothin' I say, Kate. I was just a security guard."

"But you said they fired him because he was talking about ghosts. Right?"

"Aw, I don't know nothin' about it, Kate. Not really. I should've kept my big mouth shut. It's just that . . . that was the rumor."

Kate walked back to the car in order to think. After a few more minutes, the Tri-County Cloggers arrived and tromped inside, freeing Mrs. Brennan to leave. But Kate no longer felt like asking her about the library or the Whittakers or anything else. She gave both Molly and her grandmother a quick hug good-bye and hurried inside.

Kate spent the next thirty minutes trying to log on to her computer to write an e-mail to her father. After much frustration, she did manage to send off a message via the American Schools Abroad Program's website.

Then Kate reached her arms up and stretched. She leaned her head so far back that she was looking upside down, and right at June. Kate snapped upright, turned, and glared at her mother. June was on the landing with another FedEx package. Kate snapped, "How long have you been standing there?"

"I didn't mean to startle you," June said.

"Good job!"

June held out the package and spoke in a gentle voice. "Kate, we got this today. It's from Asia."

Kate snatched the package away, ripped it open, and dumped out its contents. She knew immediately what those contents were—the letters she had written to her father, at least a year's worth. They were bundled together under a sheet of paper bearing the letterhead of the American Schools Abroad Program. It read:

To: Miss Kate Peters
Re: Mr. Charles Peters

Be advised that Mr. Peters no longer works for the American Schools Abroad Program. We do not know his current whereabouts.

Kate stared at the pile of letters, each filled out in her own handwriting so meticulously and so hopefully. Tears filled her eyes and spilled out onto the top one.

June placed a hand on Kate's shoulder and tried to think of some comforting words to say. But before she could, Kate took hold of the hand and removed it. Then Kate gathered up the pile of letters and walked into her room.

WEEK FOUR

29

A Plea
to Help the Indigent

The students who exited the Whittaker Magnet School on Monday afternoon had changed in one dramatic way: They were all dressed exactly alike. The boys now wore tan slacks, blue blazers, and striped ties. The girls now wore frilly white dresses.

Kate and George emerged last, looking out of place in their jeans and T-shirts. As they walked past the office, Cornelia stepped out and blocked their paths. "Why are you two out of uniform?"

"We're still trying to scrape together the money," George answered. "Would it be possible for us to return our copy of *The Whittakers of King's County: A Biographical History*?"

Cornelia leaned over him. She answered coldly, "All sales are final."

George started to walk away, but Cornelia's big hand stopped him. She checked her watch. "I'll tell you what, let's settle this matter right now. Come with me." She grabbed each child by an elbow and steered them across the lobby to Elevator #3.

Kate and George stood like shackled prisoners in the elevator and rode up to the eighth floor. Cornelia forced them to walk ahead of her into the County Commission Room. To Kate's complete surprise and utter horror, the room was filled with people she knew: Ma and Pa, dressed in their most outrageous clogging outfits; the other four Tri-County Cloggers; Mr. Kagoshima; and, lastly, LoriBeth Sommers.

"Uncle George," Kate whispered. "Am I losing my mind? What are they all doing here?"

"They're here for a rehearsal maybe? For the First Lady's visit?"

Cornelia made Kate and George stop in front of the dais. She announced, "I would like to take a minute of everyone's valuable time in order to make a plea for charity. It is important that we who *have* give to those who have not. These children standing before you lack even the basic funds to buy their school uniforms."

Cornelia reached over to the table and grabbed a large plastic cup. She held it up so that all could see the writing on it: BUD WRIGHT'S SWIM-WITH-A-DOLPHIN AQUATIC PARK. She then handed the cup to Kate. "You may circulate among the generous people who have come here today. I'm sure they will help you."

Kate looked out over the crowd. The first people she made eye contact with were Ma and Pa. Each of them was holding up a dollar and waving it cheerfully.

"We don't have to take this, Kate," George whispered. "We can leave right now. Just walk out, and I'll follow you."

But Kate responded coolly. "You go sit down, Uncle George. I'll take care of everything."

Several people along the aisle stuffed dollars into the cup. LoriBeth Sommers, with a triumphant smile, fished out a dime and tossed it in. Mr. Kagoshima put in a dollar. "I'm sorry," he told her. "I wasn't listening. What is this for, Kate?"

"It's for you, Mr. Kagoshima. It's to help pay your expenses for bringing the Lincoln Band to Whittaker."

Mr. Kagoshima blinked. He took the cup wonderingly. "Oh, really? Well, then, thank you, Kate."

"Thank you, sir." Kate then joined George in a seat near the back.

Susan Singer-Wright banged her gavel to start the meeting. "We are here today to organize a very special program for the First Lady's visit." She consulted a schedule. "We will begin the program with our national anthem played by the Lincoln Middle School Band under the direction of their conductor, Mr. No-ree-oh Kah-go-shee-ma. Is that correct, sir?"

Mr. Kagoshima half rose. "That is close enough, ma'am."

Susan smiled. "I must say that it is a nice touch that you are a multicultural conductor."

"I try, ma'am."

"It says here that you will be joined at the fifth bar of the song by the vocals of Miss LoriBeth Sommers. Where is Miss Sommers?"

LoriBeth stood up, waved, and smiled. A skinny girl with close-cropped brown hair, she was dressed all in green, except for a brown belt and a pair of brown slippers.

Susan smiled back and told her, "You might want to wear something else for the First Lady, honey." She looked back at her schedule. "We will then have a performance of native American folk dancing by the Tri-County Cloggers."

Ma and Pa started whooping. The rest of the Tri-County Cloggers joined in. Cornelia stared at them until they stopped.

Dr. Austin raised his hand. "I wouldn't call it 'native American.'"

"Why not?" Susan asked.

"Because they are not Native American Indians."

George arched one eyebrow toward Kate to acknowledge the redundancy.

"Call it 'authentic American folk dancing,' instead," Dr. Austin suggested.

Susan picked up a pen and amended her text. "Whatever you say, Dr. Austin." Then she added, "Heidi will perform next. I'll leave that to Mrs. Whittaker-Austin to describe."

Cornelia pointed a big finger at the schedule. "Dr. Austin and I have decided that the message of *Orchid the Orca* is too important to be lumped in with all these other activities. Therefore, Heidi's performance has been relocated to this room. Just after the First Lady meets with the dignitaries and just before she goes up to the roof, she will experience Heidi's stunning performance." Cornelia stopped to look at Bud Wright. "During which, Orchid will plead for the government to end her loneliness."

Bud shouted, "Amen to that!"

The meeting ended immediately after so that the performers could rehearse. Kate and George tried to leave quietly, but Cornelia was waiting for them at the door. "How much money did you two collect?"

"I collected a little bit," Kate said. "But I set the cup down and lost it."

"What?"

"Or somebody stole it. Sorry."

Cornelia pulled herself up to her full height. "All right. I've done all I'm going to do for you two. You don't appreciate a thing!" She looked at Kate. "You couldn't pass a test if your life depended on it." Then she turned to George. "And you! Have you suffered brain damage? What has happened to your test scores?"

Kate could feel George start to tremble beside her.

Cornelia lowered her voice to a menacing whisper. "Your parents signed a contract. I might add, they signed it without reading it. Failure to honor that contract will result in the loss of your house to the county. And you know what that would make you? . . ."

Cornelia turned on her heel and left.

Kate was not at all affected by Cornelia's threats, but she took one look at George and saw that he was falling apart. "Don't listen to her, Uncle George," she whispered. "She's just a big bully." Kate grabbed George by his skinny shoulders and squeezed him hard, as if she were literally holding him together.

30

The Attempted Destruction
of a $5,000 Instrument

Cornelia hurried upstairs and burst through the door
ready to direct the rehearsal for the First Lady's performance. She first sought out Bud and Susan and placed
them in charge of security badges for the event. She
spoke to them sharply for two minutes about the cre-
dentialing procedure.

Kate's first assignment from Cornelia was to bring
up the rolling refrigerator from the basement. She was
on her return trip in the service elevator when her ears
picked up the unmistakable sound of clogging. The
elevator doors opened and she beheld all six of the Tri-
County Cloggers in full swing. They were rehearsing
one of their routines on the newly finished rooftop

stage, which seemed barely able to endure such a pounding.

Kate rolled the refrigerator past the erect, watchful figure of Mrs. Hodges and continued on to the back wall.

She heard Susan tell Bud, "Honey, I'm a country girl at heart, but this is just too cornpone for words."

"I'm sure the Doc knows what he's doin'," Bud answered.

When the cloggers stopped, Bud directed them over to Susan to collect their security badges for the big day.

The Juku Warriors were next to rehearse. George wrangled his seven charges onto the wooden stage, where Dr. Austin and Bud awaited them. Dr. Austin spoke to their smiling faces with chilling severity. "Listen to me, all of you. This will be the most important thing you have done in your lives. Isn't that correct, Mr. Wright?"

Bud, not expecting a question to be tossed his way, was caught unawares. He told them, "That's right, you youngsters. You can help to drive up the real estate values of your homes."

Dr. Austin counted off two items on his fingers. "We will begin with the prefectures of Japan game; then we will do the GRE vocabulary words. Remember, we want to show the First Lady how much fun we have. It will be like Bubble Time. Do you remember Bubble Time? It will be just like that."

Dr. Austin and Bud hopped down from the stage, leaving George with the Juku Warriors. One by one, they started to cry.

Cornelia spotted Kate standing by the back wall. She pointed at the stage and commanded, "Get up here! Now!"

Cornelia then gestured for George to join her. "I've decided we need a patriotic tableau onstage, and that you two will be in it. Since you're so good at standing around doing nothing, you will stand on either side holding flags. Do you think you can do that simple thing without losing the flags or getting them stolen?"

Kate was secretly thrilled to be moving closer to the action. She answered with cool detachment. "I think we can."

"For now, you'll have to pretend that you're holding flags." When Kate and George did not react, Cornelia screamed, "Pretend that you're holding flags!"

Kate and George extended their arms and curled their fingers around imaginary flagpoles while Cornelia positioned them on the stage. She then blocked out the positions of LoriBeth Sommers and the members of the Lincoln Middle School Band.

Cornelia looked at Mr. Kagoshima, pulled two fingers behind her head, and snapped them forward like a fly fisherman. When he did not understand her gesture, she yelled at him, "Begin! Begin!"

The Lincoln Middle School Band played. After five bars, LoriBeth Sommers began to sing. Kate listened to her miserably, growing more and more depressed with each bar. All she could think of was Lincoln Middle School and the fall musical and the role that she had been born to play—the role that the evil interloper LoriBeth Sommers had all but locked up. Kate let her imaginary flag droop as much as she dared.

At the lowest point of her misery, Pogo appeared at her side. Kate mumbled, "I hate her. She's stolen my life at Lincoln. She's stolen my part in *Peter Pan*. She's even stolen my boyfriend."

Pogo tilted her head quizzically.

Kate pointed at LoriBeth Sommers and added emphatically, "Her. I hate. I hate her."

Pogo whispered:

"Jack be nimble, Jack be quick!"

Then she disappeared.

Kate listened to LoriBeth hit her famous high note. She raised her eyes to meet George's and mouthed the words, "Play ball!"

Then Pogo was back. She appeared off to the side of the stage holding a manila envelope. Kate watched her slide a book out of the envelope and place it on Lori-

Beth Sommers's music stand. Kate knew the book from elementary school. It was *The Story of the Star-Spangled Banner*. Kate thought, *What on earth is she doing with that?*

Cornelia was issuing orders at a frantic pace, fine-tuning the patriotic tableau. She barked at Kate and George, "Hold those flags higher!"

She told Bud, "Lower that girl's music stand, Bud! It's covering up her face."

Bud waved. "Okay." He stepped forward, tucked the *Star-Spangled Banner* book under his armpit, and lowered the music stand six inches. Before he replaced the book, however, he examined it briefly. A strange look came over his face, and a strange glow lit up his eyes.

While Cornelia conferred with Dr. Austin, Bud turned to Mr. Kagoshima and said in a very peculiar voice, "Sir? Mr. Japanese man? Oh, sir?"

Mr. Kagoshima looked up from his music. "Are you talking to me?"

"Sir, is that a tuba over there?"

Mr. Kagoshima followed his gaze to an empty folding chair, upon which sat the Lincoln Middle School Band's only tuba. "Yes," he replied. "It is."

"I'm wondering something. Do you think my head would fit into the opening of that tuba?"

Mr. Kagoshima was now totally baffled. "I-I really don't know."

Bud held up one finger, said, "I'll be right back," and ran to the exit.

Kate, still pretending to hold her flag, sidled over to George. She whispered urgently, "What is he doing?"

"I'm not sure. But I'll tell you one thing. I don't think Mr. Bud Wright is currently the captain of his own ship."

Bud burst back through the doorway carrying a blender full of protein shake.

Everyone on the roof turned to look at him. It was Susan who asked, "Bud, honey? What are you doing?"

Bud spoke, but it wasn't to Susan. "First, we need a little lubrication!" He stood at attention, raised his right arm high, and poured the contents of the blender over his head.

"Bud!" Susan shrieked. "Have you lost your cotton-pickin' mind?"

He shouted, "Bud? Who's Bud? I'm Tubby the Tuba!" He pranced over to the chair that held the tuba. He stuck his head down and his rear up. Then he started to chant, "I'm Tubby the Tuba, oompah-pah! I'm Tubby the Tuba, oompah-pah!"

He pushed his head into the tuba opening, put his arms on the sides of the chair, and raised himself into a shaky handstand, like an out-of-shape acrobat. The weight of his ample backside now pressed straight downward, and his head disappeared into the opening with a *thwunk*, followed by a wet cracking sound.

Dr. Austin stared at the tuba and the pair of legs waving from it. "Quick!" he screamed at Pogo. "Go downstairs and get a hacksaw!"

A group of adults rushed over and tried to extricate Bud's head. Susan screamed, "Merciful heavens! He's gonna die in there!"

Pogo produced a hacksaw from under her dress. She gave it to Dr. Austin with her left hand. Kate and George observed that her right hand was holding something else under her dress. "It's a book," George whispered. "She has a book under there!"

Dr. Austin positioned the hacksaw blade above the neck of the tuba and started to saw.

Upon seeing this, Mr. Kagoshima shouted, "No! No!" He forced himself between Dr. Austin and the tuba. The two men faced off in a circle of frantic would-be rescuers.

Dr. Austin raised the hacksaw high. "Get out of my way!"

Mr. Kagoshima assumed an awkward karate stance. "That's a five-thousand-dollar instrument!"

"Get out of my way or you're fired!"

"You already fired me. I work at Lincoln now."

Cornelia ran into the circle and bumped Mr. Kagoshima out of the way. Then she grabbed the tuba, and Susan grabbed Bud. They each pulled like two sides in a tug-of-war. After three mighty heaves, Bud's head popped out, spraying blood from his nose.

Pogo ran up to Bud with a roll of paper towels. She quickly wiped his face clean of the blood and the remnants of the protein shake. Only Kate and George saw a book fall out from under her dress, *Perrault's Mother Goose*. Pogo flipped the book open with her foot and then pressed the paper towel roll against Bud Wright's nose, turning his gasping face toward the open pages. She then scooped up the book, slid it into an envelope, and ran away.

A few seconds later, Bud Wright was his old self, muttering, "Thank you, ladies. I musta blacked out there for a minute."

Dr. Austin raised his hands in relief and gratitude. "Thank you, everyone! What a freak accident! You never know *what* someone can slip and fall into, do you? We must all be more careful with drinks up here. Now please, back to your rehearsal."

Dr. Austin cast a glance at the back wall. Mrs. Hodges was standing there, ramrod straight, a look of supreme satisfaction on her face. He met her gaze and pointed down in the direction of his office.

Kate and George saw the gesture. Unnoticed in the buzzing crowd, they hurried to the mushroom cap, slipped inside, and beat Dr. Austin to the secret room by twenty seconds.

Dr. Austin closed the revolving door behind Bud Wright and Mrs. Hodges. He informed his bleeding friend, "I'm not sure you blacked out up there, Bud."

Bud was still applying pressure to his nose, but he managed to speak. "I didn't?"

Dr. Austin struggled with his next words. He looked at Mrs. Hodges. "No. I'm not exactly sure what happened. But I am prepared now to take Mrs. Hodges's theories a little more seriously."

Mrs. Hodges did not speak. She did not have to. Dr. Austin spoke for her. "I am ready, regrettably, to approve a *limited* burning of Cornell Whittaker Number Two's antiquarian book collection."

He ticked off his conditions to the black-clad librarian. "First, you are not to do it alone. You could be the next victim of this...demon. I want someone to work with you. Pogo, maybe. She's the only one around here who can keep her mouth shut. Second, I want you to take precautions. The construction workers left protective equipment behind. I want you to wear it. I can't run the risk of any more 'accidents.'"

"Certainly," Mrs. Hodges answered. "When shall we begin?"

Dr. Austin reached into his desk drawer and slid out an appraisal sheet from the Antiquarian Book Auction. He looked at the first item and winced as he read it silently: "Sir Arthur Conan Doyle, *The History of Spiritualism*, $7,500."

He told her bitterly. "Tonight. You can begin tonight, after everyone leaves."

At home, Kate and George sat on their back porch analyzing Bud Wright's mysterious behavior and Dr. Austin's meeting that followed. June opened the door to listen, but Kate told her, "This is a private conversation, June."

"I've already heard some of it, through the door. I'm worried about you. I really want to know what's going on."

"Nothing is going on."

But George said, "Some people have been acting really weird at the library, June."

"Mr. Barnes and Mr. Wright?"

"Yes." George looked at Kate, but Kate was staring at the ground. "June works there, Kate. She's seen things, too. She's heard things." He looked up. "Right, June?"

June shrugged. "Pogo has said some things to me. Things I don't understand."

George gave Kate a look that said, "There you go." He asked June, "Did she say anything about Jack?"

June turned pale. She finally whispered, "Jack and Jill went up the hill."

Kate pursed her lips and nodded firmly, like she had just made a decision. "Uncle George, can you leave us alone please? I need to speak to my mother privately."

George's eyes widened in surprise. "Sure," he muttered. Then he stood up and walked quickly into his side of the duplex.

June sat down in George's spot and waited.

Kate began, "This can't go on, June. I'm treated horribly at that place. I don't care what kind of 'condition' you have. You're my mother. You need to do something about it."

June waited a long time before answering. "We don't have any money, Kate. So we don't have any choices."

Kate turned and spoke through clenched teeth. "You *chose* to get divorced, June. That's why I don't have a father. You act like you're the victim of everything. Well, you're not. You've made your choices, and I'm the one paying for them."

"I didn't choose to get a divorce. It was all your father. He wanted out. He left me."

Kate tried again. "Okay. So you chose to get married, then, and to have me. Will you at least admit to that? Didn't you have something to say about that?"

"Yes."

"Well, then, June, that makes you responsible for me. You need to help me. Now."

June met Kate's gaze. "I know you're angry. You have many reasons to be angry. Good reasons. I thought this magnet school was a great opportunity for you. I really did."

Kate interrupted to ask, "And was it a great opportunity?"

"No. It wasn't. I was wrong. It's only made you miserable. And slightly green."

Kate looked at the backs of her hands.

June squeezed her eyes closed. "I want you to know that I am trying very hard these days. It may not show. But I'm trying to be there for you."

Kate thought about getting up and going inside. Instead, though, after picking her words carefully, she said, "I know you tried that one time, at the science fair. I never thanked you for that. So, thank you." She added, "But that's not enough, June. You have to try harder."

"I know," June agreed. "And I will. I'll try harder."

Kate stood up and shivered. "I guess that will have to do for now. I'm freezing. Good night."

"Good night."

Kate went inside, but June did not. She sat alone on the porch, in the cold night air, under the blackening outline of the oak tree. Her thoughts swirled and crashed around inside her head, like the ghosts in the Holographic Scanner.

31

A Silent Scream

On Wednesday afternoon, Kate reported to the County Commission Room for her job as personal assistant to Heidi. She watched Heidi rehearse her entrance—as a smiling and waving orca—from a closet next to the dais.

Heidi stopped practicing long enough to snap at Kate. "You are late! I need my makeup case. Go get it!"

Kate looked around the room idly. "Where is it?"

"I don't know where it is. That's your job. Try Whit's office."

Kate shook her head adamantly. "No way. I'm not going in there."

Then Heidi actually smiled. "You're not afraid of Whit, are you?"

"Don't make me laugh."

"Well, then..."

Kate shrugged, exited the room, and turned right. Cornelia was dead ahead, outside of Whit's office. There was no avoiding her.

Cornelia passed Kate in the hallway and commented, "Still no uniform, I see."

"I'm saving every penny," Kate assured her. "I'm even skipping meals."

Cornelia ground her jaws, but she let the matter drop and continued on her way.

Whit was standing in front of a mahogany desk in an office that was an exact copy of his father's. Kate took two steps inside and told him, "Heidi said she left her makeup case in here."

Whit looked around lazily. "That must be it, there on the floor." He pointed to a spot right in front of him, but he made no effort to pick it up.

Kate walked quickly to the spot, but Whit was quicker. He darted to the door and closed it. He told her, "Wait. I want to watch you pick it up."

Kate looked down at the makeup case. Then she looked up at Whit. "Forget it. I'll just tell her you're still using the eyeliner."

She started back toward the door, but Whit blocked her. He pointed his finger at her and snarled, "You really think you're something, don't you? You don't even belong here. I know all about you. You got in because that goofy little uncle of yours lives at the same address."

Kate answered, "You're right. I don't belong here. And, might I add, you *do* belong here. Now get out of my way. This is sexual harassment, and I don't have to take it."

Whit remained in place in front of the door.

Kate approached him calmly. Then, in one deft maneuver, she grabbed him by the lapels of his blue blazer and pushed him back onto his heels. She pinned him against the wall, with his legs twisted crazily, like a Halloween skeleton. Whit squealed, "This is assault! You are assaulting me!"

Cornelia threw open the door, nearly filling its frame, with Heidi peeking around from behind her. "What on earth is going on here?" Cornelia bellowed.

Kate released her grip on Whit's lapels and he slid down the wall, landing upright. Before Whit could speak, though, Kate said, "I want to file a complaint against Whit Austin for sexual harassment."

Cornelia snapped, "That never happened!"

"Yes, it did."

"I was just in this room with him. It never happened."

"It happened after you left."

Cornelia's voice got suddenly reasonable. "Very well, then. Produce your witnesses."

Whit scurried over to his mother's side and waited for Kate to answer. She admitted, "There weren't any witnesses."

"So," Cornelia concluded, "it's the word of the worst student at this school against the word of the most admired young man in this county." She looked at her watch. "We have no time for this. We're due on the roof."

As the three of them turned to leave, Heidi looked back at Kate and complained, "Mother, she's not even a good gofer. Can I get somebody else?"

Kate stepped out into the hallway and watched them walk away, arm in arm, until they disappeared up the stairwell. She grabbed hold of the railing and looked out at the great chains that held the chandeliers. She reared back her head, opened her mouth, and screamed a silent scream until ropes of blue veins popped out on her neck.

From three floors below, across the expanse of the square, a figure moved in the shadows. Pogo had seen and heard everything. As Kate walked away, Pogo repeated to herself:

"Kissed the girls and made them cry.
Kissed the girls and made them cry.
Kissed the girls and made them cry."

32

A Primer on Football
from an Unlikely Source

As soon as Cornelia and the children emerged from the stairwell onto the roof, a tall, awkward boy stepped in their path. The boy opened his mouth to speak, but nothing came out.

"Yes?" Cornelia snapped at him. "What is it?"

The boy stammered, "I'm William Anderson, ma'am. I'm an eighth grader."

"I know who you are. What do you want?"

"I want to volunteer to help for the First Lady's visit, for the big performance."

"We have everybody we need."

But Dr. Austin suddenly appeared among them. "Not so fast, Mrs. Whittaker-Austin. We may have use for a volunteer after all. Especially a tall one. Do you remember a problem we had last week, and our discussion that followed?"

"No. About what?"

"About a possible solution to that problem." Dr. Austin looked up at the boy. "Excuse us, William. We will need to discuss your generous offer and then get back to you. For now, go enjoy today's Story Time performance."

William backed away. "Yes, sir, Dr. Austin. Thank you. And thank you, ma'am."

After several deep breaths to calm herself, Kate walked up the twelve cement steps to the roof. She opened the metal door and stood for a moment, surveying the crowd. But her survey ground to a halt at the sight of Bud Wright's face. He was standing off to one side wearing a high white neck brace. He had two swollen ears, two black eyes, and a very large, very red nose.

Dr. Austin walked up the three steps to the wooden stage, posed for a moment, then told the audience, "Congratulations for coming here. While foolish parents are damaging their children's knees at football practice, you are improving your children's brains at the Whittaker After-School Preparatory. But don't take my word for it!" He stepped back as the Juku Warriors bounded up to join him. "Listen to this!"

The performance began with a round-robin spelling

of *supercalifragilisticexpialidocious*. But then, instead of sitting down, the Juku Warriors broke into another song. This time, to Kate's delight, it was a song from *Peter Pan:* "I Won't Grow Up."

Dr. Austin stepped forward, smiling stiffly, and shooed them away. He told the crowd, "They're inveterate pranksters." Then he followed them off, casting a deadly glance at George.

The Juku Warriors sat with Math 6, freeing George to saunter over and stand by Kate. She looked at him with a mixture of puzzlement and newfound respect. "Uncle George? Did you teach them that?"

George smiled, pleased with himself. "I taught them that. With a little help from June."

"Really? June?"

"Yup."

Cornelia walked up onto the stage. "And now, the moment you have all been waiting for. Heidi Whittaker Austin, soon to perform before the First Lady of the United States, will perform for you today. She will read the children's classic *Polar Bear, Polar Bear, What Do You Hear?* Afterward, you will work with your parents to find the *p* sound on the worksheets."

Cornelia gave the audience the applause sign, and Heidi assumed her starting position. As Cornelia stepped offstage, Dr. Austin whispered, "I know just the job for William Anderson. Come with me."

The two disappeared down the cement block stairwell just as Pogo appeared from behind it. She worked her way stealthily to the book cart. Kate and George watched as she switched Heidi's copy of *Polar Bear, Polar Bear, What Do You Hear?* with a second copy from a manila envelope. Then she worked her way around the perimeter of the crowd until she was standing next to Kate.

Kate whispered, "Pogo, what did you just do?"

Pogo whispered back:

> "Curly Locks, Curly Locks,
>   Will you be mine?
>   You shall not wash dishes,
>   Nor feed the swine."

Kate looked at George, then said, "Pardon?"

Pogo added:

> "She won't get up to feed the swine,
>   But lies in bed 'til eight or nine."

"She's talking about Heidi," George said.

Kate asked her, "Are you talking about Heidi?" But Pogo did not reply.

Kate and George exchanged a baffled look. Then they turned together to watch the performance.

After a curtsy and an energetic wave, Heidi skipped over to the black cart and selected a book. She then skipped toward the group of children, calling, "Hello!" and smiling brightly. She opened the book and began, "Polar Bear, Polar Bear, what do you hear?"

But then she stopped. Her hands snapped the book closed like she was killing a bug. Her head tilted upward and her eyes glazed over in a way that Kate and George now recognized.

George inclined his head toward Kate. "That's not Heidi anymore, is it?"

Kate could only manage, "Oh my god."

Heidi stared at the *Polar Bear* book curiously, like she had never seen it before. She looked at the audience and back at the book. Then she intoned, in a surprisingly deep voice, "Hmm. What is this? This won't do. This won't do at all. This is a baby book."

She threw down *Polar Bear,* scattering the cinders and making some children laugh. She returned to the black cart and scanned the other titles on the lower shelves. At last, she picked up *The NFL's Greatest Running Backs* and showed it to the crowd.

She struck a pose, a very girlish pose, with her hair tossed back and her hand on one hip. Then she started talking demurely. "I am Heidi, the Swiss Milkmaid. How do you do? But what if I got tired of being Swiss?

Or of being a milkmaid? Or, even worse, what if I became lactose intolerant? What would I do then? I know! I could play in the National Football League."

She backed over toward the wall, turned, and struck a new pose. Her fist went down into the cinders and her rump went up in the air, in a perfect football player's three-point stance. Then she shouted, "Give me the ball, Coach! Give me the ball!"

She yelled, "Hut!" and sprinted forward face-first into the cement blocks.

She turned back to the audience.

A red welt began to blossom on her forehead. The Juku Warriors laughed and clapped. Mrs. Hodges leaned forward, her gray stripe of hair temporarily blocking Kate and George's view.

"Uh-oh," Heidi said. "No gain. Second down and ten to go." A rivulet of blood trickled out of her nose. "A lot of girls never do figure out what that means. It means that it's my second chance to gain ten yards. And here I go."

She put her head down and, once again, ran full tilt into the wall. She staggered backward. Blood was now leaking from a cut over her left eye. The kids were all cheering now. But some of the parents stood up, unsure of what to do, wondering if this was all part of the show.

Heidi put a hand up to her mouth, fiddled around for a few seconds, and pulled out a tooth. "Third down and ten. I'd better make it this time, or Coach may sit me on the bench." She crouched unsteadily, wound up, and again hurtled forward into the reddening wall.

She turned back on wobbly legs and babbled, almost incoherently, "Oh no, Heidi the Milkmaid! Now you'll have to punt!"

Then she collapsed in a heap.

The kids screamed with delight. The parents, however, almost as one, covered their children's eyes and rushed them toward the elevator.

Pogo took off like a fleet-footed mouse. Under the guise of helping the prostrate Heidi, she slipped out a book from under her dress and opened it. A few seconds later, she slid it back and disappeared into the stairwell.

Kate took off right behind her, calling to George, "Keep your eye out for the Austins! *Semper Paratus!*"

Kate followed Pogo down four flights of stairs with a flood of thoughts, troubling thoughts, coursing through her brain. She exited the stairwell on the fifth-floor landing, looked left and right, then set off toward the applied sciences section. She found Pogo in a far corner, leaning casually against a bookshelf. Pogo bobbed lightly and waved.

Kate walked toward her. "Everybody's still up on the roof, Pogo. Why aren't you?"

Pogo smiled happily and shrugged.

"I really want to know, Pogo. Why are you down here, all alone?"

Pogo bounced and answered:

> "Here I am,
> Little jumping Joan.
> When nobody's with me,
> I'm always alone."

Kate's eyes scanned the nearby shelves. "Where's the book that you had with you?"

Pogo stopped bouncing. She looked down at the floor.

Kate moved closer, cutting off Pogo's escape. "I've been thinking some strange stuff. I want you to hear what I've been thinking."

Pogo fidgeted with her dress.

"I've been thinking stuff like: You knew that I hated Heidi. And you knew that I hated LoriBeth Sommers."

Pogo broke away from her spot, but Kate moved into her path. "Walter Barnes picked up a book that was meant for Heidi, didn't he? And Bud Wright picked up a book that was meant for LoriBeth. Right?"

Kate twisted forward until her face was directly in front of Pogo's. "Do you have anything to say to me about these strange thoughts?"

Pogo finally looked up at her. She answered defiantly:

> "Wake up bright
> In the morning light
> To do what's right
> With all your might."

Kate shook her head no. "But this is not right, Pogo. Heidi, LoriBeth, they're *my* enemies. Not yours."

Pogo knitted her brow in thought.

"I fight my own battles. I always have. I'm proud of that. Do you understand?"

Pogo thought for a moment longer, then nodded.

Kate pointed at her own chest. "Kate Peters, alone, fights Kate Peters's battles. Got it?"

Pogo continued to nod.

Dr. Austin and Cornelia, returning to the rooftop via the service elevator, had to push their way through the mob of fleeing parents and children. They looked at each other, puzzled, until the mob cleared enough to reveal the bloody wall and the body that lay beneath it. Cornelia started screaming and pointing frantically at Heidi.

Dr. Austin, however, did not get frantic at all. He understood clearly what had happened in his absence. He stepped aside, located Mrs. Hodges, and walked toward her.

As the chaotic scene played out around them, and as George Melvil drifted imperceptibly closer, Dr. Austin leaned forward and spoke with perfect composure. "The First Lady of the United States is on her way to a building that is currently being haunted by demons, Mrs. Hodges. Now please tell me what I can do about that."

Mrs. Hodges reached into a deep pocket and pulled out a folded sheaf of papers. "We must expand the book burning. Priceless books be damned! We must get all of the demon-possessed books into the furnace before they attack again."

Dr. Austin nodded calmly.

Mrs. Hodges unfolded the papers. They contained a long list of book titles, not only from the private collection of Cornell Whittaker Number Two, but children's books from the general library collection. She informed him, with great satisfaction, "We will start with these."

33

The Problem Gets Worse, Much Worse

Cornelia was waiting for Kate on Friday morning, posed ominously at the end of the *Andrew Carnegie in Hell* mosaic like an avenging angel.

"Due to Heidi's unfortunate accident," Cornelia snarled, "she will not be making any public appearances for a while. This means that you, as her understudy, will read the part of Orchid the Orca. That is all." Cornelia started away. Then she stopped. "Wait. That is *not* all. You have been transferred over to Whit as his personal assistant. You will report to him after school."

Kate's first impulse was to refuse, regardless of the consequences. But her second impulse, and the one that won out, was to accept the new assignment calmly. Kate knew she could punch out Whit's lights if she had to, and she was now determined to stay near the center of the mystery that was unfolding around her.

Her first after-school encounter with Whit occurred in the County Commission Room. Without a word, and without looking at her, Whit handed her an index card with a book title printed on it. She assumed that she was to get the title from the stacks and took off to find *Genetic Mapping: The Path to Superior Human Beings.*

Kate found the title on the fifth floor. When she came back up the stairs, she ran into George, June, and the Juku Warriors on the landing.

George looked at the book and asked, "What do you want with that thing?"

"It's for Whit."

"Whit?"

"Yeah. I'm his personal assistant now."

"No!"

"Yeah." Kate looked for Whit through the Plexiglas window. "I'm on my way to give it to him."

George shook his head. "No, Kate. Let me take it. I'm going in there anyway."

Kate looked at him closely. "Are you sure?"

"I'm sure. Why don't you go take a break?"

"I do need to go to the bathroom."

"Here's your chance. Let me have the book."

Kate handed it over. "Thanks, Uncle George."

"No problem." He took the book and started in, but he paused to hold the door for June and the Juku Warriors, and then, seemingly out of nowhere, Pogo.

June took the children to the back, but Pogo hovered near the front, bobbing around aimlessly. George watched her and wondered, *Why is she in here?*

Whit was seated on a folding chair in the first row, draped in his father's blue shower curtain, as his mother trimmed his hair.

George walked calmly up to the dais and placed the book on the slanted face of the podium. Then he started to walk calmly back, but he had to leap out of the way as the door flew open.

Dr. Austin entered, took in the barbering scene before him, and warned his wife, "That shower curtain had better be returned to my office."

She assured him, "It will be."

Then he pointed at George. "George Melvil. I want the Juku Warriors to perform today. I think the Harvard representatives will be impressed with them. Don't you?"

"Oh, yes. Yes, sir."

Dr. Austin's eyes narrowed. "But no more singing!"

"Oh, no. No, sir."

Pogo darted behind them and slipped out the door. George watched her through the Plexiglas as she hurried away. He walked back to June and whispered, "Pogo's up to something. I know it. I have to find out what."

June's eyes widened in fear.

"Cover for me, okay? I'll be right back."

June kept her teeth clenched. "Okay. But be careful." She watched her little brother circle and then exit the room, walking as quickly as he dared.

George caught up with Pogo on the roof just as she was pulling back the mushroom cap. When Pogo spotted him, she gasped aloud and clutched at her throat.

George, by way of apology, started twisting his hands into expressive shapes, like an interpreter for the deaf. "Sorry! Sorry, Pogo. I...I want to know what you're doing now. Okay? I like to know things like that."

Pogo stared at him, puzzled.

"I...I need your help, Pogo, to figure this all out."

Pogo scrutinized his face and followed the twists and turns of his hands. She pointed at him and said:

> "Georgie Porgie,
> Pudding and pie."

George flipped his hands outward in confusion. But then he directed them back at himself. "Yes. Georgie.

That's me. Me wants to know. I mean, I want to know. Please help me."

Pogo thought for another moment. She muttered:

> "To do what's right
> With all your might."

Then she led him down the hole.

Once inside the secret room, Pogo guided George to the Holographic Scanner. He stared down into its glass plate and waited.

Pogo snatched a book from the half-empty case. She handed it to George with great urgency.

George recognized the book, *Perrault's Mother Goose*, but he puzzled over its meaning. He pleaded with Pogo, "Will you talk to me about this?"

She would not.

George set the book on the glass and pressed his hands to his temples. "Okay. Let me try to talk this out myself. You know? To think out loud? Maybe you can tell me if I'm right or wrong?"

Pogo cocked her head.

"The demon will go into *any* book you put on the scanner—like *Brown Bear, Brown Bear* or *The Three Billy Goats Gruff*—and then come back out after he's done his evil work?"

Pogo shook her head no very rapidly, like quivering gelatin.

George tried again. "Okay. The demon will go into any book you put on the scanner, but...But! He will only come back out into this one?" He pointed at *Perrault's Mother Goose*.

Pogo stopped quivering. She nodded an emphatic yes.

George's face lit up. He pumped his fist. "Yes!" Then he begged her, "But why, Pogo? Please, tell me why."

Pogo pushed past him, turned her back, and set to work at the scanner.

George waited for a moment longer and then gave up. He said, "Thank you, Pogo. Thank you for talking to me. I'd better get back to my job."

Pogo didn't look up.

George hurried out. In his excited state, he did not notice the title of the book that Pogo had placed, with practiced care, onto the scanner. It was *Genetic Mapping: The Path to Superior Human Beings*.

Twenty minutes later, the County Commission Room was filled with an assortment of adults and children. Prominent among them were four representatives from Harvard University.

Dr. Austin and Cornelia huddled near the door with the Harvard group. Cornelia asked them, "Isn't it remarkable that the next great student from Whittaker would be our own son?" She didn't wait for an answer. "The Whittakers, as you may know, comprise the upper class of King's County—" But she paused when she saw Kate walk in. "You there!" she called. "Find your mother and help her dust the lobby." She turned back to the Harvard representatives with a smile. "We must, of course, train the future domestic class, too."

Kate took a quick look around. George was sitting in the back with the Juku Warriors. She snuck over to him and whispered, "I have to go down to the lobby. To train for my future career. Keep your eyes open up here. *Semper Paratus*, right?"

"Right."

Kate started out just as the crowd quieted and Whit walked to the podium. He frowned when he saw the manila envelope. He tilted the envelope toward him, slid out *Genetic Mapping: The Path to Superior Human Beings*, and opened it.

After a moment of silent reflection, Whit closed the book emphatically. Then, as the puzzled crowd looked on, he removed his blue blazer and began tying it into tight knots. He then did the same thing to his tie, and then his shirt.

Down in the lobby, Kate had dutifully joined June to help with the dusting. The can man was asleep in a chair with a newspaper over his face, so Kate dusted around him. She continued her work, lost in her own thoughts until, a few minutes later, she heard a great commotion and looked up. Way up. To the eighth floor.

She spotted George hustling the Juku Warriors out of the room and running with them toward Elevator #3. She could hear the children's shrieking voices, but she couldn't tell what they were saying.

The four Harvard representatives ran out of the room right afterward. They turned left and sprinted for Elevator #2.

Then Dr. Austin burst through the door. He grabbed on to the railing and yelled across the chasm, "Hodges! Hodges!"

Mrs. Hodges appeared at the seventh-floor railing. "Mrs. Hodges! Get your equipment," he ordered. "The time has come!"

Mrs. Hodges darted away toward the stairwell as Dr. Austin took off running for Elevator #1.

Kate tried to watch in four directions at once. Elevator #3, with George and the Juku Warriors, was descending well ahead of the other two.

When the doors of Elevator #3 opened, Kate heard the children laughing wildly and shouting about "the funny man."

George said, "Yes, he was a funny man. Wasn't he?"

Kate ran up to them. "Uncle George, what happened?"

George rolled his eyes up. "Oh, nothing."

The Juku Warriors yelled, "The funny man took his clothes off!"

"Oh yeah, well, aside from that, nothing happened."

"Uncle George, come on! Please!"

"Well, let's just say Whit was not himself. For one thing, as the children have pointed out, he took all his clothes off."

A little boy shouted, "He was a monkey!"

George smiled at him. "Oh, yes, I nearly forgot that part. He climbed up on top of the podium. Then he started shrieking, in some kind of monkey language."

The boy shouted to Kate, "He was a funny man!"

George shook his head. "Then, well, I can't tell you the rest."

"Uncle George!"

"I'd rather not go into the graphic details in front of the children," he whispered.

George turned the Juku Warriors over to June as Elevator #2 arrived with the Harvard representatives. Dr. Austin's elevator reached the lobby ten seconds later.

The Harvard group sprinted past Kate and George, with Dr. Austin in pursuit just ten yards behind. Kate and George watched them all run through the entranceway and out into the street. The Harvard representatives were clearly faster and were pulling steadily away from Dr. Austin.

Kate turned and pleaded, "Uncle George! Come on!"

George checked to see that they were far from the children. Then he confided, in a low voice, "Do you remember that time when I was in third grade, and you were in fifth grade, and our whole school took a field trip to the zoo?"

Kate remembered. "Yeah."

"Do you remember when we went into the monkey house?"

"Yeah. I remember how bad it smelled."

"Okay. Now. Do you, by any chance, remember what the bad monkeys, specifically the bad boy monkeys, were doing to themselves?"

Kate's jaw dropped. "No!"

"Yes."

"No way!"

"Yes. Way." George cast his gaze upward toward the County Commission Room and intoned, "Welcome to the monkey house."

The Harvard group ran past the front in the other direction. Dr. Austin ran past, too, trailing now by a wide margin.

"I don't think Whit's getting into Harvard," George added. "Not in this lifetime. Unless of course it's as a specimen in their anthropology department."

Then they heard Cornelia screaming. They looked up in time to see Pogo run in a panic from the County Commission Room to Dr. Austin's office.

To the left, they saw Mrs. Hodges come crashing out of the service elevator. She was dressed in elbow-high gloves and thick protective goggles. She propelled a black cart before her like a sled down a snowy hill, rounding one corner and smashing through the door of the County Commission Room.

Back across the square, Pogo dashed out of Dr. Austin's office holding the blue shower curtain before her. Cornelia met Pogo at the door, snatched it away, and ran back inside. She returned seconds later, hustling Whit toward her husband's office with the shower curtain now wrapped around him.

Kate spoke slowly and deliberately. "Uncle George? Do you remember that book I gave you?"

George gulped. "That genetic engineering thing?"

"Yes. Did you, by any chance, give that book to Pogo?"

"No. I gave it to Whit. Like you said. I put it on the podium."

"Was Pogo in the room?"

"Uh. Yes."

"Did Pogo then leave the room?"

George looked up. "Yes again."

Mrs. Hodges careened back through the door with a manila envelope now sitting atop her cart. She steered the cart to the service elevator and punched at the button with a gloved hand. The doors opened, and Mrs. Hodges pushed the cart in, but it came rolling right back out, followed by Pogo.

Mrs. Hodges shouted, "Pogo! Get out of my way! I command you to get out of my way!"

But instead, Pogo rushed the cart and grabbed the manila envelope. Mrs. Hodges grabbed it back. They wrestled desperately until the envelope ripped away into Pogo's hands, leaving a large antique book in Mrs. Hodges's hands.

Pogo stumbled sideways into the railing. The metal squealed once and then gave way completely. A three-foot section snapped off and hurtled, eight stories, to the lobby below. It landed with a loud clatter, dangerously close to Kate, George, June, the sleeping can man, and the returning Dr. Austin.

Pogo pinwheeled her arms wildly, reeling back and forth on the edge of the precipice. She regained her balance, though, and backed away from the hole with a look of fear and confusion on her face. She continued to back up until she disappeared into the elevator.

Mrs. Hodges then stepped toward the hole with a

stiff-legged gait, like a zombie platform diver. She inched out over the eight-story abyss so that only the heels of her black shoes remained on the landing. She peeled off her gloves and goggles, dropping them and the antique book into the empty space in front of her. Then she declared, in a booming theatrical voice, "Jack fell down and broke his crown, and Jill came tumbling— *Ahhhh!*"

Mrs. Hodges raised her arms and took off flying. Momentarily. Then she started to fall. She fell for a long, long time, her arms and legs moving in slow motion through the air like a swimmer's. She hit the lobby floor without the slightest bounce and stuck there, like a wad of black putty.

34

A Possible Perpetrator
of the Crimes

After a moment of stunned silence, Dr. Austin approached Mrs. Hodges in small fearful steps. He said, "Get back all of you. I'll call Dr. Cavendar. He'll take care of her." Then he added loudly, "I think she's going to be all right."

Cornelia ran up to him and was about to speak when he barked at her, "Where's Dr. Cavendar? Where's Bud?"

Cornelia whispered, as best she could, "I don't know. Listen: Whit is in the Hummer. We're on our way to the emergency room."

Dr. Austin ordered her, "Get the blue shower curtain!"

"I can't. It's wrapped around Whit."

"What?" Dr. Austin exploded. "Then get it off of him!"

"He ruined his clothes. It's all he has to wear."

Dr. Austin clenched his fists and hissed, "Bring me my blue shower curtain! I need it! Now!"

Cornelia stomped away just as Pogo emerged from the service elevator. She circled carefully around the prostrate Mrs. Hodges, as if looking for something.

Kate startled her with an urgent whisper in her ear. "Pogo! You promised me! You said you wouldn't do this again!"

Pogo's body stiffened, but her eyes continued to search.

"You promised that you would let me fight my own battles. Do you remember that?"

Pogo's eyes shifted to Kate. She shook her head, bewildered. "Georgie Porgie, pudding and pie." Then she pointed over Kate's shoulder.

Kate turned and saw that she was pointing at George. Her uncle was standing five feet away from them and looking down at Mrs. Hodges's body. His lower lip was quivering. Kate didn't understand, and then she did. "Oh my god. Uncle George! You did this for Uncle George?"

Pogo nodded and bared a set of large and slightly crooked teeth.

Kate stared deeply into Pogo's brown eyes, trying to

choose the right words. "Listen to me, Pogo. Uncle George is in total agreement with me on this." Kate had a moment of doubt, but she continued. "I'm sure he is. He doesn't want you to do things like this for him." She glanced at George and back again. "I know you meant well, Pogo, but there's a dead person over there. You didn't want to kill Mrs. Hodges. Did you?"

Pogo shook her head vehemently no.

Kate exhaled, relieved. "But that's what happened. Once you set this... thing in motion, you can't control what it will do."

Kate took Pogo's elbow and turned her toward George. "My uncle doesn't need to hear that you did this for him. Okay? Ever. He can be very sensitive about these things."

Pogo nodded slowly in agreement. Then she broke free and wandered over to the sawed-off piece of railing. She picked it up and turned it over and over, looking from its serrated edges to the broken body of Mrs. Hodges and back again. As she did, a deeply troubled look spread across her face—clenching her jaw, narrowing her eyes, and furrowing her brow.

Cornelia stormed back through the lobby holding the blue shower curtain. She snarled at Dr. Austin. "Here's your precious shower curtain. Now may I take your naked son to the emergency room?"

Dr. Austin gripped the shower curtain tightly. "Yes! Do what you want. Go."

He looked past his wife to the glass entrance doors. Bud Wright, Sheriff Wright, and Dr. Cavendar were walking in together. He shouted, "Dr. Cavendar! Thank god. Mrs. Hodges has fallen, Doctor. You have to help her."

Dr. Austin then told everyone else, "Clear this lobby! All of you! Go home. Can't you see that this woman needs air?" He jumped up and herded people toward the entranceway. As Kate moved to the exit, she noticed an oval of red oozing from beneath Mrs. Hodges.

Kate found June at the end of the *Andrew Carnegie in Hell* mosaic. However, despite a careful search among the fleeing library patrons, she was unable to find her uncle.

George Melvil had not evacuated the building as ordered. He was lying flat on the second-floor carpet, with his face pressed against the rail, at the exact spot where he had connected the wires and pulleys of the flying machine.

One floor beneath him, in the lobby, Bud Wright asked Dr. Austin, "Okay, Doc. You're the boss. What do we gotta do first?"

"Let's get Hodges downstairs. Then we need to

think of a story. We need to find a perpetrator for this crime. And fast."

Bud stooped over and strained to get a grip on Mrs. Hodges.

"I agree," Dr. Cavendar said. "And look over there, Doctor. It seems that the lobby is not completely empty."

George froze in place, fearing he had been discovered. But he quickly realized that they were not talking about him. George leaned forward and saw another figure. The can man was still in the lobby, and he was still asleep.

"I am thinking, Dr. Austin, that this one might prove to be useful," Dr. Cavendar said.

"Yes, he might, indeed. But Pogo is still our safest bet. She is, after all, mute."

Bud grunted. "Give me a hand here, Doc." He pointed out the can man to his brother. "You watch him, Bubba."

Dr. Austin helped Bud drag Mrs. Hodges across to the service elevator and down to the basement.

George shifted his position. He watched Dr. Cavendar wander over to the bloodstained area of the lobby. He saw him pick up two objects, with some difficulty, and lug them to the elevator doors.

As soon as Dr. Austin and Bud returned, Dr. Cavendar confronted them with the first of the objects. "Look what I found. This is conclusive evidence. This piece of railing has been cut, right here, with an electric power saw, probably old Mr. Pogorzelski's."

"Pogo!" Dr. Austin shouted. "I knew it." He glanced at the bloodstains. "Mrs. Hodges knew it, too. She warned me that Pogo's been using those power tools at night."

Dr. Cavendar set down the railing and held up the second object. It was an antique book, now stained red with blood—*Perrault's Mother Goose.*

"Look at this. I found it on the floor where the body landed. I found this same book on the roof the day the unfortunate worker had the coronary occlusion and dragged the others to their deaths. How curious that it reappears today."

Dr. Austin's eyes filled with the light of revelation. "Yes! Walter Barnes, Bud, Heidi, Whit... What did they all do? They all picked up a book."

Dr. Austin seized the book from the old doctor. He held it high. "This book will now be in my possession twenty-four hours a day. This is the break we needed! This is how we'll trap the demon!" His eyes darted across the lobby. "Now let's find, arrest, and lock up our perpetrator."

George shifted again. He watched Drs. Austin and Cavendar hurry into the lobby office and sit at a terminal while Bud and his brother shook the can man awake.

The sheriff forced the can man to his feet and hand-cuffed him as Drs. Austin and Cavendar emerged carrying a single sheet of paper.

In his darkest and most menacing voice, Dr. Austin informed the can man, "First of all, may I remind you that you are on probation for assaulting my wife. Secondly, may I remind you that you are homeless, out of work, and probably mentally ill. We are going to send you to jail for the rest of your life. We may even send you to the electric chair in Milton if you do not sign this statement."

Dr. Austin held the paper up before the hapless man's eyes and ordered: "Read it aloud, so we can all hear!"

The can man focused and read, as best he could. "'Miss Pogorzelski has been trying to kill Mrs. Hodges by sawing through parts of the railings with power tools at night. She has also been trying to kill Mrs. Cornelia Whittaker-Austin by getting me to ram my supermarket cart into her Hummer H2. She also tried, and succeeded, in killing Mr. Walter Barnes by inducing a heart attack in the old gentleman. She is clearly a homicidal maniac. Sincerely, your name.'"

Dr. Austin indicated that the sheriff should unlock the handcuffs. He then produced a pen and pressed it into the can man's hand. He was in the process of guiding the pen to the paper when the can man ripped his hand away, stared hard at the pen, and tossed it far across the lobby.

Dr. Austin shouted at him. "You *are* mentally ill!"

The can man then surprised them all by speaking in a voice that was strong and full of conviction. "I betrayed somebody once, and I've never forgiven myself. I won't do it again."

Dr. Austin said, "Then *you* will be found guilty of the crimes enumerated on this statement. Is that what you want?"

"If it's that or my honor? Yes, that is what I want."

Dr. Austin concluded, "He's as crazy as Hodges. Sheriff Wright, take him away."

The sheriff handcuffed the can man again and force-marched him through the entranceway.

Dr. Austin turned to the two others. "Never mind him. We'll sort this all out later. For now, let us focus on our main objective—destroying the demon!" He looked at them with his eyes shining. "Mrs. Hodges did half the job for us. She got us the book! The question is, gentlemen, who is going to do the other half of the job?"

Dr. Cavendar demurred. "That would not fall under my duties as county coroner."

Bud protested, too. "Don't look at me, Doc. That demon busted me up good already."

Dr. Austin assured them both, "No, no, gentlemen. You have both done your parts. I was thinking of someone else. Someone who always gets the most difficult jobs done, and in the most spectacular fashion."

Bud smiled. "I think I know where you're going here, Doc."

George strained forward to hear Dr. Austin's final words. "Yes, gentlemen. I think it's time we called in Ashley-Nicole."

35

Quod Erat Demonstrandum

Molly got dropped off in front of Kate's house on Saturday night. She was again carrying her flute and her grandmother's scrapbook; Kate was again carrying Cornell Whittaker Number Two's diary.

The two girls walked around to the back porch hoping they could talk privately. If they were hoping to avoid George, however, they were soon disappointed. He joined them ten minutes into their conversation, shortly after Molly had delivered a Lincoln Middle School update that had depressed Kate greatly. Molly reported that Derek Arroyo had been spotted, by Lisette herself, holding hands with LoriBeth Sommers.

At the exact moment of George's arrival, Kate was simulating hanging herself from one of the porch rails, while Molly was playing a half-tempo rendition of "Captain Hook" on her flute. Rather than disturb the girls with chatter, George had opted to drift across the back porch toward them, in a graceful, rhythmic way that very much resembled dancing.

At the end of the song, Kate straightened out her bent neck, closed her flapping jaw, and asked him, "What was that?"

George looked to his left, and then to his right. "What?"

"That…locomotion you were doing there. Was that dancing?"

"No. I can't dance."

Molly set down her flute and told Kate, "He's right. He can't."

Kate persisted. "Come on, Uncle George. That was pretty good. Where did you learn to do that?"

"I didn't learn it. I was just faking. I really can't dance."

Molly started disassembling her flute. "He really can't."

But Kate was not convinced, and she continued to regard him curiously.

As Molly bent to pick up her case, she spotted a figure by the back gate. Her lips pulled back in distaste. "You are not going to believe this."

Kate looked up and saw William Anderson. He

waved happily. "Hi, Kate! I was just checking to see which house was yours."

"What do you mean, William?"

"I mean, I was trying to figure: If your house was, like, the fourth from the corner from the front? Then which one would it be from the back?"

"Do you mean, like, this was some kind of scientific thesis that you were testing?" George asked.

William answered happily, "Yeah!"

George grinned. "If it's the fourth one from the front, then it's the fourth one from the back, too, William."

William admitted, "Yeah, I can see that now."

"QED."

"Huh?"

George explained, "QED. It's Latin. You write it after you prove a thesis, after you demonstrate the one true answer. *Quod erat demonstrandum*. It means 'Which was demonstrated.'"

"It does?"

Molly suggested, "Could you two do this somewhere else?"

But William continued. "Hey, do you guys remember *our* Latin motto?"

They did, but they did not respond. William finally answered himself. "*Semper Paratus*. Do you guys remember that?"

"He's not going to go away, you know," George muttered to Kate. "You may as well invite him up."

Kate couldn't bear to look at Molly when she said, "Come on up, William, and join us."

After a few failed attempts, William managed to unlock the gate and walk up to the porch. When he spotted Molly's flute case, he asked her, "Hey, Molly, are you in the big show for the First Lady?"

Molly looked askance at him. "Yeah. Why? Are you?"

William told all three of them, "Yeah, I am. Dr. Austin and Mrs. Whittaker-Austin found a part for me."

Molly faked a smile. "Lucky you."

"Yeah! I know. I really wanted to get into the show."

George asked him, "What part did the Austins give you?"

William extended his long arms. "Mrs. Whittaker-Austin asked me if I could hold a pole, for a long time, without dropping it and messing everything up, and ruining all the hard work everybody had done."

George looked at Kate. "That sounds like the invitation she gave us."

"You're holding a flag," Kate said, "like we are, in the patriotic tableau."

"That's fine with me. I just want to be there to see what happens."

Kate had to smile at his open enthusiasm. Then she sat back on her haunches, held up the diary, and said, "I have to put this book back on its shelf tomorrow. The Austins are going to miss it, and they're going to blame Pogo. So this is it, you guys. This is our last chance."

After a tense pause, George asked, "Have you read every word in the diary?"

"Yes. I have. Several times." She opened to the last page. "Here. I found this at the end. See if it makes any sense to you." Kate cleared her throat and read, "'Despite all my expenses and all my efforts, I have not been able to join them. They will never let me join them. So be it.'" Kate closed the book and turned to her uncle, hopefully.

George grimaced. "Okay, I'm going to try an experiment here. I'm going to try thinking out loud, just brainstorming. Okay? Here goes."

George clenched his eyelids together. "There were guys in this London Spiritualism Society. They succeeded in reaching another plane. They did it by escaping into a book. It was the book that Cornell paid way too much for and brought back here." George opened his eyes.

Kate said, "One book?"

"Yes. Just the one. *Perrault's Mother Goose*. They were in it, and Cornell knew it. He tried to join them, but he failed. So he said the heck with them. He let his favorite student inventor, Ashley-Nicole Singer-Wright, plaster holographic stickers on his books, including the, uh, *occupied* one." He looked at Kate. "And they all escaped."

Kate stared at him. "That's an answer. But do you think it's the one true answer? Do you think that's really what happened?"

George could only shake his head. "I don't know. I'm just thinking out loud. Maybe there was only one ghost in the book. Maybe Cornell *really* got swindled. Maybe he only got one ghost for his money."

The back door to the left side of the house opened, and June stepped out. Everybody else froze. June told them, "You don't need to stop talking. I've heard every word you've said." She looked at the tall boy. "Hello, William. I'm June Melvil, Kate's mother."

William gulped. "Hello, ma'am."

June looked around the group. "It sounds like you kids are trying to scare yourselves. With what? A ghost story?"

George told her, without hesitation, "This is not a ghost story, June. This is real."

"How do you know it's real?"

"I saw it. I saw it with my own eyes."

"You saw what?"

"I saw a demon, or a ghost, enter a person, take over a person completely. Then I saw it leave. Into a book."

"That sounds really crazy, George."

Kate jumped to her uncle's defense. "Do you want to talk about crazy, June? How about this: Walter Barnes, Mr. Bud Wright, Heidi, Whit, and Mrs. Hodges. All of them picked up a book and started acting the same way. You saw them! How would you describe the way that they were acting?"

June answered her quietly. "Crazy?"

Kate slapped the porch boards with finality. "Thank you!"

George's eyes rolled up, as if looking into his own brain. "But here's the part that I don't understand: The demon can attack people out of any book, right?"

Kate answered tentatively, "Right."

"Any book with a holographic sticker on it."

"Right."

"So why can't it escape back into any book with a sticker? Why does it have to go back into that old *Mother Goose*?"

Kate shrugged. "Maybe it doesn't *have* to. Maybe it *wants* to."

June added, "Maybe he's looking for some—" But she stopped herself in midthought. She studied all the faces on the porch, one by one, culminating in Kate's. "I'm sorry. I shouldn't be eavesdropping on you. I shouldn't be intruding on your time. This should be your time only." Then she turned and walked back inside.

WEEK FIVE

36

Ashley-Nicole

As soon as they stepped out of June's car on Monday morning, Kate and George spotted a police cruiser. Sheriff Wright was in the driver's seat, training a pair of binoculars upward at the Whittaker Building.

Kate followed the line of the binoculars to the roof. "Look! It's Pogo, Uncle George. I can see her up there. She's holding her power saw!"

George said, "Maybe she's threatening to jump."

"No, not Pogo." Kate shook her head. "She wouldn't do that."

"I have no idea what Pogo would or wouldn't do."

"She needs my help," Kate decided.

Kate pushed her way past the Mushroom Children in the entranceway. She ran downstairs to Math 8 and told him, "They want me in the Protein Lab to test a new formula. I'll be gone all period."

Math 8 smiled his consent. Then he removed her test booklet from the day's pile.

Kate sprinted to the service elevator and pressed the button for the roof. Fear rose in her as she ascended the nine floors. She gritted her teeth, and stamped, and pounded her fist against the elevator's steel walls, urging it to move faster. When the doors opened, she burst out and ran toward the front roof wall, toward the spot where she had last seen Pogo. Then she heard a crash.

Kate stifled a gasp. But she had run only three steps more when she saw a black dress to her left. Kate skidded to a halt on the cinders and changed direction. "Pogo! Thank god you're all right."

The normally pale librarian was bright red with exertion. She looked at Kate and panted, "Do what's right with all your might." Then she leaned over the roof wall and pointed down.

Kate leaned, too, and looked over. She saw a swath of machine parts spread out all around the loading dock. Pogo reached under her dress and pulled out a brass plaque. It read ASHLEY-NICOLE SINGER-WRIGHT, SIXTH-GRADE SCIENCE WINNER.

Kate asked, "The Holographic Scanner? Is that the Holographic Scanner?"

Pogo nodded.

Kate looked down again at the hundreds of glass and metal shards, and red and blue snippets of wire. All she could think to say was, "So, that's the end of that. Huh?"

Pogo answered, "Jack fell down and broke his crown." Then she pushed away from the wall and sprinted toward the front of the building.

Kate took off running behind her shouting, "No, Pogo! Don't do it. Don't jump!"

But to Kate's great relief, Pogo stopped at the mushroom cap and sat on it, like a frog on an aluminum toadstool. She reached down, picked up a red-and-black power saw, and cradled it in her arms like a favorite doll.

Kate joined her silently for a moment and listened to the sounds of the street below. Then she asked, "Pogo, what do you do with that saw?"

Pogo hugged the power tool tighter.

"I mean, do you suddenly wake up somewhere and realize that you just sawed something?"

Pogo nodded yes.

"And when you do, do you always have the *Mother Goose* book with you?"

She nodded yes again.

"So, it was the demon? The demon was making you saw things?"

Pogo answered:

"Jack be nimble, Jack be quick."

"You always call the demon 'Jack.' Did he tell you to call him that?"

Pogo nodded and added:

"It made the children laugh and play,
   Laugh and play,
   Laugh and play."

Kate smiled. "Yeah. I'm sure." Then she added sternly, "But Jack did bad things, too. And he made you do bad things."

Pogo moved her mouth to answer, but then the stairwell door banged open, revealing Bud Wright and his brother.

Pogo set down her saw. She whispered:

"There's a big fat policeman
   At my door, door, door.
   He grabbed me by the collar,
   He made me pay a dollar."

Bud and his brother advanced ominously. The sheriff held out a paper and attempted to read from it. "Miss

Poga-Poga-zoo-ski. I've got a warrant here for your arrest."

Kate spoke for her. "Her arrest? That's ridiculous. What for?"

"For the attempted murder of Mrs. Mildred Hodges by sawing through a railing."

"*Attempted* murder?" Kate sputtered. "You mean, Mrs. Hodges is still alive?"

The sheriff looked at Bud, who answered, "Of course she's alive. She's fine. Doc Cavendar got her back on her feet in no time."

"But she fell eight stories to a marble floor!"

"She had a little fall. It just knocked the wind out of her, that's all."

"If she's fine, then where is she?"

Bud grimaced behind his cervical collar. "How am I supposed to know? Maybe she took a day off."

"She never takes a day off."

Bud indicated to his brother to get busy. "You'll have to take that up with Dr. Austin, kid."

The sheriff handcuffed Pogo and pulled her off the aluminum cap. He told her, "You have the right to remain silent…"

Kate watched the two men march Pogo away. Then, with her heart pounding and her mouth cottony dry, she bent back the cap and slipped down the ladder. She pushed through the door and returned Cornell

Whittaker Number Two's diary to its shelf—its now-empty shelf.

At the start of fourth period, Science 8 read an announcement: "Dr. Austin has canceled school tomorrow. He wants all students to watch the news to learn about the First Lady's historic visit to the Whittaker Magnet School and to write a five-paragraph essay about it. He also wants you to point out to your friends and relatives that the Whittaker Magnet School is the only school in King's County ever to be visited by a First Lady of the United States."

Science 8 then walked back and handed Kate a separate printed announcement from Susan Singer-Wright. It read, "All involved in the performance for the First Lady must report to the County Commission Room immediately."

Kate got up to leave; Science 8 smiled.

Kate rode upstairs, entered the County Commission Room, and turned to walk toward the back. But she saw that the last row was occupied by three people and an assortment of medical equipment.

Heidi and Whit Austin were seated on a bench against the wall. Between them sat an elderly nurse dressed in white tights, a white uniform, and a white triangular hat. Heidi's eyes were two large black circles, like a raccoon's. She had an ice pack affixed to her jaw, held in place by a Velcro sash. Whit had an IV pole next to him, with a hanging bag, from which a clear liquid was dripping. He stared straight ahead, openmouthed.

Susan Singer-Wright began the meeting with a quick rap of the gavel. She led the group through a rereading of the timetable for the First Lady's visit. The only new business came when Cornelia entered the room with a shopping bag.

Cornelia took the microphone and announced, "Since certain students who are part of the patriotic tableau cannot afford the Whittaker Magnet School uniforms, I have designed a special costume for them for this performance. Would the students who cannot afford uniforms please come forward."

Kate caught George's eye across the room. He shrugged at her and started to the front, so Kate did the same.

Cornelia reached into a shopping bag and pulled out two sets of yellow silk pants followed by two sets of purple-and-yellow-striped shirts.

George whispered to Kate, "They look like the uniforms of the Swiss Guard."

"Who?"

"The guys who guard the pope?"

Kate disagreed. "No. They look like the uniforms

of the guys who guard the Wicked Witch of the West. Remember? In *The Wizard of Oz*? They had those stripes?"

"Yeah. Yeah. Those, too."

Cornelia handed one uniform to Kate and one to George. She was about to speak to them, but Susan cut her off with a delighted squeal. "Ashley-Nicole!"

Kate and George turned to the door and saw a smiling young woman enter, followed by two somber Technon Industries engineers. The young woman's blond hair was tied back in a ponytail. She wore black shoes and tights, a red plaid skirt, and a white blouse buttoned to the top.

"Well, by golly, look who's here," Susan bubbled. "All the way from the Massachusetts Institute of Technology. And I thought you were decorating for some big homecoming mixer!"

Ashley-Nicole answered in a high voice. "I am, Mommy. I have to be back by tomorrow night."

"Tomorrow night!"

"Yes! I'm in charge of the balloons."

Bud Wright and Dr. Austin hurried over to greet her. Bud hollered, "Hi, honeybun."

"Hi, Daddy. What happened to your neck?"

"This? Aw, it's nothing. Thank you for getting here so fast."

"Anything to help, Daddy. You know that."

Dr. Austin took her hand and pumped it. "This school will always be indebted to you for coming, Ashley-Nicole." His eyes darted around the room. He lowered his voice. "How about if you and your father and I adjourn to my office."

Kate and George exchanged a knowing look and prepared to move out.

One of the Technon Industries engineers spoke up. "We will need to accompany Miss Singer-Wright to any meeting regarding Technon Industries products."

Dr. Austin looked at Bud. "You will? Well, all right. Let's all go, then."

Kate and George hopped up.

Kate announced, to no one in particular, "We'd better go try on these uniforms."

George said, "Yeah. I can't wait to see what mine looks like."

They exited casually, walking through the door clutching their new uniforms like prizes. At the foot of the stairwell, they turned to check behind them; then they took off running up the steps. They were crouching in place behind the low bookcase in time to see Dr. Austin lead his group of five inside.

Ashley-Nicole passed through the rotating door tentatively, but then she squealed with delight to see her old Laser Cannon again. The silver-and-black weapon now stood between the tall bookcase and the desk. The Technon engineers produced two legal pads and waited.

Dr. Austin got right to the point. "Ashley-Nicole, we want to use your Laser Cannon to solve a very specific problem."

"What's that, Dr. Austin?"

"We want to destroy a book and its contents."

Ashley-Nicole scrunched up her nose. "A book?"

"Yes. We want to destroy a book. One book in particular. A children's book."

"Can't you just shred it? Or burn it?"

"No. I mean, yes, we could just burn the book. But, you see, the *contents* of this book must be destroyed, too. I've given this a lot of thought, Ashley-Nicole. Surprise is the key element. The contents must be taken by surprise by the remote tracking feature of the Laser Cannon."

Ashley-Nicole adjusted a dial on the Laser Cannon. She asked flatly, "How far away will the target be?"

"It will be right here. In this room. On top of a cart."

"You said that the target is a book. Do you know the dimensions of the book?"

"It's a large children's book. An antique. Maybe nine inches by twelve inches by an inch thick."

Kate poked George in the ribs. She whispered what he already knew. *"Perrault's Mother Goose."*

Ashley-Nicole thought for a moment. "These 'contents' that you're concerned about, would they be vulnerable to the heat ray of a laser?"

"Yes, I believe they would."

Ashley-Nicole looked at the Technon engineers and winked. "Dr. Austin, I've done enough top-secret work to know that I shouldn't ask too many questions. So I will ask only one: Are you sure you need the Laser Cannon for this job? It's designed for use across a fifty-mile battlefield, you know."

"Yes, of course I'm sure. Absolutely. It's the perfect weapon for the job."

Ashley-Nicole winked at the Technon men again. "Okeydokey. I'll calibrate it for the job that you described. We'll need to make a few modifications, but I am sure we can destroy one children's book on top of one cart."

Dr. Austin was jubilant. "Excellent, Ashley-Nicole! I knew we could count on you."

Bud added, "That's my honeybun!"

Ashley-Nicole pointed out to them both, "Of course, collateral damage could be a significant factor."

Bud adjusted his neck brace. "How's that, honeybun?"

"Innocent bystanders could get killed."

Dr. Austin and Bud looked at each other. "That's not good," Bud commented.

"No," Dr. Austin agreed. "Ashley-Nicole, what can we do to protect, say, three people here in the room when the Laser Cannon does its job?"

Ashley-Nicole tapped her two pointer fingers together. "Hmm." She looked at the Technon men. "Here's what I think we could do."

Both engineers started writing. "We will have Technon install a safety barrier of a perioplastic that is very hard, has opaque properties, and is reflective on its energized side only."

Dr. Austin and Bud both nodded appreciatively. Then Dr. Austin asked Bud, "What did she say?"

Bud turned to Ashley-Nicole. "Honeybun, what'd you just say?"

"Oh, Daddy! Technon will install a protective wall for us. It will be like a two-way mirror. That way we'll be able to see what happens when the Laser Cannon hits the target."

Dr. Austin clapped his hands together. "Oh! Good. That's good." He pushed on the rotating door and gestured them all out. "In fact, it's perfect. The perfect plan!"

Kate and George waited for thirty seconds. Then they grabbed their striped uniforms and retraced their steps, up to the roof and down to the County Commission Room.

They had hoped to slip back in quietly, but Cornelia spotted them from the dais. She interrupted Susan Singer-Wright by calling out, "You two! How did my new uniforms fit?"

Kate and George froze; then they turned toward Cornelia. George started to shake, but Kate steadied him with her left hand. With her right hand, she answered for them both by sticking up her thumb and smiling hugely, like she had just pulled out a plum.

37

Library Forgiveness Day

That evening Kate was very surprised to hear that June had called Mrs. Brennan and had invited her and Molly to dinner. She was annoyed, though, when the doorbell rang and June came out of the bathroom with her hair still wrapped up in a towel.

Kate snapped, "You're the one who invited them, June. Didn't you know what time they would be here?"

June ignored Kate's comments and, to Kate's further mortification, answered the door as she was. She shook hands with Mrs. Brennan and told her, "I'm June Melvil, Kate's mother. I should have invited you here over a year ago. Please forgive me."

"Don't be silly," Mrs. Brennan answered. "We're all busy people. It's nice to finally get together."

As they walked into the parlor, June confessed, "I haven't been that busy. I haven't even had a job until recently. Now I'm working at the library to help pay for Kate's fees."

Mrs. Brennan replied, "Perhaps Kate has told you: I worked there for years. I was the director of Library Services."

"Yes, I know. I'm also embarrassed to say that I still have an overdue library book."

Mrs. Brennan laughed. "Don't worry about that. Just wait for a Library Forgiveness Day."

June, Molly, and Kate all looked puzzled. Mrs. Brennan asked, "Have none of you ever heard of a Library Forgiveness Day?"

Kate answered for the group, "No. Never. What is it?"

"It's an idea to get books back. A good idea, I think. Libraries set aside a day when they are willing to forgive all the fines that are owed to them."

June was surprised. "No matter how much?"

"No matter how much."

"But then the libraries don't get their money," Kate said.

"No, they don't. But they get something that is more important to them. After all, libraries aren't about fines; they're about books."

Kate commented, "That's pretty cool."

George came in through the back door and joined them in the parlor. June took the opportunity to stand up and excuse herself, saying, "I'll be back in two minutes."

Mrs. Brennan smiled a welcome to George. Then she fished a large white envelope out of her bag. "It's funny, Kate. Until our conversation the other day, I hadn't thought about Pogo in years. And now, this very morning, I received this."

She turned around the envelope to show that it was a FedEx overnight package.

Kate leaned forward. "What's in it?"

By way of answering, Mrs. Brennan dumped out the contents. Kate, Molly, and George beheld a flood of pages from children's books. The pages were isolated, unrelated, and from dozens of different books. They tumbled out in all sizes, conditions, and colors.

Mrs. Brennan explained. "It's Mrs. Hodges's secret collection. She razor-bladed every one of these pages out of a children's book."

Molly sputtered. "Why?"

"If she were here, she would say it was to protect you children."

"From what? What's on them? Anything good?"

Kate, Molly, and George rifled through the pile. But all they saw were witches, Halloween pumpkins, and friendly ghosts.

Mrs. Brennan grinned. "I thought you children might like to see everything that you missed growing up."

Kate asked her, "So how did you get this again?"

"It came from the library shipping room. From Pogo."

"How do you know it was from Pogo?"

"She included this note." Mrs. Brennan pulled out an index card. On it was written, in Pogo's neat hand:

See-saw, Marjorie Daw.
Jimmy shall have a new master.

Molly twisted her mouth. "What on earth does that mean?"

"I don't know," Mrs. Brennan admitted.

Kate thought for a moment, then she interpreted for them. "She's talking about what happened to you, Mrs. Brennan. She's saying she's sorry that you got driven out by the Austins."

Molly sounded doubtful. "Where do you see that?"

"You don't. You just have to know Pogo." Kate then looked at George, wondering how much she should reveal to the guests. She limited the news to "Pogo is gone now, too."

Mrs. Brennan raised her eyebrows. "No!"

"Yes. Pogo and Mrs. Hodges and Walter Barnes. Your entire staff is gone now, Mrs. Brennan, except for little Jimmy Austin."

"Why?" Mrs. Brennan shook her head, unable to comprehend. "What is going on in that place?"

Kate lowered her voice. "Mrs. Brennan, please. What do you know about Ashley-Nicole Singer-Wright? Who is she?"

A chill rippled across Mrs. Brennan's shoulders. "She...she's a genius. A genius in applied science. She's the girl who put the Whittaker Magnet School on the map, I'll tell you that. She owned fifteen patents by the time she entered high school. Where, by the way, she only remained for two years. Every major university was after her. She chose MIT, I believe."

"She didn't look like a genius. She looked really... normal."

"I suppose she is as normal as she could be, for a girl whose science fair projects are the deadliest weapons ever invented. The last thing old Mr. Whittaker did before he died was give Ashley-Nicole the school science fair ribbon. It was the third straight time she had won.

"He was very proud of her. He said in his speech that he could now die in peace because he had seen the second coming of his father, Cornell Whittaker Number One. Of course, that didn't sit too well with Cornelia. That's why she's been pushing that Whit creature so hard to be the new heir to the throne. But from what I've heard, he's an empty suit. The only things he invents are his accomplishments."

Kate laughed ruefully. "No argument there."

Mrs. Brennan looked up. Her mouth and her eyes both widened.

June had reentered the room.

Kate, George, and Molly soon all wore the same look of total surprise.

Kate spoke for them all. "What did you do to your hair?"

June's hair was no longer dyed blond. It had suddenly reverted to its natural brown. Nor was it combed to hide her face. It was brushed back behind her ears, just as it had been ten years before.

June explained. "Nothing. For a change. This *is* my hair."

"I think it looks good," Molly told her.

Mrs. Brennan added, "So do I."

"You may have seen me like this before, Mrs. Brennan." June turned to Kate. "And this may explain why it was so difficult for me to go back into that building, Kate. I used to bring you there every week. I was one of the founding parents of Toddler Time, now known as

Story Time. It was something we loved to do together, my little girl and me."

"Good heavens!" Mrs. Brennan blurted out. "It was you!"

June turned back to Mrs. Brennan. "That's right. I was the grown-up who went crazy that day. They tell me I was swinging by one arm from a chandelier."

Kate and George leaned forward until they were nearly falling out of their seats.

June looked right at Kate. "We were sitting in a circle for Toddler Time. You and me and all of the other parents and their children.

"The book was *Peter Pan*! *Walt Disney's Peter Pan*. The Little Golden Book version. And it was your turn to hold the book and show the pictures. For some reason, you were too shy that day. You handed the book to me and said, 'You read it, Mommy.'

"That's all I remember. Until the fireman pried my hand loose from the chandelier and carried me down the extension ladder. Then I remember grabbing you and all our things and running from the library."

Kate was speechless.

June looked down. "Our world fell apart after that. Your father got called in at Technon. He lost his security clearance. He lost his job.

"Your father was very particular about things—his clothes, his cars, his wines. He was very particular about his wife, too. She couldn't be a raving lunatic who made a public spectacle of herself."

Kate was trying not to cry. She choked out, "Did you explain what happened?"

"Unfortunately, yes. I did. I told him the whole truth. I probably should have made up a story. I should have said that I had suffered a nervous breakdown or something. I think he could have handled that."

"Well, what did he say?"

June shook her head slowly, reliving the painful memory. "He said a lot of things. He said I was lying. He said I was on drugs. He said I had some genetic mental illness from Ma and Pa.

"Within a week he had packed up all his fancy stuff and moved out. He took that job with the American Schools Abroad Program, I suppose, to get as far away from me as he could."

George finally found his voice. "You, June? You were possessed? By Jack?"

June replied, with an intensity and purpose in her voice that none of them had ever heard before: "Jack and Jill went up the hill."

38

A Historic Visit
from the First Lady
of the United States

The sun rose in a bright blue sky on Tuesday morning, the morning of the First Lady's visit to the Whittaker Building.

June drove Kate and George downtown at 9:00 A.M. Ma and Pa trailed behind in their van, transporting the other four members of the Tri-County Cloggers. All six cloggers were dressed head to toe, hats to boots, in their most spectacular outfits.

Kate and George climbed out of the Geo Metro at a distant parking spot along the River Road. They stared at each other's yellow silk pants and purple-and-yellow-striped shirts for a long moment, making horrible faces.

June locked the car and walked up to them, nervously tying and retying a black scarf under her chin.

She was wearing a blue pantsuit that Kate did not recognize. June's face, beneath her natural brown hair, was white with fear.

Kate surprised June by taking her left hand. Then she took hold of George's right hand. She led them up the long hill to the Whittaker Building, moving grimly and silently, five paces ahead of the jangling sequins and clanging spurs of the Tri-County Cloggers.

The group approached a security checkpoint outside the main entrance. Agent McCoy himself stopped them. He compared their identification cards to a computer printout. Without a word, he unclipped a velvet rope and indicated that they should proceed to the entrance. There, another agent opened the doors and watched them file past the fiery mosaic of *Andrew Carnegie in Hell.*

Dr. Austin and his wife were in the lobby, busying themselves by making last-minute adjustments to the table display of *TBC: Test-Based Curriculum.*

June untied her scarf, slid it off, and dropped it ceremoniously into a garbage can. With her restored brown hair and her rediscovered blue suit, she now looked exactly as she had on that fateful day in the lobby ten years before.

Dr. Austin stopped straightening his books and stared at her. His calm expression became troubled.

Cornelia looked up from the table and snapped at

June, "Get upstairs and set out those folding chairs." She informed Kate and George, "Pogo's not here to help you. You'll have to cover her duties, too. You can start in the basement. Bring up the refrigerator with the soda cans."

George bristled at the rude treatment, but Kate took it in stride. She exchanged a quick smile and a wave good-bye with June. She walked toward the service elevator looking up and thinking of her mother in a whole new way—as the woman who had swung on the Whittaker Library chandelier.

As soon as they reached the basement, Kate and George spotted a cooler bearing a purple-and-yellow sign. The sign read THIS ONE! in Cornelia's large handwriting.

George said, "She forgot to add 'You idiots!'"

Kate picked up the sign and studied it with interest. "Uncle George? Why would anyone go to the trouble to do this?"

"I don't know." George thought about it. "To keep us from taking the wrong cooler?"

"Okay. But this one obviously has four hundred and eighty cans of soda in it. What's in the other one?"

"Nothing. Presumably."

"Then why bother writing a sign?"

George studied the sign, too. Then he smiled slyly. "Let's go find the other one."

They checked in the kitchen and in the furnace room with no luck. Then they snuck into old Mr. Pogorzelski's workshop. The second cooler was hidden in there, in a back corner, covered with a roofing tarp.

Kate and George pulled off the tarp together. Then they let out a simultaneous shriek. They grasped onto each other and peered through the glass top in open-mouthed horror.

Neither could speak for several seconds. Finally Kate managed to say, "Oh my god. Tell me I'm not seeing this."

"Sorry," George stammered. "But I'm seeing it, too."

Just inches below them, in the frosty cooler, were the bodies of Walter Barnes and Mildred Hodges. They were frozen together, their limbs entwined in an embrace they would never have shared in life.

Kate thought long and hard. Then she said, "Uncle George, I don't think we were supposed to see this."

George gulped his agreement.

"Furthermore, I don't think we have to take any more crap from the Whittakers, or the Austins, or the Whittaker-Austins, ever again."

George tried to smile.

"The only question is: What do we do next?"

George flailed his arms and head, trying to shake out his fright. He thought for a moment longer, then he answered with a large measure of sarcasm, "I'm not sure

I understand Mrs. Whittaker-Austin's sign. I think maybe she wanted us to *switch* the two coolers."

Kate laughed and clapped her hands. "You're right. That is probably what she meant. But we were too stupid to see it at first." She leaned over to grasp the cooler. Then she had a moment of doubt. "Wait a minute. Can we really get away with this, Uncle George? What if someone checks it?"

George was ready with an answer. "If we turn down the temperature, it will be so foggy that no one will be able to see in."

Kate stole one more glance at Walter Barnes and Mildred Hodges. Then she reached for the thermostat. "Let's do it."

Kate and George parked the frosty refrigerator in its designated spot on the roof and returned to the lobby. Dr. Austin and Cornelia were still standing in place at the *TBC* table.

Cornelia snatched up a shopping bag and shook it at Kate. "Here! Take this orca costume. Then get yourself up to the County Commission Room. I want you hiding in the closet listening for your entrance cue." She held up a sheaf of stapled papers. "This is your script. Try to memorize it. Try not to destroy my book completely."

Kate accepted the bag and the script without comment. Once inside the elevator, she examined the large head, gaping mouth, and black-and-white flippers of the Orchid the Orca costume. George just stared at it.

"Don't say a word," Kate warned him.

George looked away. "There are no words."

At the eighth floor, the doors opened onto another strange sight. William Anderson was standing at the railing outside Dr. Austin's office. He was dressed in a white smock with a white painter's cap. At his feet were two cans of opened paint, one blue and one red. His arms held an aluminum extension pole with a narrow paintbrush attached at the end.

Kate called out to him in a stage whisper, "William!"

"Oh! Hey, Kate!"

"William! What are you doing?"

"Turns out I'm not in that patriotic thing with you guys after all. I've got a special job right here."

"As what? A painter?"

He corrected her. "A pretend painter. When the First Lady and all of them get here, I'm supposed to pretend like I'm painting George Washington's head. You see, that way, they'll think I've finished the whole thing except the head."

"Did Dr. Austin think of that?"

"Yeah. He did."

"I knew it. Okay. Keep your eyes open. Remember: *Semper Paratus.*"

William smiled happily. "Yeah. *Semper Paratus.*"

Kate held one finger to her lips, indicating the end of the conversation. The three of them then leaned over the railing and waited for the scene to unfold below.

Outside, a large contingent of reporters and onlookers strained to get a look at the occupants of three black Lincoln Town Cars as they pulled up to the Whittaker Building.

The first person to step out was Agent Pflaum. He carried a long black bag with the word BioSensor emblazoned in red on its side. He looked around carefully and then opened the door of the second car, the First Lady's car.

The people in the crowd cheered as the First Lady stepped out, turned, and waved to them. The First Lady was a familiar sight to all. Her pleasant face and soft voice had been beamed into American homes for three years. She looked and acted like what she was—a former first-grade teacher.

The door to the third car opened and Rosetta Turner emerged. She waited for the First Lady to finish her smiling and waving; then she guided her subtly, by the elbow, toward the glass entrance.

Dr. Austin, Mrs. Whittaker-Austin, Bud Wright, and Susan Singer-Wright stood waiting at the end of the *Andrew Carnegie in Hell* mosaic.

Cornelia's voice resonated down the entranceway. "Welcome, Madam First Lady, to the magnificent library built by my—"

But Rosetta cut her off. "We'll do all of the introductions upstairs."

Agent McCoy approached the Austins and the Wrights with a piece of paper. "This is your official timetable. The day is going to proceed minute by minute, exactly like this. There will be no surprises. Should myself or any of my agents be compelled to spring into action, you are to follow our directives immediately and without question."

Dr. Austin took the paper and nodded his acknowledgment.

Agent Pflaum then led the way to the service elevator. He unsheathed his BioSensor and trained it on the doors. The doors opened just as he pronounced it, "Uninhabited."

McCoy growled, "We can see that, Agent Pflaum."

Rosetta guided the First Lady into the elevator. McCoy turned to the Austins and Wrights and told them, "You'll have to ride up in another one."

Dr. Austin didn't hesitate. He took off at a run and led his group to Elevator #3. They arrived on the eighth floor just seconds after the First Lady's group and managed to head them off at the entrance of the County Commission Room.

This time Rosetta Turner did make proper introductions, based on identification badges, of the Austins, the Wrights, and the county commissioners. The First Lady smiled graciously at all. Then she gravitated toward the children wearing headbands and *gi*s. They were posed in a small group, each holding a copy of *Green Eggs and Ham*.

The First Lady kneeled next to one little girl. She put an arm around her, smiled, and said, "This is one of my favorite books, too. Tell me what you like best about it."

The little girl smiled back and replied, "It contains excellent modeling of the phoneme-grapheme representation *g-r.*"

The First Lady stared at her blankly until Rosetta took her elbow, raised her up, and moved her deeper into the room.

39

Orchid the Orca

George and Kate positioned themselves near the back, trying to look inconspicuous in their yellow pants and purple-and-yellow shirts. George muttered, "Hey, do you want to break into 'Dingdong! The Witch Is Dead'?"

"No. I just want to get this over with. My god, Uncle George. This getup is bad enough. Next I have to put on that ridiculous orca costume."

George gripped her arm and told her sincerely, "You're a great performer, Kate. It doesn't matter what you wear. Whatever you do will be great."

Just then Dr. Austin walked to the center of the dais and raised his hands for silence.

"Thanks," Kate whispered. "I'd better get into my closet now." She slunk off.

The people in the room quieted and looked at Dr. Austin. He began, "Madam First Lady, distinguished guests: Like me, you may have grown tired of reading about how students in Asia and in Europe are ahead of our own students in reading, history, science, and mathematics.

"I decided to do something about it. My *TBC: Test-Based Curriculum* has sparked a revolution in America's schools. Nowhere are the results more evident than here at the Whittaker Magnet School.

"At Whittaker we consistently outscore every other state in this nation on standardized tests. In fact, we outscore every other state on their *own* state tests. Our next goal, with the president's help, is to spread the word that our methods will work in *all* of America's schools."

Cornelia stepped up behind her husband. She raised one hand and gave the applause signal to the county commissioners, the Juku Warriors, and their parents.

Agent McCoy watched her closely.

Dr. Austin then followed his introductory remarks with a glowing description of the Whittaker After-School Preparatory.

George listened for his cue. Upon hearing the

words "the Juku Warriors," he arranged his seven charges into a straight line and walked them to the front. He awaited his next cue, which was "GRE vocabulary," after which he was to lead them in a round-robin spelling of *antidisestablishmentarianism.*

But George had no intention of doing that. When the cue came, he whispered, "A-one and a-two," and the Juku Warriors again broke into "I Won't Grow Up."

The First Lady was clearly delighted. She clapped merrily as the Juku Warriors executed a ragged bow.

George leaned over so that all seven children were looking at his face. Then he whispered to them, "Okay, guys. It's Bubble Time. Who here remembers Bubble Time?"

He backed away slowly, slipped out the door, and hurried up to the roof.

Dr. Austin announced to the crowd, "A little silliness to warm things up. Now, to get down to business: Our little spellers here at Whittaker have progressed beyond words that appear on the Graduate Record Exam. But don't take my word for it, listen to them."

Dr. Austin turned and pointed at the Juku Warriors. All seven had welled up with tears. One by one, they started to cry noisily, waving their arms, stamping their feet, and looking around angrily for their parents.

Dr. Austin remained pointing at them, a weak smile frozen on his face. Finally, Susan Singer-Wright came to his rescue. She ran out and shooed the children off the dais, turning and calling to the First Lady, "Aren't they precious? Don't you just love them at this age?"

The First Lady smiled back sympathetically.

Dr. Austin glared at the Juku Warriors with the bitter look of a man betrayed.

Susan announced the next person to speak: "My own dear husband, local businessman and entrepreneur, Mr. Bud Wright."

Bud walked to the front as genially as his injuries would allow. He began, "Madam First Lady, we're in a library, and I'm here to talk to you about a book. It's a new children's classic called *Orchid the Orca.*" Bud paused to hold up a copy.

"It's all about a big, lovable fish named Orchid, who eats lots of free shrimp all day and gets treated like a queen. She knows it, too. It's just the federal government that don't."

Rosetta Turner directed a steely gaze at him.

"So—let me introduce the author of this children's classic. She's our own Cornelia Whittaker-Austin."

Cornelia stepped forward and took Bud's place. She began with an awkward curtsy toward the First Lady. "Madam First Lady, as Bud told you, I am the author of the children's classic *Orchid the Orca*. Because the actress who would have played Orchid, our own Heidi Whittaker Austin, took ill, we will not be treated to her extraordinary performance today. I hope that you, Madam First Lady, may invite her down to the White House so that you can see it."

Rosetta held up her watch, a Rolex Cellini this time, and stared at it pointedly.

"In the meantime, as they say on Broadway, the show must go on." Cornelia paused for a moment to steal a glance into the back. Heidi and Whit were sitting on either side of their nurse. Heidi was staring straight ahead; Whit was drooling.

"I will read the beginning of my text, and then a substitute for Heidi Whittaker Austin will read the part of Orchid the Orca."

She cleared her throat productively and began. "Orchid the Orca swims in a big, safe public swimming pool. She gets lots of food and excellent medical care. But, sometimes, she is lonely.

"She watches all the mommies and daddies and boys and girls who come to visit her. She watches the ladies with their husbands. She watches the girls with their boyfriends. And she knows there is something missing in her life. Even though she likes helping the children learn all the county science requirements in one fun stop, and even though Mr. Bud Wright takes excellent care of her, she has one request that she would like to make of him."

Cornelia paused and looked to the side. Kate, upon hearing her cue, opened the closet door and stepped out dressed in the black-and-white orca costume. A tittering sound rippled through the audience, like a suppressed wave. Even the First Lady stifled a laugh.

Kate took three steps forward and stopped. She looked around for George, and then for any friendly face, but she could not find one. She tried to remember her lines, but she could not recall the first word. Her mind began to race. She found herself thinking about the Juku Warriors, with their No. 2 pencils; and the Mushroom Children, with their green faces; and William Anderson, with his changing addresses.

She peered through the orca head until she spotted the guest of honor. She took another three steps in that direction, prompting Agent McCoy to cast a cautionary glance at Agent Pflaum.

Kate stopped directly before the First Lady, closed her eyes, and pleaded with all the pent-up longing in her soul: "Set me free! Please! Set me free! I am trapped in a tiny pool and made to perform like a clown. I'll never see any of my friends again or do any of the things I love again. Please! Please! Send me back to the ocean where I belong. Set me free!"

Bud bolted upright in his chair, straining his neck. He pointed vehemently to Susan to do something. Susan hopped up, stepped forward, and smiled brightly at the First Lady. "I guess she just forgot her lines!" She then grabbed Kate by a black-and-white flipper and started pushing her toward the closet.

But Kate ripped free from her grasp. She turned to the First Lady, pumped her flipper into the air, and shouted, "Free Orchid the Orca! Free the Mushroom Children! Free Pogo and the can man!"

Then she ran for the door as fast as her costumed legs would allow her. Once in the hallway, she ripped off the orca head, unzipped the front, and threw the rest of the costume to the floor like a molted snakeskin.

Agent McCoy left his station and approached the Austins and the Wrights. He demanded to know, "What was that all about?"

Bud answered, laughing as best he could through his neck pain, "The poor kid! She forgot her lines. She just started yellin' stuff. Crazy, loco stuff."

Agent McCoy stared at Bud, then at Dr. Austin. After an icy look of warning, he turned to go back to the First Lady.

Susan Singer-Wright composed herself and walked as close to the First Lady as the Secret Service would allow. She smiled her widest smile. "Does the First Lady have any questions at this time?"

The First Lady did. She asked Susan, in a high, strong voice, "When can I visit the children in their classrooms? I'd like to see what they do on an average day."

Susan pictured the twelve empty classrooms in the basement. She fixed a frightened stare at the First Lady, as if she were looking at an oncoming train. But just then a thunderous, syncopated pounding began on the roof, directly over their heads.

Susan raised up one braceleted wrist toward the ceiling and shouted above the din, "Oh! I wonder what could that be?"

The First Lady smiled at her but did not respond.

Susan shouted again, "Maybe it's some authentic native American folk dancing. How does that sound?"

There was no response to that question, either, but the First Lady's entourage did get up as one, exit the County Commission Room, and proceed to the service elevator.

Agent Pflaum scanned the elevator for life-forms.

As the First Lady waited, she watched a tall boy in a painter's cap. The boy was dabbing at a ceiling mural with a small brush tied to an extension pole. The First Lady favored him with a smile. Then she turned her gaze to a square-cut hole in the center of the ceiling mural. Within the hole, the First Lady could see the underside of a wooden stage. It appeared to be moving slightly, sagging and rising under the force of many unseen, pounding feet.

Agent Pflaum gave an "All's clear" hand signal, upon which the group entered the elevator and rode up to the roof.

40

A Performance
with a Few Surprises

Cornelia's patriotic tableau was standing in place. Mr. Kagoshima, LoriBeth Sommers, and the Lincoln Middle School Band were arrayed behind the new, highly polished wooden stage. Center stage was currently occupied by the six Tri-County Cloggers, whose synchronized, stomping feet were making the boards quiver. The sides of the stage were festooned with red, white, and blue bunting hanging from vertical poles.

George stood stage left, holding an American flag. Kate stood stage right, holding a special flag designed by Cornelia. It contained the words THE WHITTAKER BUILDING and THE WHITTAKER MAGNET SCHOOL in alternating bands of purple and yellow.

Mrs. Brennan had accompanied Molly as a band chaperone. She was sitting on a folding chair, one of the hundred chairs arranged in a semicircle behind the First Lady's section.

One additional person—neither part of Cornelia's patriotic tableau nor part of the audience—was in attendance. Ashley-Nicole Singer-Wright, dressed exactly as she had been the day before, was standing by the stairwell just one foot away from a black library cart.

The First Lady waved to all in attendance and took her seat amid the din of the clogging. Agent Pflaum sat to her left, and Rosetta Turner sat to her right.

Dr. Austin posed before the stage and waited. The dancing and whooping of the Tri-County Cloggers clearly went on for longer than he or anyone else expected.

Dr. Austin finally turned and gestured at Ma and Pa to wrap it up. They finished with a six-person "Whoop!" that visibly startled the First Lady, after which she and her entourage applauded.

Dr. Austin held up his hands. "Now, let me introduce some of the fine young people we have here in King's County." He turned and raised his arms up and down to the Lincoln Middle School Band members, indicating that they should stand. The forty band members set down their instruments, stood up, and faced the

First Lady. "Madam First Lady, all of these youngsters that you see before you took the test to get into the Whittaker Magnet School, and they all failed. That is how high our standards are." He motioned for them to sit back down.

The First Lady shifted uncomfortably. Rosetta Turner held up her wristwatch again and pointed to the time.

Dr. Austin nodded rapidly. "So, with no further ado, let me introduce the band director. Here he is."

Mr. Kagoshima stepped forward tentatively, not at all sure that he had been introduced.

Dr. Austin snapped at him. "Quickly, man. The First Lady is on a timetable."

Mr. Kagoshima walked to his spot in front of the band. He gestured to LoriBeth Sommers. She walked center stage to a point equidistant between Kate and George. The Tri-County Cloggers rearranged themselves along three sides of the square, posing like country-and-western chess pieces.

Then Mr. Kagoshima raised and lowered his hand. The orchestra started to play, LoriBeth Sommers started to sing, and the Tri-County Cloggers started to clog.

The combination was dreadful. The Juku Warriors made a great show of covering their ears. The First Lady's face contorted in pain.

Mr. Kagoshima raised his hand higher, trying to control the band members, trying to get them in sync with LoriBeth Sommers and the cloggers. But the cloggers took this as a signal to clog even harder.

Kate and George exchanged a fearful look. The stage boards were clearly moving, vibrating up and down, rippling like a suspension bridge in an earthquake.

Just as LoriBeth threw herself into the highest note of the national anthem, the center section of the stage splintered apart, its wooden boards snapping like Popsicle sticks. The Tri-County Cloggers all dived for safety. And while the band played the last notes of "The Star-Spangled Banner," LoriBeth Sommers disappeared through the hole.

The First Lady's smile tightened. No one moved until Agent McCoy jumped to his feet. He stepped forward to examine the hole, but Dr. Austin cut him off.

Dr. Austin turned on his brightest smile. Then he threw out his arms and yelled, "How about that finale! I told you we had a few surprises in store for you today!"

Agent McCoy answered him hotly. "No, you didn't."

But Dr. Austin talked past him, to the First Lady. "Don't worry. It's all part of the show. We rigged up a special stage!"

Agent McCoy peered past him at the hole. Dr. Austin explained, "She's completely fine! She landed on a . . . trapdoor, padded thing, right below there."

To prove this, he stepped back himself and leaned over the edge of the hole. He called down, "Ha-ha, young lady! That was a good one. Ha!" He made a thumbs-up sign into the hole. Then he yelled to the audience, "She's smiling back and laughing."

Susan Singer-Wright stood up and started to laugh uproariously. She was followed by Bud and, to a lesser extent, Dr. Cavendar. Then Susan hurried to the stairwell, bugging her eyes out at Dr. Austin, as if to say, *Do something!*

Kate lowered her flag and took three cautious steps toward center stage. She stared down through the opening. At first, she could only see a wedge of the eighth floor. She then spotted an aluminum extension pole, and then the green-clad arms of LoriBeth Sommers clinging to it. LoriBeth's mouth was open, and she appeared to be screaming, but no sound was coming out. As Kate watched, the pole swung away, and LoriBeth vanished.

One floor below, William Anderson had been watching closely as the wooden stage started to splinter apart. He thrust his painter's pole into the hole in a desperate attempt to shore it up. To his great surprise, LoriBeth Sommers burst through, hit the pole, and grabbed at it. William leaned down on the pole, using the railing as a fulcrum. He slowly guided LoriBeth over the railing, to a hard landing on the carpeted hallway.

William pulled the pole back and let it fall noisily to his side. Then he took off running. By the time Susan Singer-Wright reached the bottom of the stairwell, William was cradling LoriBeth in his long arms and muttering, "There, there. You're okay now."

Susan stared at them with immense relief. She stooped down and, with William's help, pulled Lori-Beth to her feet. LoriBeth, her mouth still frozen in a screaming position, pressed her face into William's side. He held on to her tightly until she was able to stand upright on two very wobbly knees.

"Thank you so much for your help, but I'll take over from here," Susan told William. "You go on upstairs and enjoy the rest of the presentation."

William started to back away, but LoriBeth wouldn't let go of him. William assured her, "There, there. You're safe now," until LoriBeth finally released her grip, although her jaws remained locked two inches apart. Susan then guided her around the corner and into a nearby office.

41

The Secret Service
Springs into Action

Upstairs, Dr. Cavendar approached the First Lady's entourage and explained, "I am going down to see the girl, but only to congratulate her and maybe to check her blood pressure."

Bud said, "I'll go with you, Doc."

Dr. Austin, still laughing about the surprise, added, "Me, too!"

He turned to Cornelia, put his mouth up to her ear, and hissed, "Stall them. For god's sake, stall them!" The three men half walked, half ran to the service elevator.

Cornelia beamed her brightest smile at the First Lady. The First Lady and her entourage stared back blankly.

Cornelia then asked, "Would anybody like a beverage?"

The First Lady bent and whispered something to Rosetta Turner. Rosetta signaled Agent McCoy to come over. She spoke to him; then he walked up to Cornelia. "The First Lady would like a beverage."

"Ah! Excellent." Cornelia looked around for the rolling refrigerator. She spotted it off to her left, where Kate and George had parked it. She curtsied to the First Lady, walked over, and opened the lid. Then she let out a horrified scream.

Agent McCoy unholstered his revolver.

Rosetta leaped to her feet. "What is it? What happened?"

Cornelia slammed down the lid, spun around, and asked, "Does the First Lady drink regular or diet?"

Rosetta walked toward Cornelia, answering warily, "The First Lady is opposed to empty calories. She is also opposed to artificial stimulants. She will have a sugar-free, caffeine-free beverage."

"Oh? I'm sorry," Cornelia explained. "We only have high-sugar, high-caffeine beverages." Rosetta stepped closer to the refrigerator, but Cornelia blocked her view. "Would she prefer a Mountain Dew, a Surge, or a Jolt Cola?"

Rosetta decided, "The First Lady will pass for now."

She gave up trying to see past Cornelia and returned to her seat.

At that moment, inside the refrigerator, Mrs. Hodges's eyes, dead for four days, suddenly snapped open. They gazed outward with a mischievous twinkle. Then one thin hand disengaged itself from Walter Barnes, reached up, and opened the frosty lid. The hand tapped on Cornelia's back rhythmically, like a secret knock.

Cornelia turned, annoyed at the interruption. Then she saw who was interrupting. Before she could scream again, the hand grabbed the front of her blouse and pulled her halfway into the cooler.

Cornelia stayed that way for several seconds, looking as if she was trying to decide between the three types of beverage. When she finally straightened and turned back around, she had a new, strange light in her eyes.

She rasped out, in a voice somewhat higher than normal, "Don't move, children! I'll be right back for a very special Story Time." Then she bounded off toward the stairwell.

Kate and George exchanged an excited look. George pointed to himself. He mouthed the words, "I'll go," and took off after Cornelia. He slipped through the door and raced down the steps, leaping the final three to the landing. He spotted Cornelia running around the eighth-floor railing and into Cornell Whittaker Number Two's office.

George followed as fast as he could. He sprinted to the office door and fearlessly slipped inside. Then he crouched low and crawled across the carpet toward a large mahogany desk.

George peeked up over the desktop. The bookshelf along the rear wall was now open, revealing the secret room. George slid his chin along the top of the desk to a point where he could see inside.

He watched Cornelia flip over Cornell Whittaker Number Two's heavy wooden trunk like it was made of Styrofoam. She ripped a yellowed piece of tape from the bottom, revealing an iron key. She let the trunk crash back upright, thrust the key in, and opened the lid.

Cornelia stared into the trunk for ten seconds. Then she reached in and removed several fantastical items—a long black necromancer's robe, a floppy black hat, and a magic wand.

She quickly donned the robe and hat, but then, just as quickly, she snatched the hat back off. As she did, her blazing eyes turned toward the opening, prompting George to dive for cover under the desk.

Cornelia hurried into the outer office, ransacked

the desk drawers, and pulled out an electric hair trimmer. She stomped back into the secret room, found an outlet, and plugged it in.

Then, as George watched in amazement, she shaved her own head. Several yards of long blond hair, one thick strand after another, plopped down into the opened trunk and onto the floor.

It was all over in a minute. Cornelia pulled the hat onto her head and ran back out, wand in hand. George ducked and scooted around a corner of the desk as she bounded by.

Twenty seconds later, Cornelia made a sudden, splashy return to the rooftop. She threw open the door and skipped clumsily toward the First Lady's area, popping her wizard's hat on and off of her exposed scalp. Some of the children started to laugh; some started to nuzzle nervously into their parents' sides.

She spoke over the head of the First Lady, directly to the children. "Greetings! I am Cornell Whittaker Number Two. Do you know what that makes me?" She held up two fingers. "That makes me twice as many as Cornell Whittaker Number One."

Cornelia broke off to laugh at her own joke.

George slipped back through the door, unnoticed. He walked casually through the crowd until he was standing next to Kate.

Kate whispered right away, "That has to be Jack, right?"

"Oh yeah. That's Jack."

Kate was baffled. "So, what happened to Cornelia? She didn't pick up a book. Did she?"

George shook his head and frowned. "No. Cornelia hasn't gone near a book."

"The last thing she did was go to the cooler. She saw the bodies. Right?"

"Right." George looked up at the sky. Then he looked back down at Kate with the answer. "Jack wasn't in a book! He was in Mrs. Hodges!"

Kate was appalled. "But she was dead!"

"So's Jack. He doesn't care. Do you remember when Mrs. Hodges fell to the lobby floor? The *Mother Goose* book fell with her. Do you remember who picked it up?"

Kate racked her brain. "No."

George scanned the roof, looking for a possible answer. His gaze stopped at Ashley-Nicole. Kate looked in the same direction. They both gasped. There, on the top shelf of the book cart, was a manila envelope with a distinctive shape inside.

Dr. Austin raced out of the service elevator and looked around. The first thing he saw was his wife dressed in Cornell Whittaker Number Two's wizard robes. He turned to the stairwell and made eye contact with Ashley-Nicole. She patted the manila envelope and smiled at him.

Dr. Austin nodded and jerked his head several times in Cornelia's direction. Then he strolled over toward Agent McCoy and commented loudly, "Look at that, will you? She's wearing a wig. A funny baldness wig!"

Cornelia pointed to him. "We had so hoped that the roof would be ready this summer for a Story Time with phonics. Right, Dr. Austin?"

Dr. Austin nodded yes, rapidly, and smiled his toothy smile at Agent McCoy.

Cornelia thrashed the air angrily with the wand. "But then those three snoopy men, those construction workers, they slipped to their deaths. They delayed Dr. Austin's plans to tell you nice stories with nice phoneme-grapheme combinations." Her frown slowly turned into a smile. "And yet! All is not lost. For I will tell you a story like that today."

Cornelia looked at the First Lady. The First Lady smiled back, but she fidgeted in her seat. Cornelia adjusted her cap theatrically; she pretended to sharpen her wand, like a pool cue. Then she struck a dramatic Story Time pose, with her head back and her arms outstretched.

By now, Dr. Austin had heard enough. He gestured to Ashley-Nicole, pointing at the manila envelope. No one but Kate and George observed as Ashley-Nicole picked up the envelope and carried it over to him.

Cornelia began in a flamboyant tone, reminiscent of Walter Barnes during his first and only Story Time performance. "Today, we are doing the *m* sound. The *m* sound as in *magic*." She flourished the wand, and a plume of blue flame shot out of its tip, causing the audience members to gasp, Agent McCoy to stand up and place his right hand on his revolver.

Cornelia acknowledged the rapt attention of the crowd with a sly smile. "The *m* sound as in *mouse*." She hunched over and pulled her hands inward, simulating a mouse eating cheese. Her voice got as high as it was able. "I'm a tiny little mouse! Squeak! Squeak!" Some of the children giggled.

Then the little mouse stopped eating. It seemed to expand and grow erect, to double or triple in size. Cornelia's voice dropped down, nearly as deep as her own. "The *m* sound as in *moose*. I'm a great big moooooose."

More of the children laughed. The First Lady, who had been smiling stiffly, turned toward the children and smiled naturally.

Then Cornelia stretched even taller, up toward the sky, like a moose on its back legs. She pantomimed looking for something in the heavens. "Where did it go? Where can it be? Is it too bright to see it? Ah, well, we shall have to make do. For our next *m* sound is the *m* sound in *moon*!"

Cornelia spun 180 degrees, pulled up her wizard's robe, and pulled down her drawers. She let out a high-pitched, demonic cackle while she shook her enormous posterior back and forth ten feet away from the First Lady's face.

Agent McCoy leaped between Cornelia and the First Lady, his revolver drawn. But he quickly lowered his weapon and looked away, completely flustered. He commanded, "Agent Pflaum, see to your charge!"

McCoy yelled to a group of four other agents, "Apprehend her!" The agents hesitated a moment, then threw themselves on top of Cornelia, pinning her to the ground and slapping four sets of handcuffs on her wrists and ankles. One agent managed to pull her robe back down as she cackled, over and over, "Jack and Jill went up the hill!"

In the midst of this chaos, Dr. Austin circled the squirming pile formed by his wife and the Secret Service agents. He carefully removed *Perrault's Mother Goose* from its envelope. Then he slid it under the pile, directly under his wife's face, and waited.

Almost immediately, her old voice returned. She started bellowing in outrage. "Get off of me! All of you! Get off of me!"

The agents managed to get enough of a grip on Cornelia to raise her three feet off the ground.

Dr. Austin, pretending to help them, yanked the book away and slid it back into its envelope. Then the agents started to carry Cornelia toward the service elevator, like a rescued whale. But Agent Pflaum, in scrambling to do his duty, tripped one of them, and the whole pile went crashing down again.

Kate and George ran to the stairwell. They saw Dr. Austin hand the envelope to Ashley-Nicole with the breathless words, "We got him. He's in here."

Ashley-Nicole replied, "Okeydokey. I'll take this down to the target area. You and Daddy bring the cart when you're ready." She took the envelope and walked quickly to the exit.

Dr. Austin spun around, panting wildly, and beheld the scene on the roof: Four Secret Service agents were struggling to hoist his wife up again and drag her away; Agent Pflaum and Rosetta Turner were forming a human shield around the First Lady; the Lincoln Band members, the Juku Warriors, and the guest families were staring, transfixed, at the epic struggle to subdue Cornelia.

Dr. Austin ran to a spot in front of the First Lady's group. He shouted at the top of his lungs, "I can explain this. All of this has a simple explanation. Here is the simple explanation." Dr. Austin froze in the position of a man about to speak, but no words came from his mouth.

Rosetta Turner brushed past him and marched across the roof on a mission. She announced, to everyone, "I am going to find out what is going on here!" She grasped the lid of the cooler and threw it open. Then she leaned back and gasped, "Oh lordy."

Agent McCoy ran to her side. He took one look and made a command decision. "That does it!" He spun around. "Agent Pflaum, listen to me. Take the First Lady, find a vacant room, and hide her in it! We're getting her out of here."

Rosetta slammed the lid of the cooler. She hurried over to the edge of the rooftop and looked down at the throng of reporters and TV crews. She called out, "Wait a minute. What are you doing?"

Agent McCoy punched at a cell phone. "I'm canceling the rest of this visit. I want the helicopter. Now."

"Hold on. Please. There are fifty reporters down there. We can't give them a big panicky scene to broadcast on the six o'clock news."

Agent McCoy pointed at the First Lady, retreating down the stairwell on the arm of Agent Pflaum. "We're *not* staying on this roof."

Rosetta whispered to him, "I don't know what, in god's name, is going on here. And neither do you. So let's just take a few more minutes to find out. We can't leave here without some answers."

McCoy walked over and glanced down at the swarming press corps. He looked back at Rosetta and tacitly agreed.

Dr. Austin and Bud approached, both smiling. But before either could utter a word, Agent McCoy demanded to know, "Tell me, Doctor, why do you have dead people in a cooler over there?"

"What?" Dr. Austin sputtered. "Oh, that! Why, that is just a mistake. A ghastly mistake. You see, Dr. Cavendar is the county coroner. He keeps bodies here sometimes, as evidence. This is a county building, you know. Those are his bodies."

McCoy pushed past them without another word, followed by Rosetta Turner. They entered the waiting service elevator, closed the doors, and started down.

Dr. Austin spoke through clenched teeth. "Now's our chance, Bud. Let's get downstairs. Ashley-Nicole is waiting." They ran toward the stairwell, toward Kate and George. Dr. Austin yelled, "You two! Quick! Hold that door open!"

Kate and George jumped to the task. The two men picked up either side of the black book cart and carried it carefully down the stairs between them.

While all this was going on, the rest of the people

on the roof hadn't moved an inch. June and Mrs. Brennan remained in the seats they had occupied throughout the entire bizarre proceedings. Molly had joined them right after her band performance. William Anderson, to Molly's chagrin, had joined them after Susan Singer-Wright sent him upstairs.

Kate now sprinted over to them, followed by her uncle. She announced with great excitement and with great import, "Let's go! Something big's about to happen! Follow us!"

June, William, Molly, and Mrs. Brennan hopped to their feet, not at all sure of what Kate had said, but sure that they wanted to follow her. The six of them hurried across the black cinders toward an aluminum mushroom cap.

42

The Death of the Demon

Kate bent back the top of the mushroom cap. She, George, Molly, and William dived quickly onto the ladder rungs, like rabbits down a hole. Mrs. Brennan hesitated. Kate called from the bottom, "Hurry, before they get here!"

Mrs. Brennan looked fearfully at June. June said, "I'll go ahead of you, Mrs. Brennan. You stay one rung behind me. That way I can steady you all the way."

Mrs. Brennan nodded to June and struggled onto the ladder after her. They descended the eight rungs in tandem and stepped off into Kate's welcoming grasp.

The three then entered through the rotating door and joined George, William, and Molly, crouching behind the low bookcase.

The first thing Kate noticed was the new plastic shield. It curved from their bookcase to the other side of the room, a see-through semicircle eight feet high and four inches thick. "Uncle George," she whispered. "What is that thing?"

"That's the protective shield they were talking about. It's some space-age NASA plastic. Sorry, that's redundant."

Kate's eyes then fell on the opened trunk and the long blond hair piled around it. "Look! Over there!"

They all craned forward to see the piles of hair, but then froze in place at a sharp sound. The door to Cornell Whittaker Number Two's office had just opened. Kate hissed, "Everybody down."

The six intruders crouched behind the bookcase. Only Kate dared to lean to her left and peer out.

The door to the secret room opened shortly after, held by Dr. Austin, and Ashley-Nicole wheeled the black cart inside. The manila envelope sat on the top of the cart. She was followed by Bud Wright, who panted after her in a voice filled with fear, "You be careful there, honeybun."

Ashley-Nicole answered without a care. "Oh, Daddy!" She steered the cart around the shield and parked it in front of the antique desk.

Then she cinched a piece of white twine to the base of the cart and backed away slowly, unrolling the twine as she went. She backed all the way around the shield and halted at its far end, directly in front of the Laser Cannon.

Ashley-Nicole turned a handle on the Laser Cannon. The weapon rose up, like a submarine periscope, until the muzzle of the cannon cleared the top of the shield. Then she flipped a switch and the silver-and-black weapon hummed to life.

She told her father and Dr. Austin, "It only takes thirty seconds to warm up. But remember, it takes a full ten minutes to cool down."

Dr. Austin repeated her words, as if trying to memorize them. "Ten minutes to cool down."

Ashley-Nicole smiled. "Okay, Dr. Austin, let's activate your son's tracking device."

Dr. Austin seemed genuinely puzzled. "What?"

"Didn't your son, Whit, install the tracker in the Laser Cannon?"

"No. Not at all. His mother got the Technon people to install it and put his name on it."

Now it was Ashley-Nicole's turn to look puzzled.

Dr. Austin explained simply, "He's no *you*, Ashley-Nicole. He's not even a *me*."

Kate stole an angry glance at George.

Dr. Austin said, "All I care about now is that this weapon works. Do you think it works?"

"If Technon invented it, it should work."

"But it didn't work at the science fair."

"Oh, I know why. I recalibrated the tracking mechanism. They weren't off by much." Ashley-Nicole flipped open the protective metal box that housed the red button. She asked her father, "Would *you* like to push it, Daddy?"

Bud stammered, "No. No, let's get this crazy thing over with. This is plumb loco."

Dr. Austin agreed. "Yes, please, Ashley-Nicole. If you can make this work, we may have time to save the day. The First Lady's still in the building. She's scheduled to be here for another hour. Please, hit that button."

Ashley-Nicole smiled her brightest smile, said, "Okeydokey," and pressed it.

The Laser Cannon's tracker rotated slowly toward the antique desk. Ashley-Nicole picked up the white twine, waited for the right moment, and tugged it, causing a sudden movement of the black book cart.

The Laser Cannon whined softly and emitted a thin red light. The light landed on the manila envelope. It vaporized the thick paper immediately, in a puff of black smoke, leaving the book laid bare on the cart.

Dr. Austin leaned forward, breathless, and stared at the book: *Perrault's Mother Goose*, first London edition, estimated value $50,000.

Three seconds later, the book ignited, too. It seemed about to disintegrate, just like the envelope, but before it could, something within it stirred. Something within it was alive and was trying desperately to get out.

The book emitted an unearthly glow; then it started to stretch and bulge. A bubble rose from it like a rising red sun. The energy pulsing inside the sun seemed uncontainable. Even Ashley-Nicole recoiled. She ducked down behind the shield, followed closely by her two companions. Kate stood her ground for a few seconds longer, transfixed. But then, just when an explosion seemed imminent, she dived for shelter, too.

The room suddenly felt superheated and sucked dry of oxygen. The air itself turned a hellish red, and then cooled, startlingly fast, into the thickness of a gray London fog. Kate and her group lay flat on their backs, stuffed into the small space, breathing only fitfully in gulps.

Then above them the heavy air started to swirl like a great soup. It turned slowly at first, but it quickly accelerated to a dizzying speed. White wisps of light appeared in the grayness. They grew in brightness and in speed and began to carom off the ceiling and the walls, bouncing everywhere in swift, sharp vectors.

Kate stared open eyed, lost in the spectacle above

her, totally beguiled and mesmerized by the white wisps.

And then the faces started to appear.

Kate saw the ghostly faces of children whirling around her, disappearing and reappearing, like images in a kinescope. She saw hundreds of children's faces, some from her own lifetime, some from two centuries before.

Kate did not recognize the faces of her Toddler Time friends from ten years before, but June did. Kate did, however, recognize the last sequence of faces. It began with Pogo, both as a young girl and as an adult; then the wide-eyed Walter Barnes; then the oompah-pahing Bud Wright; then the bloody Heidi the Milkmaid; then the screaming-monkey Whit; then the high-flying Mrs. Hodges. The last face was one familiar to them all. It was Cornelia Whittaker-Austin dressed as old Cornell Whittaker Number Two.

Then, just as quickly as they had emerged, the ghosts disappeared. They sucked back into the red sun like a rewinding video. After a moment of calm, the sun began to bulge once more. But this time, its energy could not be contained. The red bubble stretched for ten more seconds until it reached critical mass. Then it exploded in a blinding flash of light and a red wave of ectoplasm.

Everyone in the room lay low for several minutes. The people behind the bookcase struggled to control their heavy breathing, but they need not have bothered, as the terrified pantings of Bud Wright and Dr. Austin filled the room.

Ashley-Nicole stood up first. She studied the target sight and announced, "Okeydokey. That should do it." She took hold of the thick, curving shield and slid it toward the corner, commenting, "This is a remarkably light material, but superstrong."

Dr. Austin and Bud struggled to their feet, grimacing and sweating.

Ashley-Nicole reminded them. "Just let the Laser Cannon cycle down on its own before you cut the power. Okay?"

Dr. Austin and Bud could only stare at her and blabber.

Ashley-Nicole waited a moment, smiling patiently, until Dr. Austin finally managed to articulate, "Ghosts. They were ghosts. It was a ghost."

Ashley-Nicole laughed with delight. "Didn't you know about the library ghost, Dr. Austin? All the kids did."

"They knew?" Dr. Austin sputtered. "They knew about this? Why didn't they ever say anything?"

She laughed again. "Dr. Austin! You know they were never allowed to say anything!"

Ashley-Nicole kissed Bud on the cheek and added, "Anyway, who would have listened to them?" With a last wave to Dr. Austin, she headed through the rotating door and back to her homecoming mixer.

Dr. Austin and Bud struggled mightily to compose themselves. Finally, Bud looked at the empty book cart and said, "Well, that's it. Whatever it was, it's dead. It's finished." The two men exchanged a tense look. Bud asked, "Is it too late, Doc?"

Dr. Austin was adamant. "No, it's not too late." He held up one hand and ticked off his reasons: "The First Lady is still in the building. She knows nothing about any of this. The ghost is dead. Everything is fine. It's not too late. Come on, Bud!" Dr. Austin ran out through the rotating door with Bud at his heels.

Kate popped her head up right away, followed by the others.

June spoke first. "I saw it, Kate. Did you see it?"

Kate assured her, "Yes!"

George added, "We all saw it, June."

Kate asked, "But *what* did we see, Uncle George?"

He answered in a measured, awed voice. "We saw a supernatural being, a demon, if you like."

June asked Kate, "Did you see the faces? Did you see the children?"

"Yes! Yes! Who were those children?"

George answered for her. "Every kid Jack ever possessed, I guess. All stored within him, within his memory, like on a holographic tape."

Kate, George, and June went on like that for several minutes:

"Did you see Mrs. Hodges?"

"Yes. And Pogo?"

"Two different Pogos, at two different ages."

"Did you see Walter Barnes?"

Finally, Molly couldn't take any more. She held up her hands in a giant Y until they stopped speaking. She asked, on the verge of hysteria, "Would someone please explain to me what the hell just happened here!"

Kate gestured toward George, indicating that he should reply. He tried to encapsulate the story for them. "You just witnessed the destruction of Jack. He was a supernatural being, the ghost that has haunted this library. After hundreds of years and countless possessions, he finally ran into a being more powerful than himself—Ashley-Nicole."

Molly and Mrs. Brennan looked at George long and hard—first trying to understand him, and then trying to believe him.

William shook his head admiringly. "Wow. So that was the ghost."

Everyone started to talk at once until, suddenly, the approaching sound of clinking metal sent them scrambling back into their hiding place.

Susan Singer-Wright entered the secret room.

Kate, George, and June peeked around one side of

the bookcase; Molly, Mrs. Brennan, and William peeked around the other. They watched, breathlessly, as Susan stepped around the Laser Cannon and sat down behind the desk. Then Susan pulled out a cigarette and stuck it between her lips.

The Laser Cannon's tracker whirred into action. As Susan watched curiously, it ignited the tip of her cigarette, like a gallant gentleman. Then her hair stood straight up. Before she could even scream, the Laser Cannon superheated her body from within, causing it to implode in a burst of deadly black smoke.

Susan Singer-Wright, alive just one second before, was now a smoking, charred skeleton draped in silver necklaces. Her left hand, still wearing its wedding rings, held out the cylindrical remains of a cigarette, like a macabre antismoking poster.

Kate and the others followed the entire horrific sequence of events, wide eyed, mesmerized by the grisly sight.

But they had to rouse themselves a few seconds later. A quick scuffling sound in the outer office was followed by the commotion of Dr. Austin and Bud running back in.

"She's gotta be somewhere!" Bud panted.

Dr. Austin told him, "She is. That Agent Pflaum is hiding her. But *we* know this building better than he does. Come on!"

Dr. Austin started to run back out. But he stopped when he noticed that Bud was not following.

Bud was gazing across the room. He asked, "Say, Doc, what's that thing in the chair over there? Looks like some kind of science experiment." Bud's curiosity drew him slowly toward the desk.

Dr. Austin looked hard at the contents of the chair. He realized that it was not a science experiment. His mouth fell open; then he started screaming.

Bud turned back, panicked, and started to scream, too.

Their screaming voices drowned out the soft whir of the Laser Cannon's tracker as it clicked back into action.

Dr. Austin saw the glow of the laser just in time. He hit the red button and killed the light a second before it reached Bud.

Bud did not even notice. He moved closer to the desk to get a better look. "This might sound crazy, Doc, but it looks a little like Susan."

Dr. Austin was way ahead of him. "It is Susan! Look at her cigarette. Look at her jewelry."

"It is?"

"Yes! Obviously!"

"It's my Susan? My wife, Susan?"

Dr. Austin grasped Bud by the shoulders. "Yes! My sincere condolences. But please, Bud, let us think here.

Let us think about what your Susan would want us to do under these tragic circumstances."

Bud stared at him, confounded. "I don't know. What would she want us to do?"

Dr. Austin clapped him on both shoulders. "Now you're talking! First, she would want us to get rid of that machine. It's now her murder weapon."

Bud looked from Susan's skeleton to the Laser Cannon, and back to the skeleton until he understood. "Oh yeah. We need to get rid of that crazy contraption."

Dr. Austin pointed at the Laser Cannon. "Unplug it, wheel it down to the basement, and push it into the furnace. That will destroy all the electronics inside. Then it'll just be a big glob of metal with no fingerprints on it."

"But what about Susan?"

"I'll get the shower curtain. We'll cover her and leave her here, just until we find the First Lady."

Bud mumbled, "Until we find the First Lady."

"We can't let the First Lady leave! Not until we've explained everything that happened. We have to tell her the whole truth." Dr. Austin walked daintily forward. He turned Susan's chair so that it faced the wall. Then he helped Bud wheel out the Laser Cannon, adding, "And I think I know just what to tell her."

———

Kate, George, June, William, Molly, and Mrs. Brennan expelled a loud, collective breath. They all rose to their feet again.

"We are incredibly lucky we stayed back here," George said. "Those morons forgot to shut off the Laser Cannon. It could have tracked over here and zapped all of us."

Kate asked, "Is that lady dead?"

"She's about as dead as you can get. Excavated Egyptian mummies look better than that."

"Then we'd better get out of here." Kate turned to the oldest member of the group. "Mrs. Brennan, can you go back up the ladder?"

"Yes, if I have to. If my life depends on it. But couldn't we just walk through Mr. Whittaker's office?"

Kate looked at the rotating door. "Yeah. Maybe we could. Let Uncle George and me check it out first."

But before Kate and George could move, they heard another sound. All six looked at each other in alarm. Then they all crept, quietly and efficiently, back behind the bookcase.

Kate raised her head. The first thing she saw was the barrel of a BioSensor. It was followed by the trembling arms of Agent Pflaum. He entered the secret room with the First Lady three feet behind him. She was no longer smiling.

Agent Pflaum stopped suddenly. He aimed the BioSensor at the back of the smoking chair and checked the weapon's digital readout. He announced, "It's okay, Madam First Lady. Whatever is on that chair is not a living life-form. We're safe to hide in here."

Agent Pflaum started to get the First Lady a chair, but he got his foot tangled in a piece of white twine. This action caused the book cart to move. It bumped the desk just hard enough to make the chair spin around slowly.

Susan Singer-Wright's still-smoking skeleton rotated and came to a halt, face-to-face, with him.

Agent Pflaum screamed and dropped his BioSensor on the First Lady's foot. The First Lady looked down at her foot and cried out in pain. Then she looked up and saw the skeleton. She, too, screamed.

Agent Pflaum fumbled into his holster, attempting to pull out his revolver, but he dropped that, too.

The First Lady dived for the floor and snatched it up. She jumped to her feet holding the weapon in both hands. She took aim at Susan Singer-Wright's skeleton and started firing. Screaming and firing. She fired until the bullets ran out, causing the skeleton to spin around and around and around in the chair.

Just as the revolver's chambers were emptied, Bud Wright and Dr. Austin ran back in with the blue shower curtain.

The bullet-riddled chair was still spinning.

Bud looked from Dr. Austin, to Agent Pflaum, to the First Lady of the United States. He asked her simply, "Madam First Lady, why are you shooting at my wife?"

43

An Alleged Incident
That Never Really Happened

Kate rose to her knees and peeked above the bookcase. The four people standing before Susan Singer-Wright's smoking corpse had not moved much.

Agent Pflaum remained frozen in his spot, staring in horror at the skeleton in the chair.

The First Lady, still clutching the revolver, was muttering under her breath, disjointed statements such as "Reading is fundamental" and "Breakfast is the most important meal of the day."

Bud Wright was listening to her, and nodding, with a confused look on his face.

Dr. Austin was clutching and unclutching his blue shower curtain, hoping there still might be a way to remove the body.

Then Agent McCoy's voice called from the outer office. "Pflaum? Are you in there?"

Rosetta Turner appeared in the doorway. "Madam First Lady, are you all right?"

The First Lady said, without emotion, "I believe we need to educate every child."

Rosetta answered tentatively, "Yes, ma'am."

Rosetta took two steps into the secret room and stopped still. Her face paled, and she gasped, "Oh lordy."

From her hidden perch, Kate watched as the First Lady's chief of staff absorbed the various elements of the gruesome scene. Then, slowly, she removed the revolver from the First Lady's grip. She told Agent McCoy, in a low voice, "I'll take care of the live lady; you take care of the dead one."

Agent McCoy took control of the revolver. "Okay. Agent Pflaum? Agent Pflaum! Snap out of it!"

Agent Pflaum rotated his whole body to stare at his superior. "Yes, sir," he croaked.

"Take that shower curtain. Cover that corpse with it, and wheel it out of here."

Dr. Austin told them, with quiet determination, "No. This is my shower curtain. You can't take it."

"This is a matter of national security, Doctor. We'll get you another shower curtain."

Dr. Austin was unmoved. "But it won't be *this* one. No. You can take her in something else."

Agent McCoy stared at Dr. Austin in disbelief. Then he snatched the shower curtain away, thrust it into Agent Pflaum's hands, and pushed him toward Susan's corpse. "Get her out of here!"

"But, but where? Where should I put her?"

Agent McCoy looked at Rosetta.

Rosetta covered the First Lady's ears. "We have two corpses up in the cooler already."

McCoy ordered, "Take her upstairs and stash her with the other two." He helped Pflaum tuck the shower curtain into the sides of the chair. Then he helped him guide the chair out. Susan's bracelets jangled with every bump.

Bud watched his wife go. He muttered, "Good-bye, little buttercup."

Rosetta turned to her boss. "Are you feeling any better, Madam First Lady? That dead lady has gone away now."

The First Lady's smile twitched.

Agent McCoy returned quickly with two other agents, a man and a woman. He told Rosetta, "These agents will take the First Lady upstairs. We've secured the roof for the helicopter's arrival." The man and woman each took an elbow and guided the First Lady through the door.

As Kate leaned left to watch them, her sweaty hand

slipped on the floor and she nearly fell. She held her breath and ducked, fearing she had been heard.

But Rosetta was addressing Dr. Austin. "Tell me, Doctor, how many witnesses were there to this unfortunate event?"

Dr. Austin pointed at Bud. "Just the two of us."

Rosetta exchanged a purposeful look with Agent McCoy. "Then we need to talk about some matters, some national security matters."

Dr. Austin understood immediately. "Yes, of course."

Kate moved to get a better view. She straightened herself up as slowly as an opening flower. She turned her head so that only her right eye appeared above the bookcase.

Dr. Austin was now standing directly in front of Rosetta Turner. He snapped his lapels and spoke with his old authority. "Not only does this unfortunate event look bad for the Whittaker Magnet School, it also looks bad for the First Lady of the United States."

Rosetta selected her words carefully. "I knew you would understand. After all, the First Lady is known for advocating two things: better schools and gun control."

Rosetta held both hands in front of her, in a shooting position. "Now, the way I see the situation is this: The First Lady fired a gun into a corpse." She looked over at Bud. "Am I correct in saying that, sir? Your wife *was* dead when this accident occurred?"

Bud answered, "Yeah. I guess so."

Rosetta turned to Agent McCoy. "Then there is no question that it was simply an *accidental* discharge of a *legal* weapon into a *nonliving* thing."

Agent McCoy shrugged. "No question."

Rosetta turned back to Dr. Austin and Bud. "Still, to the media or to a political rival, this would not look good. Are you following me, gentlemen?"

They nodded.

"In Washington, perception is reality. We four can redefine what happened here, and we can present it to the media together. Are you still with me?"

"Yes!" Dr. Austin answered. "Absolutely!"

"So, this alleged shooting incident never really happened."

"No, it never did," Dr. Austin agreed. Then he added, "And this crazy 'ghost in the building' incident never really happened, either."

"Ghost?" Rosetta shook her head and turned to include McCoy. "I think we can agree on that, too. Nobody here believes in ghosts."

McCoy nodded his assent.

But suddenly, from behind the low bookcase, a sharp voice startled them all. "Oh no! No, you don't!"

June scrambled to her feet and harangued them with all the force she could muster. "This really happened! People have been telling me it didn't happen for ten years. But it did happen! And no one is going to say it didn't."

Rosetta exchanged an astonished look with McCoy. She whispered, "Who are you?"

"I am a witness. I saw everything."

Kate straightened to her full height and moved next to her mother. "Me, too."

She was followed by George. "So did I."

Rosetta stepped toward the bookcase. "Lord almighty! How many of you are hiding back there?"

George told her, "Six, ma'am."

Molly rose and helped her grandmother to her feet. William then stood up awkwardly to complete the picture—the very upsetting picture—that now confronted Rosetta Turner.

Rosetta asked, "George Melvil, what exactly did you see?"

"More than any sixth grader should have, ma'am."

Rosetta looked down the line of witnesses. "All of you?"

"All of us," Kate answered.

Rosetta seemed to meditate for a moment, with her eyes closed. Then she opened them, whipped out her

WebWizard X, and held it high. "All right. Let's talk about what is best for *all* involved here. Dr. Austin, can we use your office? I will need access to a printer."

Dr. Austin glared at the new witnesses. "Yes, I suppose so. If we have to."

"Please go down there, all of you, and wait for me. I need to speak privately to Agent McCoy."

Dr. Austin raised his hand. "Certainly. But before we do, is there any chance that I could talk to the First Lady one more time?"

"None whatsoever. Absolutely none. It is a complete impossibility."

He lowered his hand. "Thank you, anyway."

Dr. Austin quickly led Bud and the six witnesses out of the secret room as Rosetta and Agent McCoy leaned their heads together.

44

A Deal with
the Devil's Advocate

In the time it took for Rosetta Turner to walk down the short stretch of hallway, she had typed up an official statement on the WebWizard X. Upon entering Dr. Austin's office, she waved the WebWizard at his laser printer, causing it to switch on and to roll out four copies.

Rosetta held the copies up to the group. "What I have in my hand is the official statement describing what happened here today. It contains no mention of guns; it contains no mention of ghosts."

She passed out the copies to Dr. Austin, Bud, June, and Mrs. Brennan. "In exchange for signing the statement, I am offering each of you one wish. That's the deal, people. You sign, and one wish of yours comes true."

Rosetta took a place near the door with her Web-Wizard X in hand. Then she pointed at a spot two feet in front of her on the floor.

The group members all looked at each other in confusion, until she said, "Line up!"

Bud Wright and Dr. Austin moved quickly. Bud, in spite of his neck brace, managed to get to the spot on the floor first, elbowing ahead of Dr. Austin. June and Mrs. Brennan hung back politely.

Rosetta checked her watch and frowned. Usually a woman of a few well-chosen words, she spoke slowly and elaborately. "I am *not*, mind you, your fairy godmother. I cannot turn a pumpkin into a carriage, or better yet into a Ferrari 456. I *am* the First Lady's chief of staff. As such, I can make things happen for you in Washington, D.C.

"That being said, I want you all to pick something good. I want you to leave here happy and determined to keep up your end of the bargain. Wishes can come true, but they can also come untrue. You will discover that, should you ever break your word. Don't forget what happened to that pumpkin carriage at the stroke of midnight. Now, assuming that we understand each other, let's get started."

Rosetta looked at Bud, and he spoke up right away. "I want the Department of the Interior to approve my Ivy League Estates housing development."

"I see. And what about those chipmunks in the woods?"

"What about 'em?"

Rosetta consulted her WebWizard X. She started hitting buttons and reading screens. "All right. Here's what we can do: We can *move* the chipmunks to a national park." Rosetta turned the tiny display screen so that Bud could see it. "There's a national park in Wyandot County, just seventy-five miles from here."

Bud was wary. "And they wouldn't come back?"

Rosetta fixed a meaningful look at him. "Not unless we brought them back."

Bud gulped. "Okay. That sounds good to me. Where do I sign?"

Rosetta held out the paper for him to sign. Bud hooted, "It's moving day for Chip and Dale!" He turned and offered to high-five with Dr. Austin, who ignored him.

Dr. Austin spoke eagerly to Rosetta, "I'm next!"

"All right. What does the good doctor wish?"

"I wish for the president of the United States to come to the Whittaker Magnet School."

Rosetta eyeballed him. "Let me ask you something: If the president comes to visit this school, will there be students in it?"

Dr. Austin squinted. "Do you want there to be students in it?"

"Yes."

"Then, yes! Absolutely."

"Will they be healthy-looking students?"

Dr. Austin squirmed. "They will. They will be." He added, "Hodges was a nut with those protein supplements. I can see that now. They'll all be eating...apples and...grapes from here on out."

"And will they be exercising?"

"Oh, yes, ma'am. They'll do...jumping jacks and things like that. Outside. Every day."

"Then I'll see what I can do." Rosetta gave him the form and watched as he signed it. Then she asked, "Who's next?"

June and Mrs. Brennan each extended a hand, indicating that the other should go first. But June prevailed when she said, "No. You go. I'm not ready yet."

Mrs. Brennan said, "Are you sure, dear?"

"I'm sure. I need to talk to my daughter first." June inclined her head toward the window. Kate left the other children and joined her there. June bent close to Kate and began to whisper urgently as Mrs. Brennan stepped forward.

Rosetta looked up expectantly.

"I have a wish that is well within your powers," Mrs. Brennan said. "I want to get the Palace Theatre placed on the National Registry of Historic Buildings."

Bud snorted. "Now hold on a dang minute!"

Rosetta snapped, "You keep it zipped over there." She looked at Mrs. Brennan. "Where is this theater?"

"It's right here in town. It has been a part of our local history since eighteen forty-one."

"You're right. That is well within my powers. Just sign your name here."

Molly had listened proudly as her grandmother made her wish, but George and William had never taken their eyes off of Kate and June. George leaned toward William and predicted, "This is it. She's getting her out of Whittaker."

William agreed. "Yeah. That's gotta be it."

When June finally took her place in front of Rosetta Turner, she had Kate standing next to her, holding tightly on to her hand. Tears welled up in June's eyes, but she wiped them with her free hand and whispered to Rosetta Turner, "Can I ask for anything?"

"Anything connected with the government. That covers a lot of things."

June took a deep breath. "All right. I want you to set Orchid the Orca, and all the other prisoners of this place, free."

George and William gasped. Bud Wright started to snort.

Rosetta asked, incredulously, "What? The big fish?"

"I believe she is an aquatic mammal. I want her to be returned to the ocean."

Rosetta was clearly impressed. She switched to a secure channel on the WebWizard X and punched in numbers. "That is doable."

Bud finally found his voice. "No! That orca's my property!"

Rosetta cocked her head. "Do I hear the sound of chipmunks returning?" Bud shut up. "Sign here, ma'am. I know someone in the Department of the Interior who'd be very happy to arrange that for you." She extended the contract to June.

George, William, and Molly all looked at Kate, confounded. Kate raised her free hand into the air and formed it into a fist.

June took the contract, but she held it down at her side. "We're not finished."

Rosetta replied, politely but firmly, "The deal was one wish, ma'am."

June agreed. "And I made my wish." She looked at Dr. Austin and Bud. "It was to free all the prisoners of this place."

Rosetta considered her words. "Okay. You did say that. So, it's the fish and what else?"

"I want you to arrange for the release of Pogo, and the can man, and all of the homeless people."

This time, it was Dr. Austin's turn to protest. "Those people are criminals!"

Rosetta didn't even look at him. "Pipe down, shorty." She asked June, "What's a Pogo?"

"Her name is Miss Pogorzelski." June spelled it, letter by letter, as Rosetta input it into the WebWizard X. June added, "She works here at the library."

"All right. I can arrange that, so long as she isn't a serial killer or anything."

June looked quickly at Kate.

Kate shrugged.

June answered, "I'm sure she isn't."

"What's this can man's real name?"

June hesitated, so Kate answered, "He's a homeless person. He got arrested here last Friday."

Rosetta punched at the WebWizard X. "That should be good enough. Who else?"

"The others are all homeless, too. They've been kept in quarantine at their shelter."

"Quarantine? For what? What's wrong with them?"

"There's nothing wrong with them. The county coroner is willing to quarantine anyone who they"—she directed an accusing finger at Dr. Austin and Bud—"want to keep away from here."

Rosetta knitted her eyebrows. "Very well. I'll call that in first thing in the morning. Now please sign the statement."

June told her, "No, ma'am. You'll call that in right now."

They locked eyes; Rosetta looked away first. "All right. I'll have the Justice Department get the first two out, and Health and Human Services will get on that quarantine thing right away."

She used the versatile WebWizard X to notify all of the pertinent people. In less than one minute, she announced, "Done. The feds are on it."

June signed the contract and handed it back.

Rosetta looked down at her watch, then up toward the roof. She sighed and told the group, "It looks like we still have some time together."

Rosetta cast a kindly look at the children. "And, it seems to me, that we have a few more prisoners of this place. Don't we, George Melvil?"

George, at first, did not understand what she meant.

"You and I had a conversation once about a big mutant octopus. Do you remember that?"

George remembered. "Oh yes! We had that conversation. Yes, ma'am."

Rosetta extended her WebWizard X out to him. "Show me what it looks like."

George took the device and held it reverently in his hands, studying its features. He accessed the Internet and punched in kingscountyschools.com. Within seconds the screen displayed the black outline of the Whittaker Magnet School District.

George handed the WebWizard X back to Rosetta. She studied the screen for a long moment, her lip curling higher and higher in disapproval. She looked over at Dr. Austin. "There's no way that this is legal."

Dr. Austin was flummoxed. "It most certainly is legal! It was drawn up by the County Commission."

Rosetta winked at the children. "I'll tell you what. I'm going to have the Justice Department review this. And the Department of Education. And the Civil Rights Commission. Maybe they'll all agree that this arrangement is the fairest one for the children of King's County, but I wouldn't bet on it."

Dr. Austin raised his hand to object, but no thought came into his head, so he put it back down.

"I don't like this octopus thing you have going here. I don't like seafood of any kind." Rosetta looked at June. "I think it's time to free all of the prisoners."

A tremendous racket above caused the nine people in the room to look up. It sounded like a tornado wind, followed by the scraping of a giant chair across the roof. Rosetta said, "That's the helicopter, coming to take the First Lady away."

Rosetta counted her signed statements and her witnesses once more. When she was satisfied, she told them, "All right. This meeting is over. For the record, ladies and gentlemen, this meeting never happened. Now, I need all of you to stay put. I'll come back for you in ten minutes."

Rosetta exited and hurried down the hallway to the stairwell.

But the instant the door closed, Kate hissed at George, "Let's get up to the roof!" She turned to June, William, Molly, and Mrs. Brennan. "Wait here. We'll come back for you."

Bud held out his hands. "What about us?"

Dr. Austin seemed as perplexed as Bud. Kate instructed them flatly, "You wait here, too."

Kate and George dashed down the hallway to Cornell Whittaker Number Two's office. They reversed their usual route, passing through the office, through the secret room, and up the eight-rung ladder. Then they crouched behind the mushroom cap and scanned the rooftop.

The helicopter was enormous and black. It idled on the north side of the roof with its blades rotating slowly, scattering what was left of the red, white, and blue bunting and the phonics flyers.

Agent Pflaum was sitting on the cinders just four feet away talking softly to his BioSensor. The First Lady was several yards away, sitting very straight on a folding chair.

As Kate and George watched, four agents approached the First Lady and helped her walk to the helicopter. Two of the agents then returned for Agent Pflaum and loaded him on, too. The helicopter revved up and took off quickly, leaving only Rosetta Turner on the roof. Or so she thought.

Kate and George straightened themselves and stepped out from behind the mushroom cap.

Rosetta's eyes snapped open. "How did you two get here?"

George deadpanned, "Magic."

"I don't believe in magic."

"Neither did I, Miss Turner. Not until I saw it happen here today."

Rosetta told him seriously, "I have four signed statements that say it *didn't* happen here today. Do you remember those?"

George gulped and took a step backward. "Yes. I remember those."

They walked toward the stairwell in silence until Kate spoke. "Miss Turner, can you really do all the things you promised?"

"Yes, I can. Most of it has already been done. Instantaneously." She pulled out the WebWizard X. "We live in the information age."

"So...when can we get Pogo and the can man out of jail?"

"We can get them out right now. Your sheriff's not going to argue with the Justice Department. Not with the two dead people—make that three dead people—he's got stashed in the cooler."

"I want Dr. Austin to be there when we go to get them out. Okay?"

"Why?"

"Because nothing bad ever happens to him. He just keeps moving up. He never has a day of reckoning."

Rosetta flashed a perfect smile. "A day of reckoning? I don't know if it will be that, but all right. I'll throw that wish in, too. We'll bring the doctor with us. What about the fish guy?"

Kate decided. "He should be there, too."

They stopped at the office door. Rosetta banged on it loudly and called inside. "Let's go! All of you! We're taking a ride."

45

Freeing the Prisoners

By the time Rosetta's group emerged from the library entrance, all the news trucks and reporters had departed the scene. A lone policewoman was directing the cars of parents, such as William Anderson's, who had come to pick up their children.

William stood with his large feet on the curb, waiting while a white Volvo inched its way toward him. When he saw Kate and George, he said, "Thanks, you guys. Thanks for, you know, including me."

George muttered, "No problem, William."

"Now I know all about the ghost. Right? We proved it. QED."

George patted him on the shoulder. "Actually,

William, 'We proved it' and 'QED' mean the same thing."

Kate smiled. "I'm going to pay you a compliment, William." He looked at her expectantly. Kate jerked her head toward the glass doors. "You don't belong here."

William's face reddened. "Thanks, Kate."

William's mother rolled down the passenger side window as her car pulled up. She called out, "June? Is that June Peters?"

A twitch of fear showed in June's face, but it passed quickly. She answered, "Yes. It is. How are you, Linda? How are you, Bill?"

"We're just fine, June. How are you? We heard you weren't doing too well."

"I wasn't. But I'm much better now."

"Good. It's good to see you again."

William ducked his head and climbed into the back. The policewoman waved at them impatiently, so the Volvo pulled quickly away.

A few seconds later, the policewoman waved a pair of black Lincoln Town Cars to the curb. Rosetta opened the door of the first car for Kate, George, June, Molly, and Mrs. Brennan. As she climbed in behind them, she pointed at the second car. "There's no more room in this one, Doctor. You two follow us."

Dr. Austin asked suspiciously, "Where are we going?"

"We're going to take care of business, all of the business that we discussed in your office."

"Oh? Oh, yes. That's good." He and Bud hurried to the second car.

Rosetta's group settled in among the leather seats, TV screens, and tinted glass of the Lincoln.

George marveled aloud. "Look at all this stuff! It's a rolling White House communications center, right?"

"It is, indeed." Rosetta slid her WebWizard X into a portal. She pressed a button, and a computer screen blipped to life before them. She pressed PRINT, waited a moment, then handed Mrs. Brennan the fax that dropped from a slot.

"Look at this: We've already heard from the National Registry of Historic Buildings. Here you are, ma'am. Your Palace Theatre is now on its protected list."

Mrs. Brennan studied the fax and nodded approvingly. She asked Rosetta, "Is there any way to send this fax to the other car? I think Mr. Bud Wright needs to see it."

Rosetta pressed another button. "Yes, indeed. He needs to see it. And he's getting it right now."

Kate, George, and Molly turned around to witness Bud Wright's consternation.

Rosetta said, "Slide over here, Kate. I want you to see this."

Kate changed seats with George and watched the small screen as Rosetta supplied commentary. "This is real-time streaming video. The United States Coast Guard is at Bud Wright's Aquatic Park right now. They're loading Orchid the Orca onto a rescue helicopter, which will then transfer her to a special cargo plane. She'll be free off the coast of California in approximately four hours."

Molly and George exchanged high fives with Kate.

Finally, after listening to it herself, Rosetta let them hear a voice mail from the Justice Department. They heard a man's voice, in clipped tones: "Van 83091 is en route to the King's County Sheriff's Department. It is transporting the inhabitants of the King's County Homeless Shelter."

"I want to get all of the 'prisoners' together," Rosetta explained. "We'll release them all at the same time."

The two Lincolns pulled into a redbrick courtyard in front of the King's County Sheriff's Department.

An unmarked white van was already parked by the door. A man in a blue suit got out of it and approached the car. "Good afternoon, Miss Turner."

She responded to him familiarly, "Hello, Barney."

"I have a delivery for you. From the top. Eight

people from the homeless shelter." He handed her a clipboard.

"Thank you very much." She signed a form. "Okay. You can let them out now."

Bud's brother emerged from the Sheriff's Department building guiding Pogo and the can man by the elbows. The man told Rosetta, "This is Sheriff Wright. He received a fax from the Justice Department to release two prisoners."

Rosetta got out of the car followed by June, George, Kate, Molly, and Mrs. Brennan. They fanned out across the courtyard.

Rosetta walked up to the sheriff. She demanded to know, "What are these people's names?"

The sheriff struggled to read from a clipboard, "Miss Poga-poga-zoo-ski and Mr. Peters."

"Why were you holding them?"

"Uh, suspicion of murder, ma'am."

"Murder of whom?"

"Uh, I'm not sure yet, ma'am. I'll have to consult with these two gentlemen."

The sheriff pointed to the second Lincoln. Dr. Austin and Bud had emerged from their car and were standing, staring with distaste at the homeless people.

Rosetta declared loudly, "I think Dr. Austin and Mr. Wright will tell you that these two people could not possibly be responsible for any murders at the library or anywhere else."

Dr. Austin and Bud smiled weakly at the sheriff. Bud finally called over, "That's right, Bubba. Whatever the lady there said is right."

Dr. Austin motioned for Rosetta Turner to join him away from the others. She shook her head no, so he slinked over to her and whispered, "Listen: There are incidents that have occurred at the library that you don't know about. Incidents that have yet to be resolved. Incidents that have nothing to do with today's agreement."

"Do you mean the stiffs in the cooler?"

Dr. Austin pulled back. Then he admitted, "Yes."

"Are you looking to blame those incidents on someone who may be in this area?"

Dr. Austin squirmed. "That may be the case. Depending on the coroner's findings."

"I see. Well, let me assure you, *everyone* you see here is protected by today's agreement."

Rosetta's cell phone lit up bright blue and made a musical sound. She checked its screen, said, "Excuse me," and drifted three feet away. But she spoke loud enough for Dr. Austin to hear. "Yes, I'll hold for the president."

She covered the speaker, looked back, and asked Dr. Austin and Bud, "Now, gentlemen, am I correct in saying that these prisoners should be released?"

Dr. Austin answered with great enthusiasm, "Oh yes. Yes!"

Rosetta caught the sheriff's eye. She motioned that the eight homeless people and Pogo and the can man should be allowed to walk over to her. "Am I also correct in saying that these people are welcome in the King's County Library at any time?"

Dr. Austin answered giddily. "Yes! Why not? By all means."

The eight homeless people looked at each other and shook their heads at the craziness of it all.

Rosetta spoke into the cell phone in a low voice. Then she held it out to Dr. Austin. She apologized. "I was wrong. It isn't the president."

Dr. Austin stiffened.

"But it is the president's chief of staff."

Dr. Austin's eyes grew wide. He took the phone, but he covered it right away. "What do I call her?"

"It's a him. Call him 'sir.'"

Dr. Austin started immediately, "Yes, sir?" He continued to say, "Yes, sir," very happily for two minutes. Then he stopped. His face turned pale, and he inquired, "I'm sorry. On what condition?"

Dr. Austin handed the cell phone back to Rosetta. He searched the crowd to find a face from his past.

Dr. Austin walked up to Mrs. Brennan. "I have decided to give you your old job back, as director of

Library Services. I will be too busy to run the library system." He turned to include a wider audience. "I will be devoting myself full-time to education as a member of the Presidential Commission on Teacher Accountability." Dr. Austin then spun around on his heel and walked away.

Mrs. Brennan did not say a word back to him. She thought for a while and finally remarked to June, "Little Jimmy Austin. He is amazing. He continues to rise while everybody around him falls."

June, too, had listened to Dr. Austin's latest announcement with growing anger. As soon as she could, she motioned Mrs. Brennan over to the side of the white van, where they engaged in a prolonged conversation. Kate, George, and Molly watched them with undisguised curiosity.

June finally took Mrs. Brennan by the elbow and walked her back toward the children. Kate, George, and Molly waited for one of them to speak, but neither one would.

Molly cracked first. She demanded of her grandmother, "So? What is it? What's the big friggin' mystery?"

But before Mrs. Brennan could fashion a suitable, evasive reply, another mystery presented itself. The can man walked up, wringing his hands, and stood in front of June.

"I know what's been going on at the library, June. I saw with my own eyes what happened to those people. I know now that everything you said was true. Can you ever forgive me?"

At first, June didn't even look at him. Then she did. Anger creased the lines of her face, and she snapped, "No, I can't ever forgive you! Do you have any idea what you did to me? And to your daughter?"

The can man tried to tell her, "I don't know *why* I did what I did, June—"

But June cut him off. "I know why you did it. And so do you! You always had to have the best—the best... laptop, the best golf clubs. And suddenly you had something that wasn't the best. Me. Your wife. There was something wrong with me, so you took off."

Kate slipped in next to June and took her hand.

The can man couldn't even look at her. He mumbled with his head down, "I understand, June. I don't deserve to be forgiven."

Kate stared up at June, dumbfounded. June finally said, "All right. Go on, Charley. Say hello to your daughter."

Charley Peters slowly raised his bearded face and looked at Kate. He spoke, with desperation in his voice, "Hello, Kate."

Kate stared at him for a long time, trying to sort out all the contradictions in her head. She finally babbled,

"I-I thought you were in Japan or someplace. I wrote you a bunch of letters. I thought you were a teacher. Not a..."

Charley completed her thought. "Not a what? A homeless bum?"

"I didn't say that."

June spoke only to Kate, her voice filled with contempt. "He abandoned us, Kate. He turned tail and ran."

Charley stood there a moment longer, in abject shame, and then shuffled away.

"So?" Kate whispered. "Is that it? Will I ever see him again?"

June shrugged. "Do you want to?"

"Yes. I want to. I think."

June exhaled, long and loud. "Then maybe we can work something out. Maybe something at the library. Something that I can monitor, of course."

Kate then became aware of a bobbing presence ten feet in front of her. She looked up and saw Pogo waving and trying to get her attention. Kate waved back, so Pogo stopped bobbing. She smiled at Kate with all the gratitude she could muster. Then she told her:

> "There was a crooked man
> Who walked a crooked mile."

Kate instinctively turned her head to look for Dr. Austin. She spotted him in the back of Rosetta's Town Car. He was sitting next to Bud, talking on a cell phone, and jabbing at the air with his hand. Kate swiveled back to see Pogo, but she was too late. Pogo was gone.

Rosetta Turner rolled down the front passenger window. She called over, "I'm off to the airport now. You folks take care!"

She pointed into the backseat, with its two eager occupants. "We have just a few more details to work out about those chipmunks. The other car will take you back to the library. Can you all get home from there?"

When no one else responded, Kate answered, "Yes, we can. No problem."

Rosetta signaled for the driver to pull out. She turned back to them with these final words: "Soon, all of your wishes will come true."

46

Singing and Dancing
on a School Night

Kate was flying.

She took off straight up, secured by a bodice and a thin wire, as the audience in the Lincoln Middle School auditorium gasped in wonder and delight.

She hovered above the stage and sang "I'm Flying" dressed in the long Victorian nightclothes of Wendy Darling, the eldest of the Darling children, and the possible love interest of Peter Pan.

Peter Pan was flying, too. He soared above and around her, sprinkling Wendy and her two brothers with fairy dust, urging them to think beautiful thoughts and to rise up into the air. Derek Arroyo flew awkwardly as big brother John, while a diminutive sixth grader flitted through the air as Michael.

Below them all, behind the stage curtain, LoriBeth Sommers was running back and forth with a wire tied around her waist. The wire ran through a series of pulleys to the Velcro harness wrapped around Peter Pan.

LoriBeth strained to keep up with Peter's moves while avoiding collisions with the other stagecraft students. Among these backstage helpers was LoriBeth's hero, William Anderson. Although she still could not speak following her trauma at the Whittaker Building, LoriBeth's jaws had closed, and she was otherwise healthy. She had insisted on joining the backstage crew to be near William.

During three intense weeks of rehearsals, LoriBeth had spent every spare moment with her head cradled in William's shoulder. William, for his part, did not mind at all, and he ceaselessly reassured her with a litany of "There, theres" and "Now, nows."

At this moment, however, both LoriBeth and William were totally focused on the task at hand. They and the other "ballast" students were providing the backstage magic to keep Lincoln Middle School's production of *Peter Pan* soaring. And it had indeed soared, all week long, thanks to the virtuoso performance of its star, George Melvil.

For it was George who currently gliding through the air, dressed in green tights and singing lustily in the lead role of the boy who never grew up.

George had surprised everyone by trying out for the role of Peter Pan and bowling over the director, Mr. Kagoshima, with his powerful voice, smooth dancing skills, and superb comic timing.

Kate didn't mind losing the part to George at all, especially since she got to do scenes with Derek Arroyo. Kate and Molly spent hours discussing the ramifications: Here, Kate was playing a scene with the boy she loved, who was pretending to be her brother, while her character was in love with Peter Pan, who in real life was her uncle.

As Kate's ballast, her slight uncle had been replaced by the sturdy William Anderson. He ran beneath her during the rehearsals and the shows, serving Kate as dutifully as LoriBeth served George.

Now, on the fifth and final night of sold-out, wildly successful shows, Kate was very sorry to see it all end. But she was overjoyed to be back at Lincoln Middle School. And her performance as Wendy Darling was universally acclaimed as a triumph, second only to the performance of the remarkable sixth grader who played Peter Pan.

At a backstage celebration, Mr. Kagoshima congratulated Kate and George heartily. Then he said, "Kate, I have to get used to your new name. What is it again?"

"Melvil, Mr. Kagoshima. I'm Kate Melvil now."

"I'm happy to get you back from that crazy Whittaker School, no matter what your name is. And you and George are finally getting some color back in your faces."

June appeared behind them with Molly and Mrs. Brennan. Mr. Kagoshima included them in the conversation. "I was very pleased when the County Commission decided to change the school district lines. We gained some excellent musicians. I bet the commission would not have done that if Susan Singer-Wright hadn't left the country. I hope she stays in Korea, or wherever she is, for a long, long time."

Kate, George, June, Molly, and Mrs. Brennan exchanged furtive looks.

After the celebration at school, June invited Molly and her grandmother back to the house. The children rode with June in her new Honda Accord, while Mrs. Brennan and Molly followed. They pulled up in tandem before the freshly painted duplex.

June had repainted the exterior, choosing a snowy white for the shingles and royal blue for the trim, porch, and railing. The house cheerily reflected the light of a full moon on this cold October night.

The group gathered on couches in the living room as June served mugs of hot cider. She told

Mrs. Brennan, "I am sorry that we haven't gotten together in so long."

Mrs. Brennan waved away the apology. "I can see how busy you've been, June. The house has been transformed! It's lovely."

"Thank you."

"I've been doing some remodeling myself, you know. Evenings and weekends, down at the Palace Theatre."

June sat between Kate and George. "We've been anxious to hear about that. And about any news you can share from the library."

Mrs. Brennan sipped the cider. "All right. Let's see. Pogo is my new head librarian. She supervises two others, mostly through example." Mrs. Brennan looked right at June. "And you know that I hired Charley Peters, too."

June answered civilly. "Yes. I know. He told Kate, during our last visit there."

George quickly changed the subject. "So what about the president's visit? What's the news there?"

"Believe it or not, the president of the United States *is* coming tomorrow, October thirty-first."

"On Halloween!"

"Yes. Although that appears to be just a coincidence of scheduling. We have more Secret Service agents in our stacks now than we have book browsers."

Kate asked, "So what's left of the school, Mrs. Brennan, after the redistricting?"

Mrs. Brennan set down her cup. "Officially, twenty-eight children, when given the opportunity, transferred out of the Whittaker Magnet School. This was despite Dr. Austin's warnings to their parents that the children would never get into an Ivy League college."

"Dr. Austin is still rising, though?"

Mrs. Brennan glanced at June. "If you want to call it that. Dr. Austin is now actually living in his office. His own home is under quarantine by Dr. Cavendar to assure that Cornelia, Whit, and Heidi do not appear in public during the president's visit.

"Dr. Austin has been rehearsing for his big Story Time every day. He will perform the *p* sound for the president."

George said, "I heard a news commentator say that the president is coming here 'to lay to rest the crazy rumors surrounding the First Lady's visit.'"

Kate snorted. But then she added, sadly, "I just wish we could tell people the truth."

George warned her. "No way. That Rosetta Turner lady will undo everything, with a wave of her Web-Wizard X."

"He's right, I'm afraid," Mrs. Brennan said. "The Palace Theatre would be the Paintball Palace overnight."

"And she'd have the Coast Guard recapture Orchid the Orca," George added.

Kate clenched her jaws in utter frustration.

June spoke to her daughter. "Still, Kate, the truth has a way of coming out. Even if you have to wait for years." Then she and Mrs. Brennan exchanged another deadly serious look.

47

A Favorite Book

The following day, the day of the president's visit, saw the King's County Library Building once again surrounded by the flashing lights of police cars and the satellite trucks of the news media.

Far away from the tumult, one mile to the west, June was parking her Accord in the lot of the King's County Savings and Loan Building.

She had just taken Kate and George out for a Saturday-morning pancake breakfast. Both were enjoying the new car's roominess and its CD player; neither thought twice about this unannounced stop on the way home. All June said to them was, "Come inside with me. I have some old business to take care of."

Kate and George walked into the cool darkness of

the marble lobby. The only sound was the echo made by their own feet. Kate said, "Listen to the acoustics in here. It's better than the Lincoln auditorium. Come on, Uncle George."

George smiled and joined her in an a cappella duet of "Never Never Land."

One weekend teller and one security guard looked up from their posts outside the safe-deposit boxes. June produced a key and two forms of identification. Then she and the children followed the teller into a vaultlike room lined with rectangular faceplates.

They stopped at a faceplate bearing the number that matched June's key. The teller unlocked the faceplate; June reached in and slid out a long, low box.

June then led Kate and George to a countertop against the back wall. She said, with utter seriousness, "I want to show you something, Kate. But to see it, you have to close your eyes."

Kate squeezed her eyes shut. June took Kate's hand and placed it on a document. "Feel this. And tell me what it is."

Kate smiled. "I don't know. Is it paper?"

"That's right. That's exactly what it is. And that's all it is."

Kate opened her eyes and beheld a document. It read CERTIFICATE OF MARRIAGE.

"It is paper. Nothing more. There is nothing magic about it. If you want it to be more, Kate, you have to supply the magic yourself."

June then looked at George. "It's like a book. What is that made of?"

George answered, "Paper."

"That's right. That's all it is. But if you sit down with a book and you supply your imagination, it can become something more. It's like anything in life, you two. You get back what you put in."

Kate stared hard at the Certificate of Marriage. She thought about the father who had reappeared in her life. She thought about a frail, beaten man, so different from the one in her photos. She thought about their two awkward meetings together in the Whittaker Library lobby. They had sat and talked quietly, or not at all, for thirty minutes each time, while June stood at a distance and watched them.

June returned the Certificate of Marriage to the box. She then pulled out two manila envelopes—one large and one small—and slid them into her carry bag. She closed the safe-deposit box, returned it to its slot, and locked it with the key.

They left as they came in, tramping noisily through the corridor. But this time, Kate did not feel like singing. Her mood began to lighten, though, when they got into the sunshine and settled back into the comforts of the car.

"Today is the day!" June reminded them. "The president of the United States will be in our little town. Isn't that wonderful?"

"He's just coming to make Dr. Austin look good," Kate said. "How's that wonderful?"

June replied cryptically. "I don't know for sure. But I know this: A lot of surprising things have happened at the Whittaker Building."

As they drove east into the sun, the mood got lighter still. George announced, with mock sentimentality, "You know, I really miss the Whittakers. And the Austins. And the Whittaker-Austins."

Kate scoffed. "Yeah. Right."

"I miss Heidi. She was so gifted. And I miss Whit. He was like a brother to me."

"Please. You're bringing up my pancakes."

"And I miss Cornelia. I miss her kind words, and her generosity. Remember when she offered to give you those used milkmaid dresses?"

"I mean it, Uncle George. I'm going to hurl."

Kate and George laughed. Neither gave a thought to the items in June's bag, not even when she made a second unannounced stop.

June parked at the bottom of the hill, along the

river, farther away than usual because of the crush of presidential onlookers. She hopped out quickly, waved for Kate and George to follow, and led them along the sidewalk of the River Road.

They reached an initial checkpoint, a set of red-and-white barricades manned by Secret Service agents. Kate and George recognized one agent right away. She was the woman who had walked the First Lady out of the secret room and helped load her into the helicopter.

June reached into her bag and pulled out three badges. Each said, SECURITY CLEARANCE, LEVEL 1, followed by one of their names.

June showed the badges to the agent, who studied them and said, "I'll need to see a driver's license for you."

June complied.

The agent informed her, "I'll need to see official IDs for the kids."

June reached into her bag again, pulled out the small manila envelope, and proffered two documents with raised seals. "Here are their birth certificates."

The agent checked the names versus the names on the badges. She pointed out, "The girl's badge has a different name."

June said, "Sorry, I forgot." She dug out another document. "This is the court order to change her name.

Peters was my married name; Melvil is my maiden name. Kate changed her name to match mine."

The agent studied the document. She told Kate, "That's nice."

Then she told June, "You have to wear these badges at all times. These are Level One badges, entitling you to be on the street, but not in the building. Do you understand?"

They all answered, "Yes."

The agent stood aside and let them enter the cordoned-off street.

The first thing Kate, George, and June saw was a group of reporters clustered around Dr. Austin. They listened to him say, "We need tougher assessment standards nationwide."

But June would not let them stand there for long. She guided Kate and George over the thick wires of the TV trucks toward a second security checkpoint.

June found an opening in the crowd and waved to a figure in a high window of the Whittaker Building.

The figure waved back. It was Mrs. Brennan, the director of Library Services. On this special day, she was dressed all in black—black shoes, black stockings, and black dress. It was an outfit that a Story Time witch might wear beneath a black pointed hat.

Mrs. Brennan exited the building a minute later carrying a manila envelope under her arm. She walked up to the security checkpoint and stood before the agent in charge for the day, Agent McCoy himself.

He looked at her Level 2 security badge and then at his clipboard. "What is your name?"

"I'm Mary Brennan, the director of Library Services for King's County."

"And what is your function here today?"

Mrs. Brennan beamed with pride. "I shall have the privilege of assisting Dr. Austin in his Story Time performance. I will be passing out phonics worksheets."

McCoy looked from the clipboard to his timetable. Satisfied that she was telling the truth, he turned his attention to her envelope. "May I see that?"

"Certainly."

Agent McCoy took the manila envelope, opened it, and removed its contents. It was a children's book, the Little Golden Book version of *Walt Disney's Peter Pan*.

Mrs. Brennan informed him, "This is the book that Dr. Austin will use."

Agent McCoy answered curtly. "I am aware of that, ma'am. He is doing the *p* sound in *Peter Pan*." Then he softened his tone and added confidentially, "No more *m* sounds. Right?"

Mrs. Brennan's hand shot to her mouth. "Oh heavens no!"

Charley and Pogo emerged through the doors together and joined her. They also wore Level 2 security badges.

Agent McCoy asked, "Who are these two? And what are their functions today?"

"They work for me. They are full-time employees of the library. The lady is Miss Pogorzelski, and the gentleman is Mr. Peters. They will be serving refreshments after Dr. Austin's Story Time performance."

Agent McCoy found the names on his list. "All right."

Mrs. Brennan smiled her most grandmotherly smile at him. She inquired, softly and sweetly, "May we step out into the street for a moment?"

Agent McCoy's attention was already elsewhere. He muttered, "What for?"

"We want to see some of the excitement out here! The TV reporters and all."

"Yes, you can do that. But you will have to pass through the metal detectors again."

"All right. Thank you."

Mrs. Brennan indicated to Pogo and Charley that they should follow her. She walked across the street toward the reporters, but then she veered off to the right and headed straight to June.

When she got to within ten feet, Pogo stopped, bobbed, and waved brightly to Kate, who waved back.

Charley Peters stopped, too, but he kept his eyes fixed on the ground.

Mrs. Brennan greeted June with a big hug. Then, in the blink of an eye, like a team of magicians, they switched their manila envelopes. They did it so deftly that no one, not even Kate and George, noticed. June casually slid her new envelope back into her bag.

Mrs. Brennan held her new envelope out at arm's length, like a sacred object. She asked June, "Is it in here? Is this the one?"

"Yes. That's the one. I'm afraid it's long overdue. I'll bet I owe hundreds of dollars in fines."

Mrs. Brennan looked at her kindly. "Do you remember what I told you about Library Forgiveness Days?"

"Yes. I think so."

"They're not about money. They're not about collecting exactly what is due you. You may never collect exactly what is due you, June. I think you know that. But you will reach a point where that doesn't matter."

June nodded nervously.

"Forgiveness Days are about leaving the past behind and moving on to the future."

Mrs. Brennan turned herself so that June could see the forlorn man standing in her wake. Charley shifted his weight uncomfortably.

Mrs. Brennan whispered, "Come on, June. No

questions asked, no punishments meted out. This is a Forgiveness Day."

June put her head down. She squeezed her eyes tightly. Then she took a deep breath, raised up her head, and walked over to Charley.

Charley could not bear to meet her gaze.

June waited patiently until Charley stole a quick glance upward. Then she told him simply, "I forgive you, Charley. You've been punished, severely, for anything you've done wrong. I was the last to see that, but I see it now.

"I forgive you, Charley. I have no more bad thoughts about you. And I hope you will feel the same way about me."

Charley's eyes filled with tears. He croaked out, "Thank you so much, June. I've got no bad thoughts about you. I never had. Just crazy thoughts. I was the crazy one to think anything bad about you."

June held out her hand, Charley reached for it, and they shook, up and down, one time.

Then June walked back to Mrs. Brennan and the children. She crossed her eyes and blew a gust of air up at her own brown bangs, as if to say, *Thank god that's over with.*

Kate and George hugged her from either side.

Mrs. Brennan waited for a moment, then she

pointed discreetly to the manila envelope. She whispered urgently, "When can I open it?"

June kept her arms around the children's shoulders. "I would wait, Mrs. Brennan, until about a minute before the performance."

Mrs. Brennan looked worried. "Tell me exactly what to do again."

"Open the envelope, and leave it on the podium with just the top of the book sticking out."

"All right. I can do that."

"Remember: Let Dr. Austin pull out the book the rest of the way. Let him be the one exposed."

Kate couldn't take any more. She demanded to know. "Mom, what's going on?"

June lowered her voice so that only Kate and George could hear. "When I told you my Whittaker Library story, Kate? About you and me at Toddler Time? There was a detail that I left out. I *do* remember one thing about the experience: Jill. It was not Jack who took over my body. I am absolutely certain about that. It was Jill."

She turned to Mrs. Brennan. "Show them the book. It's safe if you do it the way that I described."

Mrs. Brennan opened the top of the envelope and carried it over to the children like it was an unexploded bomb. Kate and George peered inside. They saw a

Little Golden Book, a match of the *Walt Disney's Peter Pan* that Mrs. Brennan had carried out to June.

June repeated, to Kate and George, "It was Jill. She was inside this very book. And guess what?" Kate's and George's eyes widened. "She's inside it still."

June looked from astonished face to astonished face. "Unless, of course, you don't believe in ghosts."

Kate reached out with a trembling hand. "Can I touch it?"

"Yes. In fact, you have touched it before, Kate. It was one of your favorite books. You held this very copy in your hands when you were a toddler. You turned to me and said, 'You read it, Mommy.'"

Kate tried to cast herself back to that moment, long ago. "I gave the book to you. That means it would have happened to me. I'd have been possessed by Jill. Instead, it happened to you."

"That's right. No one would have given it a second thought. The grown-ups would have said, 'There's little Kate Peters having a little-girl tantrum.' Jill would have escaped, like she always did. She would have joined Jack back home in *Perrault's Mother Goose*."

George asked, "So why didn't that happen?"

"Because this book never made it back to the scanner. When the fireman got me down, Jill slipped back into the book. I grabbed Kate, and all our stuff, and ran out. This book was part of our stuff."

"Jill thought she'd be going right back into the scanner, to be with Jack. But, instead, she has been a prisoner for ten years in a safe-deposit box?"

June smiled. "That's right. You don't think she's mad, do you?"

Kate shook her head in wonderment. "So what about Jack? Is he really gone?"

June answered decisively. "Jack is gone. We were there when it happened. Right, George?"

George had no doubt, either. "Oh, yes. He's gone. Vaporized. That Ashley-Nicole really kills things dead."

Mrs. Brennan pointed at the Whittaker Building. "But Ashley-Nicole is not here today. And neither is her killing machine."

Kate could barely contain herself. "Oh my god, Mrs. Brennan, do you really think you can do this?"

"I know I can do it. Believe me, little Jimmy Austin will be making an unforgettable impression on the president of the United States today."

Mrs. Brennan started back with the book tucked safely under her arm.

Pogo bent down and peeked at the envelope as she walked by. She then turned to Kate, pointed at it excitedly, and called out, "Jack and Jill went up the hill!"

Kate called back, "Yes! Yes!" and waved good-bye to her. She turned to June and George. "Pogo knew!"

June smiled sadly. "Oh, yes. She always knew. She knew everything. But no one would ever listen to her."

Mrs. Brennan led Pogo and Charley back to the security checkpoint. She opened the top of the envelope to let Agent McCoy glance inside. He waved them in with the order, "Proceed to the metal detectors in the lobby."

Mrs. Brennan, Pogo, and Charley walked under the *Id pendemus* motto and past the *Andrew Carnegie in Hell* mosaic. Soon they, and the long overdue copy of *Peter Pan* and its occupant, Jill, were out of sight.

Then Kate, June, and George turned and started back down the crowded street. They stopped only once, at the spot where Dr. Austin had been interviewed. The TV crew had packed up, but Dr. Austin remained.

He and June stood and stared at each other for a long moment, amid the swirl of people with Level 1 badges, both of them remembering an incident from ten years before.

Dr. Austin looked away first. He shook his head, as if to drive away the memory. He started off briskly toward the Whittaker Building, intent on escape, but he stopped upon seeing George.

In spite of his disturbing encounter with June, and in spite of all the demands on his schedule that day, he took the time to say, "Ah, George Melvil."

George answered with uncharacteristic insolence. "Ah, Dr. Austin."

The insolence was not lost on Dr. Austin. He narrowed his eyes and replied caustically, "Apparently I overestimated you, my boy. You turned out to be a Whittaker Magnet School failure."

George snuck a look at Kate. Then he answered, "'A Whittaker Magnet School failure'? That, sir, would be redundant."

Dr. Austin blinked rapidly. He thought for a moment, then he replied coldly, "I must get ready. I am about to meet the president of the United States."

But George got in the last word, to Dr. Austin's back. "I know. To teach him about the *p* sound in *Peter Pan*."

As George, Kate, and June watched him walk away, they pictured what would happen during that Story Time: Mrs. Brennan would fold back the manila envelope and place it on the podium; Dr. Austin would pick up the envelope and slide out his copy of *Walt Disney's Peter Pan*.

Then they pictured what the vengeful Jill, released after ten years of captivity, might do within the body of the headmaster of the Whittaker Magnet School and the author of *TBC: Test-Based Curriculum*, as he performed for the president of the United States.

After a minute of this contemplation, they turned to go, working their way back through the reporters and the onlookers and the security guards. The morning sun had by now risen fully above the Whittaker Building, and they soon passed from shadow into sunlight.

As they cleared the outer checkpoint, Kate grabbed George by one hand and June by the other. She led them at a brisk pace toward the river. Every step away from the Whittaker Building lifted their spirits higher, so that soon they were practically skipping down the steep hill.

When the building was completely out of sight, Kate could no longer contain herself. She let go of their hands and took off running on her own. She threw back her head to feel the breeze in her hair and the sunlight on her face. Then she stretched out her arms and let the swirling river winds envelop her. They seemed to lift her up and pull her along as if she were weightless; as if she were sprinkled with fairy dust; as if she were flying. Quite involuntarily, she opened her mouth and started to sing.

Reader Chat Page

1. Dr. Austin and the other administrators at the Whittaker Magnet School are convinced that high scores on standardized tests and rote memorization of facts make an ideal education. Do you think success in these areas is truly a measure of intelligence? What else do you think is wrong with the Whittaker system?

2. One of Dr. Austin's many innovations was having teachers be known to students only by the subject and grade level they teach. What purpose did this serve?

3. At the beginning of the story, Kate and George have very different personalities and interests. Over

the course of their time at the Whittaker Magnet School, they grow closer and seem to take on some of each other's personality traits. How are Kate and George at the end of the story different from the way they were at the beginning?

4. What are some of the experiences that Kate and George share that bring them closer together?

5. Kate and her mother, June, also grew closer over the course of Kate's attendance at Whittaker. How does Kate feel about June in the beginning of the story, and why do her feelings change?

6. How do the First Lady and her chief of staff, Rosetta Turner, react to the practices they observe taking place at Whittaker?

7. Cornelia Whittaker-Austin, Dr. Austin, and others try to make the Whittaker Magnet School a place that is very structured and organized, with students who behave almost mechanically—but the demons in the library always seem to return to knock their system out of control. What kinds of actions do the demons cause that are normally suppressed at Whittaker?

8. If you could open your ideal school, what would it be like? What kinds of classrooms, teachers, and lessons do you think would best promote learning? How would it be different from the Whittaker School? How would it be different from the school that you attend now?

Edward Bloor
on Writing *Story Time*

My first two novels, *Tangerine* and *Crusader*, tried to deal with reality, as I saw it, in our public schools. For my third novel, *Story Time*, I was eager to do something different, or at least to approach reality from a different direction. The result is a novel that is part ghost story, with lots of supernatural action, and part satire about public schools.

Story Time is set in the Whittaker Magnet School, a grades six through eight experimental school that boasts the highest standardized-testing scores in the United States. Within this school's sterile, Orwellian environment arises a curious poltergeist—at times funny, at times malevolent—who turns everything upside down. This unfriendly ghost provokes incidents that, should the public catch wind of them, would wreak havoc on real estate values in the highly desirable Whittaker Magnet School district.

I was fortunate to teach in the public school system (nearly twenty years ago) in what now seems to be a golden age, unencumbered by state standards and high-stakes tests. Seventh-graders could read aloud and talk about *The Odyssey, Flowers for Algernon,* and *Lord of the Flies.* They could put on a drama festival in which they wrote and acted in their own plays. They could write and illustrate poems to adorn the classroom walls.

I doubt that so many fanciful activities could occur with such frequency in seventh-grade classrooms in America today. The relentless pressure from above to succeed on standardized tests, pressure originating from the president of the United States himself, trickles down through descending levels of politicians until it pours onto the heads of local principals. These hapless former teachers now find their worlds turned upside down, their livelihoods tied to their students' performances on a specific test on a specific day.

"Test-Based Curriculum," the absurd pedagogy upon which *Story Time*'s Whittaker Magnet School is founded, is already a reality in many American public schools. As a result, many children who learn to love reading today do so in spite of, not because of, what they experience in the classroom. In this topsy-turvy system, the politicians win and the educators and students lose. I believe that, in the Latin words displayed in the Whittaker Magnet School, "We will pay for it" with a less literate society. We risk producing a generation that could read for pleasure, but chooses not to.

Edward Bloor